CW00481483

The Hearts We Keep

Haley McMillan

Copyright © 2023 Haley McMillan

All rights reserved. No portion of this book may be reproduced in any form without permission from the author and publisher, except as permitted by U.S. copyright law. For permissions, contact: meggymariebooks@gmail.com

This is a work of fiction. Names, characters, businesses, events and incidents are the products of the author's imagination. Any resemblance to actual persons, living or dead, or actual events is purely coincidental.

Edited by Meghan Hurley Powell

Cover Design by Haley McMillan

Power Within Her Publishing

For Liam,

The one who makes all my dreams come true.

I hope

you are able

to remember

what was Light-woven

and beautiful.

I hope

you are able to see

to remember what was,

and carry the goodness

that you will never forget

in the direction

of what is to come.

—*Morgan Harper Nichols*

A Note from Me to You

I am so grateful and excited that you've picked up *The Hearts We Keep*. Though, before you dive in, I do want you to know that this story covers the complexity of human experiences and emotions. In this book, you'll see the characters experience great love and loss, laugh and cry, and break and heal. Despite the heaviness of topics, such as death and sexual assault, *The Hearts We Keep* is meant to remind us that we *are* capable of healing and rising and making choices that ultimately empower us to thrive.

So, as you read, please be sure to take care of yourself.

All my love,

Haley

PROLOGUE

I COME FROM a long line of nice people. You know—the kind of people that are well-regarded in the community for not being too loud, or problematic, or contrary. We are on time to work, we mow our lawns, and we make pleasant conversation in the grocery store. We make sure our children are seen and not heard. We value simple pleasures like coffee on the front porch, a good nap, and a well-tended garden.

The truth is, I was blessed with the best possible start in life. It was simple, ordinary, and good.

But this story isn't about that.

It's about what happened next. It's about the reason I'm eighteen years old, and absolutely sure that I'll never be more than half a person again.

ONE

THE SUMMER BEFORE my senior year of high school was hot. In Minnesota, we get exactly ten weeks of really warm weather, and when the days are long and the sun shines down heavily, you're sure to see plenty of boobs, bellies, butt cheeks, strappy tan lines, and skinny teenage boys showing off their budding muscles.

I, personally, was not built for summer. Apparently, my Scandinavian ancestors adapted a little too well to the frozen tundra, which is why my skin turns candy-apple red at the suggestion of sun, or anytime I laugh, cry, or bend down to pick something up. My friends used to joke that when most people's skin turns from white to tan over the summer, mine goes from blue to pink. I looked down at my exposed stomach as I lounged on the lake's only sandy stretch of beach and adjusted my sunglasses to protect my retinas from the unnatural fluorescent glare of the sun reflecting off my skin.

"Annie, are you blushing because you're embarrassed or just because you're in love with me?" a boy from my class shouted in my direction from his perch a few yards away.

The beach was heaving with young bodies, soaking up as much vitamin D and pheromones as possible before the seasons changed, and we were plunged into too many months of darkness and icy air that hurts your face as you scamper from your house to your car.

"Yes, Jordan. I'm embarrassed. Mostly embarrassed for you because you're such a dick."

My best friend Becca snorted and held out her hand to high five me—probably because she was proud that I *actually* stood up for myself for once, rather than just being the accommodating, "nice girl." She also happened to hate Jordan. In eighth grade, he tried to kiss her at her birthday party, and she never really recovered from how gross it felt. Becca likes girls now. It's a whole thing. Or *not* a whole thing, depending on who you talk to. To me, she's just Becca, and I think she's pretty great.

Unlike me and my happy apple pie family, Becca came from a long line of deadbeat assholes, who made messes and cursed and perpetuated misinformation. Unlike me, she wasn't afraid of upsetting people, or afraid of what anyone thought of her. She's better than the people she came from, but she will always be more of a badass than I could ever even try to be.

Becca's also a bombshell. She looked like she was born to be there at the beach—all tan curves and dark hair. If the boys hadn't already known better, they would have been swarming around us, vying for her attention. But sophomore year, this senior boy named Logan propositioned her about a threesome, and she broke his nose with a single punch. The boys gave her a wide berth after that, and that's how she preferred it.

Not that it made any difference to me. I was the type of girl who became really popular with the boys about ten minutes before class started when they were scrambling to finish their homework and needed fast answers. Suddenly, I blossomed from forgettable wall flower to heroic, intellectual, belle-of-the-ball. Did I oblige the lazy jerks?

Yes.

I come from a long line of nice people, remember? I didn't know how to say no to people yet. I didn't even know that 'no' was an option. And also, if I'm being honest, the attention from boys felt good even if it wasn't for the reasons that I read about when I was elbow deep in my favorite romance novels. So, I basked in the boys' attention right up until the bell rang and I was put right back into my place amongst the lesser flowers.

The afternoon at the beach was starting to drag on, and my back was starting to feel itchy from the rogue grains of sand that had made their way onto my faded pink flamingo towel. As if she could read my mind—let's be real, at this point in our friendship, she probably could—Becca rocked onto her heels and stood up, asking me if I wanted to walk down to the beach bar to top off our strawberry daiquiris.

I glanced toward the bar. Steve, the bartender, was off his lunch break. Although he was kind of a pervert, if we laughed at his dumb jokes, he sometimes threw a little shot of rum into our "virgin" drinks. He was in his late forties and shady as hell, but every teen has a 'Steve,' even good girls like me. Was this a prime example of poor decision-making? Definitely. But we were young, and permission from *anyone* middle-aged (even the men with sweaty chest hair and gold chains around their necks) felt like enough for me to justify my behavior.

Plus, I loved how Becca made me fun. Sometimes it scared me, but she made me feel like I was doing the things that meant I was 'living my best life' and not wasting my teenage years tucked away in my plaid pajama pants and journals at home. If left to my own devices, that would have definitely happened, and if it had, my life would have turned out so much differently.

We shuffled our way to the makeshift bar, which sat just between the sidewalk and the beach. It was made of weathered barn wood and decorated with the usual sculptures of freshwater fish and a big moose, because...Minnesota. Becca leaned up against the bar, her little lime green bikini barely covering her not-so-secret weapons, and I watched as Steve poured a double shot into the blender without a word. As the blender swirled the liquor together with the sugar and artificial pink color, I glanced at Steve, who had a dark goatee, a receding hairline, and an expression that gave me the impression he thought he was a lot younger and more attractive than he actually was.

"Enjoying the sunshine, ladies?" Steve asked casually, and I felt a mix of pride and disgust at being called a lady by this way older guy. I stood up a little straighter, like maybe he thought I was more grown up than I was, and then immediately felt gross for wanting him to find me attractive or even caring what he thought to begin with.

He poured our drinks, set them in front of us, and gave us a wink. Becca threw him a sarcastic smile, and I tipped him extra because I didn't know how much alcohol was supposed to cost. I didn't want to do this sly transaction wrong.

As we walked away, Becca whispered, "*Such* a creep," into my ear and then gave me an exaggerated wink.

We laughed, and some girl off in the distance squealed as a boy pushed her off the dock. Becca and I lounged under our umbrella for the rest of the afternoon, judging people, but not feeling guilty about it because sharing a mean thought with your best friend is basically the same as not sharing it at all; it just doesn't count. Everyone knows that the universe only sends you bad karma if you

6

are judgy out loud to acquaintances and strangers. Basking in that logic, we enjoyed the sweet comfort and security of an afternoon shared between loyal friends, where the only problems we had weren't really problems at all, and the future was a predictable place where ordinary things happened.

If only that had remained true.

Afternoon faded into evening, and we slipped our short shorts and tanks back on over our swimsuits as the first bonfire flames ignited along the beach. There's something about being young and innocent on a summer night. Not enough life has happened yet to make you stop believing in magic. No matter who you are, who your people are, or what you have or don't have, when the stars come out and the fire glows on your young skin and bones, you feel like at any moment, someone unexpected could suddenly fall in love with you and you could be swept up in a passionate, life-affirming romance.

At the time, I was in love with the idea of being in love because I hadn't actually experienced it yet. My whole life up until that point felt like an anticipation of those enchanting moments I had only dreamt about and read about in books. I was a freckly, redheaded, 17-year-old virgin with a few awkward kisses under my belt, waiting for chapter one of my romance novel to start.

But boys didn't tend to pursue me like they did my funnier, flirtier, curvier peers, and I couldn't really blame them. I wasn't a total weirdo, but I was a little stiff, and awkward and interested in things that weren't interesting to teenage boys, like Shakespeare and 70's singer-songwriter music and quiet contemplation. Still, I held out hope that one fine day a certain slant of light would befall me, and someone dreamy would realize that the love of his life (me) had been hiding in plain sight all along.

Of course, it didn't exactly happen that way.

I had known since elementary school who I was desperate for my leading man to be. His name was Drew Matthews, and I'm embarrassed to admit how many pages of my journals had 'Annie Matthews' written in the margins. I wasn't a stalker by any means, but I will admit that I was acutely aware of Drew's presence whenever we were in the same vicinity. It was hard not to be because he was so charismatic and handsome and talented. Like a golden retriever in a room full of bulldogs, Drew was in another category entirely—one I was young and vapid enough to imagine I would be better off being a part of. Everyone says, 'the grass is always greener on the other side,' but it takes life experience to really understand what that means.

Before that summer, Drew and I rarely spoke to each other, unless it was a word or two in a group conversation that we were both coincidentally involved in. I sometimes made eye contact with him in the hallway, and he would flash a smile, and I wondered if he felt the same jolt to his system as I did when our eyes met. I assumed he smiled at everyone, but a part of me dreamed that there might be something there that was just for me.

A girl could hope, right?

The beach was aglow, and the sand that had been burning my skin all afternoon was now cold and damp beneath my feet. The lake was still and black, and the sounds of too-loud teenage voices carried across it and were buried in the trees somewhere on the other side. The party raged on, and everyone assumed their usual roles: the attention-seeking bros doing handstands and punching each other's shoulders, the drugged-out hipsters lolling by the fire, the usual suspect lovebirds pairing up and sneaking off to the trees to make out. Then, you had me and Becca and a handful of tipsy others, chatting and watching from a safe—but still present and socially accounted for—distance.

I was beginning to think our slippery friend Steve had been extra generous with his pours. My head was starting to spin, and my muscles felt warm and loose. When Becca grabbed my hand to dance, I didn't hesitate. We danced around the fire and laughed and spun in circles and probably stumbled, but in my intoxicated mind, I was cool and fun and definitely a sexy and talented dancer. In Sober Land, I'm not actually any of those things, which is why it's no surprise that I eventually took a spin and toppled over into the damp sand. As my woozy limbs descended, the ground kept spinning and I flipped dramatically onto my back, afraid I was about to fall off the edge of the world.

I heard some 'ooo's' and laughter, and if I had been sober, I would have probably cried, but instead, I just lay there like a ragdoll and prayed for the ground to stop spinning. Becca was sitting in the sand nearby, unable to control her giggles. Before I could sit upright, big hands slid under my back and thighs, and I was hoisted up in the air like a toddler. I could smell sweat, and spicy cologne, and sunscreen and pheromones. When I opened my eyes, a dull mixture of delight and mortification washed over me.

Drew.

Drew was carrying *me*.

Drew with a chiseled jaw and perfect teeth and sandy hair and rippling shoulder caps.

Drew, the boy of my dreams, was holding my body against his body—something I had secretly imagined happening for years, just not in this completely embarrassing way.

My initial instinct was to lean into him and take in the divine moment. But reality was still floating around somewhere in my Jell-O brain, and I knew that I was making a complete ass of myself, and this would be painfully humiliating in the morning. The most perfect Prince Charming came and rescued the lamest damsel who was ever distressed.

Drew walked me over to the edge of the beach, where the sand turned into woods, and he set me down by a tree.

"Are you okay, Annie? You fell HARD!"

Umm…Drew knows my name. Yes, Drew, I have, in fact, fallen hard. Very hard.

My last shred of dignity was begging me to play it cool, but in this particular, very critical instance, my drunk brain was in the driver's seat, and she was a dipshit. "Did you see me dancing?" I slurred, just before I vomited all over myself.

I saw Becca walking toward us, and I let out a quick, "I'm sorry Drew, I love you so much."

And that's the last thing I remember about that soul-crushing night.

TWO

I DON'T KNOW who brought me home after I passed out, but whoever it was, they had to drive a long way. I'm from Concord, a small town in the middle of nowhere, but my house is about fifteen miles from said small town, in the *actual* middle of nowhere. I used to ride the bus to school sometimes, and I was always the first kid on and the last kid off. It took forever to get home at the end of the day. Lucky for me, my mom was an elementary school teacher, and my dad owned the sports shop in town, so my bus rides were few and far between. I usually got to enjoy a peaceful ride in my mom's sedan, or a clunky but comforting ride in my dad's truck.

When I turned sixteen, I bought myself a little red Ford Taurus with babysitting money, and my solitary drives to and from town became a necessary part of maintaining my sanity. I didn't have the words to articulate or understand it at the time, but I was developing into a rock-solid introvert. And not that I had ever known any different, but I did love living in the country.

There were a few other families spread out around us, but it was mostly rolling hills, trees, lakes, and farmland for miles. Our closest neighbors were the McAteers, who lived on the property just east of us. It was just a boy from my class, Shea, and his dad, John. They lived in a plain, two-story farmhouse, and we hardly ever saw them besides when they came and went from their driveway, which ran parallel to ours. All the houses around us were spread far enough apart that it was easy to exist in relative isolation. It seemed like everyone who lived out that far had a sort of unspoken agreement to not come knocking unless someone's house was on fire, or someone was dead.

I was grateful to have a secluded bubble to retreat to after spending any length of time in town, which was small enough that there was absolutely no anonymity whatsoever, and anything that happened was public knowledge within minutes. Like when Mike, the grocery store manager, had an affair with Pam from the Credit Union, and half the town knew before his wife did (including me). Besides the occasional scandal, Concord was overall picturesque and as nice a place as any. We were a tourist town surrounded by lakes and whose population basically doubled in the summer when rich people from the Twin Cities came up to occupy their summer cabins for a week and eat pizza at Zorbaz and race turtles and buy kitsch loon keychains from the local gift shops.

The locals both loved and hated the tourists. We relied on their money to keep our small businesses afloat, but at the same time, we all wanted to roll our eyes at the onslaught of requests for the 'best fishing spots' or to laugh at their overspending on outdoor gear they didn't really need. At the end of the day, we smiled and obliged because the silly requests and generous spending were a big part of what put the food on the table at our houses.

During the off-season, when the town died down to its usual dull murmur, an unfamiliar face became a rare sight to see. Just like any other small town, there was so much goodness and generosity and a sense of community in Concord, but there was also jealousy and gossip and hierarchy and an inflated sense of self-importance—and there was absolutely nowhere to hide. My family was good. My family was well-liked. And I did my part most of the time to be good and well-liked, too. But there was also a lot of pressure in being known by everyone, and I dreaded facing the public after the spectacle I made of myself at the beach. Mistakes never stayed quiet for long in Concord.

When I opened my eyes the morning after the Drew incident at the beach, there was a precious moment where my only concern was the painful pounding between my ears and the queasy feeling in my stomach. Very quickly, I remembered what a fool I had made of myself and whom exactly I had vomited on. The thought made me want to crawl inside of a trash can and set it on fire.

A knock at my door interrupted my pity party and I heard my mother's voice calling my name to check on me. My mom is sweet and unassuming, and generally gives people the benefit of the doubt—including me—but she's also not an idiot. I knew that as soon as I headed downstairs, I'd be treated to some toast, a cup of coffee, and some stern reminders of the grim potential consequences of underage drinking. It's just not something that nice girls do, after all. Mom didn't know this at the time, but I'd already experienced the worst kind of consequences—you know, public humiliation, ruining my chances with the potential love of my life, maximum level hangover—and I had already vowed to never drink again.

The morning was normally my favorite part of the day back then. The air always felt so clean and hopeful, and everything was beautiful, and anything felt possible. This particular morning felt neither fresh nor hopeful. But all the same, my youthful body and spirit still allowed me to get up and exist despite my throbbing hangover and burning shame.

Apparently, I deserved to be kicked while I was down because when I reached up to scratch an itch on my shoulder, a familiar pain seared across my skin. Evidently, despite my extensive precautions, I had acquired a ferocious sunburn at the beach the day before. I looked in my vanity mirror to assess the damage, and my nose was so pink that my freckles looked green. If you know, you know.

I determined that my best course of action was to don a large, lightweight Mickey Mouse t-shirt and some silky granny panties. This was another underrated advantage of living in the country: nobody accidentally sees your granny panties through a kitchen window, or in your backyard while you're watering plants, or while you are roller skating half-naked in your driveway. It would be a rude awakening the first time I experienced a living situation that required me to be fully dressed before leaving my bedroom.

Upon getting dressed in fresh clothes, I no longer had any excuse to delay the inevitable. It was time to take my walk of shame and scuffle my way downstairs to the kitchen where my mom awaited, fully armed with her air of superiority. As expected, mom had dry toast and coffee set out on the table, right in the seat where a bright beam of sunlight shined through the window like a spotlight, or in my case this morning, like a laser beam.

I sat down to my breakfast and my mom said calmly into the space between us, "Alexa, play 'Crazy Train.'"

The soundbot was dutiful and precise. Ozzy Osbourne's sharp vocals flooded the room and slapped my brain around in my head while I sat quietly, and humbly atoned for my sins. When the song was over, I apologized to my mom, promised to never drink again, and offered to weed the garden. When my mom was satisfied, she slid two Advil across the table and gave me a kiss on the forehead. She then disappeared upstairs to go work on the quilt she was piecing together. Some kids get lectured or grounded when they are in trouble. I like to think that's the better option. At least then you can sit and stew in your own indignation. Mom was always just direct enough to put me in my place, but just easy enough on me to make me feel the full weight of my disappointing actions all on my own.

Dad was already away doing inventory at the sports shop this morning (a Sunday morning ritual that we've never questioned) and my baby sister, Rosie, was already on her first nap of the day in her crib upstairs. Rosie was two, and a big surprise for my parents after years of trying for another baby after me. They had made their peace with having an only child, but for several weeks during the fall when I was fourteen, my mom couldn't stop throwing up. She went to the doctor expecting the worst and came out with the biggest surprise of her life. Rosie was a sweet angel, and I loved her more than I thought I could love anyone or anything. I definitely resented her for her blonde hair and long, dark eyelashes that she inherited from our dad, but when she looked at me with those sky-blue eyes that mirrored my own, I melted.

Once my mom was upstairs, I mouthed a silent "thank you" to the universe that everyone in my family was too busy living their own lives to care what I was doing (or not doing) with my day. I rinsed my plate and walked out the back door, through the narrow strip of prairie grass, into the trees and down to the small lake that our property shared with the McAteers. The lake wasn't good for fishing, or really anything except looking at and swimming in or ice skating on. There was a narrow, wood-plank dock that was technically on the McAteer's side, but I had literally never seen Shea or his dad down here, so I had kind of taken over the dock in recent years. It had become a secret spot of sorts, where I could reliably sit and daydream, stew, or throw a solid pity party in peace.

Since the lake was small and tucked within the woods, it was almost always still, even on windy days. Tiny ripples glittered in the sun, and the water reflected the blue sky in the middle and the rich forest green around the edges. I've always appreciated spaces that have just the right amounts of sunlight and shade. I needed this spot that day, and sometimes I still need it, although I think it hurts me now more than it heals me.

I sat cross-legged on the edge of the dock, the scratchy, weathered wood on my bare legs mirroring the discomfort in my brain as I indulged in my despair at officially ruining my chances with my lifelong crush. My hair still smelled a little pukey, which inspired a whole new wave of humiliation. Trying to stuff that down, my mind wandered to the fact that school was starting this week, and as far as I knew, Drew hadn't moved away in the last twelve hours and would be there laughing about me with his friends around every corner. At least Becca would be there, and I could live out the rest of my high school career quietly, but not totally alone.

While I didn't have the maturity or capacity to understand it at the time, it's clear to me now, that up until that point, I had spent most of my life waiting. Waiting for the day I would become popular. Waiting for the day I would land the perfect guy. Waiting for the day I would evolve into a confident, carefree version of myself. I didn't know who I was, or what I wanted to do with my life. And the things I thought would make me feel complete never did. Like when I made a 4.0 GPA and got invited to join the National Honors Society or that time I was invited to a popular

16

girl's birthday party in the heart of my awkward middle school years. I kept waiting to arrive, and then when I did, it never felt like enough. And I desperately wanted more for my senior year, which made my current situation all the more disappointing.

As I gazed at the water, my fantastical hopes of being on homecoming court with Drew were long gone but were also probably never going to happen anyway, so that couldn't technically be counted as a loss. When you're a teenager, it's hard to imagine a pain worse or more lasting than your own insecurity and embarrassment. It turns out there are so many more terrible things you can feel, but until the real giants appear, the molehills are still mountains. I was trapped in the prison of my limited perspective, and as far as I was concerned, life as I knew it was over.

The feeling of being untethered socially and emotionally overwhelmed me. Panic started to bubble up from my belly to my lungs, and as my breaths shortened, my face began to tingle and my thoughts became a spinning collage of 'I love you's,' cackling teenage boys, vomit, wet sand, and social isolation. Just then, a horsefly buzzed loudly around my head and bit my tender, sunburned neck. It felt like someone lit a match on my skin and I threw myself into the lake.

It was cold and quiet. For a soothing few seconds, I was cocooned in a silent security blanket made of water. I welcomed it. But, since I'm not a mermaid (much to my eternal dismay) my chest began to tighten, and I had to re-enter the world to breathe. I was glad to still be under the cool shade of the end of the dock with the water coming up around my ribcage. Normally, I would be annoyed about getting my hair wet, but after last night, it definitely needed a wash anyway, and the water felt like salve on my angry skin.

After floating on the surface for a few minutes, my mostly empty stomach started to kick up some nausea. So, I turned myself around to climb onto the dock, just as I heard a loud *thump, thump, thump,* and a large shadow arched overhead and dove into the water just beyond where I was standing. A head and shoulders popped out of the water about six feet from me, facing away, toward the opposite shore. For a split second, I was mesmerized by the dark, medium-length hair and the firm, tan shoulders, until it occurred to me who it was.

Shea, obviously.

"Oh my god, Shea, what are you doing here?!" I shouted at the back of his head (because obviously, the world revolved around me, my privacy, and my delicate sensibilities).

He whipped around and caught my eyes, clearly surprised that he wasn't alone, and looking mildly annoyed at my tone. Fair.

"I could ask you the same thing, especially considering that's my dock you're under."

Shea's voice was smooth and soft. I don't know why I expected something more abrasive—maybe because the boys I typically paid attention to were loud and flashy—but it took me by surprise. I honestly couldn't remember the last time I had heard Shea speak. We used to play together when we were little, but at some point, that stopped. I saw Shea around school, but I think I was too busy searching above my social rank to notice anyone who wasn't already shining in the limelight. Seeing him with his shirt off made me temporarily question my sanity. How could I not have noticed how hot my neighbor had gotten?

I suddenly felt foolish and exposed, but not as exposed as I felt when I realized that my thin white t-shirt was sheer when wet, and my nipples were on full display. I immediately sunk my chest down under the water and averted my eyes from Shea. I wanted to bolt, but I couldn't think of how else to get out of this situation without my granny panties staring him in the face.

Clearing my throat, I said, "Can you just leave and come back later instead?"

I didn't really care what Shea thought of me. He wasn't exactly on my social radar, and I was fine with it if, in this moment, he thought I had no charisma or common sense (I oftentimes didn't). But I drew the line at being seen in wet granny panties.

"I just finished cleaning out my car, and I'm trying to get the smell off of me. Just give me a second, your majesty."

I wrinkled my nose at his words. Gross. Shea turned his back to me. *Your majesty...* I rolled my eyes.

He dunked his head under the water once more and then swam past me and pulled himself up effortlessly onto the dock. As he walked up the path that led to his house, all I could think was, *wow, how disgusting* are *you that your car smells so bad you have to jump in a lake to get the stink off?* I didn't have it in me to think of anything nicer than that.

I gave it an extra few minutes once Shea was out of sight before heaving myself clumsily out of the water. I winced as I made my way back to the house, barefoot, dripping, and reluctantly facing the fact that I, too, smelled pretty gross.

Back at the house I took a shower and decided it was time to face my phone. I sat on the end of my bed and squinted my eyes almost all the way closed as if a creepy dead thing from a horror film was about to pop out of the screen and scream at me. Honestly, I probably would have preferred that at this point. Eight missed calls from Becca in the wee hours of the morning. She was obviously worried about me. I shot her a text:

ME: *I'm dying! tell me last night didn't happen!*

Next, I opened Instagram. To my enormous relief, I wasn't tagged in any photos from the night before. As I scrolled through, I saw myself lurking in the background of some photos, but I was so out of focus that I could only tell it was me because of the red hair and glow-in-the-dark complexion.

In the midst of my scrolling, Becca texted back:

BECCA: *I wish.*

I was about to close out of Instagram when I froze. That profile picture with the unforgettable blonde hair, those crystal eyes, and those 'you definitely want me to bite you' teeth would make me stop and click even if I was dead.

Drew posted this morning.

It was a series of photos with the caption, "About last night…"

I scrolled through photos one through nine, carefully inspecting every millimeter of the images for any hint of, I don't know, *anything*…and was relieved to be met with innocuous selfies of Drew with his friends, a photo of him doing a handstand on a dock, and one of him lying by the fire with a dog (*sigh, so cute*). There was also a group photo of several popular kids linking arms and looking like an Abercrombie ad, and I couldn't help but feel jealous of the girl tucked inside Drew's arm, Stella, who was by all accounts perfect and wildly sought after by boys. She even dated

20

Drew in an on-again, off-again sort of way that made him feel even more unattainable.

Why was life just so fucking effortless for some people?

I looked at the image for a while until I finally talked myself back down and decided to be grateful that at least no evidence of my shameful actions had made its way online. Just when I was feeling like I might be able to salvage this year after all, I flipped to the tenth and final photo in the post.

Someone had snapped a photo of Drew…carrying me. He was smiling at the camera while my head was tucked into his chest. This photo existed, and Drew shared it. All I could think in that moment was: *am I in heaven or hell right now?*

Looking back, I can't really explain what it was about Drew that had me so invested in him. I mean, besides the obvious good looks and popularity. Something about him just did it for me, and I suppose, over many years of liking him and being too shy to do anything about it, I was eventually buried under a big pile of insecurity and arbitrary limitations. He was the impossible catch. The perfect guy. Too good for me, but not so much so that I didn't still daydream about the day he would notice me. The night at the beach was embarrassing—but also, Drew had noticed me. And even more shocking than that, he posted a picture of us together.

Had he secretly been thinking about me all this time too? Was this how fate worked? Or…was this all some big joke?

Dear lord, please let it NOT be a joke.

I needed to talk. I needed my friend. I needed to know where I ranked on a scale from 'I'm a complete mockery of a human being and the world, especially Drew, is laughing at my pathetic existence' to 'Drew is obviously in love with me and wants me to have his babies.' I tried to call Becca, but she didn't answer. I left her a voicemail.

"Call me back. I need you. Love you, bye."

THREE

WEDNESDAY WAS THE first day of school, and I was as ready as I was going to be. It was the end of August and still warm outside, but the remnants of my sunburn were still evident, so I opted for a plain, long-sleeve tee tucked into high-waisted jeans. I straightened my long hair and put some light makeup on, which made me feel cute-ish but not attention-seeking. Considering my drunken escapades that had made their way onto Instagram, I definitely didn't want extra attention if I could help it. I never heard back from Becca, but she was terrible at keeping her phone on her, and I knew I'd see her at school, so I'd get her two cents soon enough.

Sure enough, when I walked through the double doors of the high school and into the familiar old buzz of hormones and fear, I saw Becca right away, leaning against her locker in skin-tight black leather pants and a crop top. *Of course.*

She snapped her gum at me and said, "Hey, loser," and gave me a hug.

Becca felt like home, and I loved her, even though—and maybe also partly *because*—she was, and would always be, WAY cooler than me. It feels pretty great when somebody who is too cool to give a shit about anything, gives a shit about you.

The differences between Becca and I were evident from the day we met on the first day of kindergarten at Concord Elementary. Once I was peeled away from my mom, I edged my way into the little classroom desperately searching for the desk with my laminated name tag on it. Relief washed over me as I found my assigned seat. I was happy to moor myself to something solid, so I could get through the day unscathed. I crossed my ankles and tucked my little-white-shoe clad feet beneath my chair and chanced a look around the room, hoping to get my bearings without accidentally making eye contact with anyone who might be mean to me or ask me my name or acknowledge my presence before I was ready.

That's when Becca walked into my life. She strolled into the room with half-brushed hair, eyes like big saucers, and a facial expression that said, 'try me.' Before I could look away, she and I made eye contact, and she smiled at me. She looked softer when she smiled.

I adjusted my braids and sat up straighter in my chair, watching out of the corner of my eye as Becca walked around the room looking for her desk. My eyes widened as I saw her peel her name tag off a desk on the other side of the room and casually exchange it with the name tag on the desk next to me. We were inseparable from then on.

Standing in the high school hallway with Becca on the first day of senior year felt just as natural as it had always been. Even though we were different, we just felt right together. Like the sun and the moon—her being the sun, of course. Becca and I looked at our schedules and were delighted to see we had first period together. We grabbed our stuff and found our seats in math class. It's rare to get a new teacher in a small town, so when a fresh young face walked in, math suddenly became a little more interesting.

Miss Jones was slender and stylish, with kind eyes, and an afro. Her whole vibe said, 'I'm cool, but also don't fuck with me.'

She was a big city girl and *fresh* out of college, which meant she was only a few years older than us. That was both exhilarating and a little unsettling as we realized how close we were to adulthood. I liked Miss Jones. I hoped she would stay.

My next class was English with my old steady, Mr. Gregory. He was the kindest, gentlest, white-haired-est man on the planet. I'm pretty sure he could have retired, like, forty years prior, but I'm selfishly glad he didn't because I was a nerd, and he always had the best book recommendations and the most thoughtful feedback on my essays. English was my sacred place and Mr. Gregory kept it Zen for me. I let out an audible sigh of relief to discover that my divine sanctuary would not be tainted this semester by anyone annoying, distracting, or overwhelmingly interesting and handsome and perfect (namely, Drew).

Mr. Gregory introduced our syllabus, and I was delighted to see we would be covering Shakespeare's *Hamlet* and diving into several short stories that were new to me. I left English feeling calm and capable and thought maybe this year might not just be salvageable, but actually really enjoyable, too.

With a bit more confidence than usual, I went to my next class, but I was still in English mode, Googling the semester's assigned reading materials on my phone as I waited for the science teacher to arrive. This was not an unusual scenario, except for the fact that I was too busy thinking about things that actually mattered to be spinning out about if or when Drew would show up. For the first time that day, I wasn't mulling over a discordant mixture of desperation to see Drew's face and mortification at the mockery I might see in his eyes when he looked at me, Annie, the girl who puked on him while accidentally confessing her love for him the other night.

I glanced up at the black and white analog clock on the wall, completely unprepared to lock eyes with Drew as he walked through the door. I sat frozen in my seat, both unable to look at him and unable to look away. I imagine my facial expression landed somewhere between hopeful and constipated.

I wasn't prepared for this. A familiar heat rose in my cheeks and burned hotter as I became acutely aware of how red my face looked in that moment. A spotlight on my shame. A clear sign to anyone looking that my emotions were out of control. The more I thought about it, the hotter my face got, as if one flame was fanning the other. There was nowhere to hide at this point, except to bury my face in my phone and do my damnedest to blend into my surroundings—a difficult thing to do when everything from your hair to your face is the color of a stop sign.

Even though I was trying to be incognito, I couldn't suppress the habit of a lifetime: I peeked up from my phone to assess the damage just as Drew glanced around the room and then looked back at me and smirked. The adrenaline hit me again. *Hard.* Right in the gut. I looked back down at my phone, scrolling desperately but not seeing anything except Drew's long body walking toward me out of the corner of my eye.

"Hey Annie, is it okay if I sit here?"

I didn't dare look up at his face for fear of literally dying.

"Um, yeah I guess," I mumbled like an anti-social troll. What the fuck was wrong with me?

Drew shifted. "It's just, all the other seats are taken, but if you want to switch seats with someone else or whatever, that's okay."

I pulled myself together. "Oh my god, no, I'm sorry. Yes, please sit down. I was just reading something interesting there, sorry to make it awkward. It's a thing I do sometimes."

Goes without saying, Annie. If he knows anything about you, it's how awkward you are.

Drew gave a half-laugh and sat down with the fluid motion of a Greek god. Energy prickled along my fingertips and spine as the reality of his presence crashed over me. He smelled so freaking good -- like pineapple and spice. If he didn't like me, then this was going to be a long semester. I almost told him he smelled good, but I was worried that my attempts at flirting would come across as psycho. I needed to know where I stood with him first before I scared him away with my confessions.

Mr. Sanders walked in and started handing out the syllabus.

"So, what were you reading?"

"What?"

"Just now, you said you were reading something interesting on your phone. Care to share?"

Holy. Shit.

Was Drew Matthews actually making conversation with me? I seriously considered lying to him about spending time Googling short stories for English class, but my brain was so frazzled that I couldn't come up with anything interesting to say instead. In moments like these, I channeled my inner Becca and hoped for the best.

"Just reading about some new reading assignments," I said, honestly.

"So, basically, reading about reading, then?" He said with a small laugh.

27

I was too busy trying to say normal things that I forgot to not look at his face. It was beaming at me, and I couldn't tell if he was genuinely interested in what I was saying or if he was ready to burst out in laughter at my expense. I assumed the latter, but then I remembered the photo he posted to Instagram of the two of us and thought there was a possibility that things weren't going as badly as I was imagining. I took a deep breath.

"Yeah, I know, probably not very interesting to anyone under age sixty-five, or with a booming social life. I get it." I looked back down at the syllabus that had, at last, landed on my side of our desk, giving me a reason to peel my eyes away from Drew's face before I could see the mocking look he was sure to deliver.

"You seemed like you had a pretty booming social life the other night," Drew said, and I flushed.

"Yeah…about that. I'm so sorry for…you know. And thanks. So embarrassing." I let out a tight laugh, hoping if I forced myself to smile, I might be able to beat my anxiety back down into my stomach where it belonged.

"No need to apologize. We've all been there. You're a pretty sweet drunk," Drew said, and then he smiled the kind of smile at me that only people with genuine confidence are capable of. The kind of people who aren't afraid to say a nice thing or a silly thing or a stupid thing for fear of what people will think. The kind of people who have never entertained the thought of embarrassment or had a reason to. It's the person he was, and the person I wasn't—not yet anyway.

Just then, Mr. Sanders started talking ad nauseum, and I didn't regain full consciousness until the bell rang for lunch. I was relieved that Drew didn't try to start a whispering conversation during the lecture, partly because I didn't have any gum so I couldn't be one hundred percent sure that my breath was fresh and also because the little banter we had shared was as much as I felt I was capable of in one day. Things were going well, and I didn't want to fuck it up by saying the wrong thing or by breathing dragon breath in his face.

"See you tomorrow, Annie," Drew said as he tossed his bag over his shoulder and walked out of the room. I was more confused than ever, but I couldn't help the smile tugging at the corners of my mouth.

FOUR

THE REST OF the day was a blur. We had a school assembly for the last two hours of the school day, and I was relieved to be sitting next to Becca in a dark auditorium where I could hide and ruminate while pretending to listen to the principal speak about our exciting academic potential and her high hopes that this would finally be the year, we would stop defacing the bathroom stalls and starting random fires. *Wishful thinking*, I mused.

The second we got the green light, the whole student body stood up and started shuffling aggressively toward the exits, like people always—for some reason—do. I made it to the parking lot and into my car without incident.

Sometimes my mom had to stay late at school to make paper flowers, paint smiley faces, sing songs, or do whatever it is teachers of small children do. On those days, it was my job to pick up Rosie from daycare. I actually had a purple car seat as a permanent fixture in my car, and if I wasn't from such a small town where everyone knew everyone's business, I would have definitely been marked as the local 'teen mom.'

I drove the three blocks to Rosie's daycare, went through the double doors, and watched her play for a minute before I let her see me. She was playing with an adorable little boy who was handing her toy after toy while she just sat like a queen on a throne. She smiled and played and said, "tank youuu," and made me beam with pride. Then the boy came in for a hug, and she shoved him off so hard he fell on his butt and cried. Maybe teenage girls could learn a thing or two from her. She looked up and saw me and her bright little smile made my heart flutter.

I collected Rosie's rainbow backpack from her cubby and grabbed her hand in mine as we walked to the car.

"How was your day, sweet girl?"

"It was great!" she said, as she tumbled along beside me.

"Mine too." I smiled as I remembered Drew saying he would see me tomorrow. The thought made my heart flutter. I buckled Rosie in her car seat and checked her seatbelt twice just to make sure she was secure. I was in such a good mood that I bent down and gave her five quick kisses on her head before closing the door.

It was a sunny day, and the dark green leaves were shimmering in the wind around us as we sped through neat patches of woods and corn fields and grassy hills. Rosie took off her shoes and tossed them onto the floor because she was two and she could do things like that. I reached back to play with her little toes while she said, "Stop it!" through gurgling giggles, which actually meant 'please don't stop it.' Then, right on cue, she shouted, "It's the big mountain, Annie!!!" as we started the final ascent toward our driveway at the top of a large curving hill.

We passed the McAteer's place right before arriving at ours, and I looked over at the house, telling myself I was glancing just out of habit and casual interest, and not because I was still sort of thinking about Shea's bare shoulders dripping with water as he emerged out of the lake. I noticed his car was there. So, he was home. *Cool. Whatever.*

I turned into my driveway and allowed myself one last glance to the left in case I might be able to catch a totally neutral and indifferent glimpse of Shea before the McAteer house was hidden behind the grove of trees that separated our properties. I saw a flash of white as Shea hurried out the back door, and I slowed my car down a little, wondering why he was in a rush and where he was headed, not that it was any of my business. At all. Suddenly, Shea's dad burst out behind him, grabbed his arm to swing him around and threw a hard punch right into Shea's stomach. Shea doubled over for a moment, but his dad lifted him back upright before reaching his arm back and punching Shea in the face.

A wave of adrenaline flushed through me as my car continued forward and the McAteers disappeared behind the trees. I knew I had witnessed something that I wasn't supposed to see. My mind was blank and staticky with shock. My parents weren't home, and I had Rosie with me, so I'm not exactly proud of my decision-making skills in that moment, but while my brain was screaming 'run away and say nothing' my hands were turning the wheel of the car back down my driveway, onto the main road, and down the McAteer's driveway.

I pulled up in front of the house and honked my horn. *What the fuck are you doing, Annie? That man is going to kill you and bury you in the grove!*

I didn't see anyone, so I honked again. "Beep! Beep!" Rosie squealed from the backseat.

A minute later, John McAteer came walking around from behind the house, red-faced and dripping sweat down the front of his white t-shirt. I noticed the blood on his knuckles that he tried to wipe onto his dirty jeans as he approached my car. Shea was nowhere to be seen. I was a sitting duck with no idea how to explain myself. John tapped on my driver's side window, and I rolled it down a few inches.

32

"Can I help you?" he grumbled. The smell of whiskey and smoke wafted off of him and made my eyes water.

"Sorry to bother you Mr. McAteer...um...my mom sent me over to see if you have any eggs today—she's baking some..."

Before I could finish my on-the-spot lie, John was walking away toward the chicken coop. He tossed a handful of eggs into a too-large cardboard box and handed it through my window.

"Thank you so much, Mr. McAteer, have a great day," I said unusually cheerfully, hoping I wouldn't give away the intense fear that was coursing through my veins. He watched my car as I backed out of his driveway and slipped back across to my own property.

I think that was the first moment in my life that I was brave, or at least, realized that I could be brave. I had never been one to put myself in uncomfortable situations for the sake of someone else. I had always avoided conflict at all costs—even if I was the one who ended up losing unfairly. And here, without even thinking twice, I inserted myself into a scary situation to protect someone I barely knew. I drove away feeling different than I had just minutes before. A new little stream of power surged through me, and I welcomed it alongside the fear, briefly.

Maybe I should have checked on Shea later that afternoon, but I didn't. I probably should have told my parents, too, but I didn't do that either. I had saved the day in a small way, and I decided to leave the rest to someone more qualified than me. Nice people stay out of other people's business, after all—or at least that was the excuse I made for myself at the time.

For a long time, I felt so guilty for not doing more when I had the chance. But I'm trying to forgive myself for that and for so many other things that came after. Adrenaline does crazy things to people. I know that now. For the first time in my life, something truly frightening had scratched the surface of the sterile, little bubble I lived in, and I had taken action. That was enough for me at the time.

Still, I couldn't stop thinking of Shea after that.

FIVE

THE NEXT DAY at school I was so busy thinking about what I had witnessed the day before, and how I had responded, that I forgot to think about Drew. Mostly. I looked for Shea in the morning, and when I saw him standing by his locker looking strong and healthy, I sighed a breath of relief and my fear and concern morphed into a burning curiosity about the goings on next door.

Shea was a little taller and broader than his dad, and he had that vibrant glow of young muscle and energy. I would definitely put my money on him in a fight. Then again, John McAteer had that murderous look about him, and I couldn't stop thinking about how Shea didn't fight back when his dad beat him up. *Why?*

Did this happen a lot? Did he know that I saw it? I mean, he had to know…I literally honked my horn in his driveway as it happened.

Either way, I felt like the best course of action was to say nothing and not make his home life my business, like a polite person would. I didn't have any classes with him so I wouldn't likely see him around anyway unless I was looking for him, which I had already found myself guilty of doing once that morning. Maybe I'd start keeping an eye out on my way home from school, just in case. It was hard to know what the right thing to do was.

So, I decided I would tell Becca what I saw after math class. Shea wasn't my business, but Becca was like an extension of me, and she had a pretty turbulent home life and might have had some perspective that I just didn't. We also needed to debrief about the night at the beach. I wasn't going to be able to think straight until I could dump all my thoughts and feelings on her.

When the bell rang, I started packing up my stuff and Becca said, "Hey, Annie, I'm going to stay after and ask Miss Jones about this homework. I'll catch you later." I sighed and hung my head in dramatic disappointment. She knew I was waiting to talk to her, but maybe after school would be better than between classes anyway. I gave her a reluctant thumbs up, and she rolled her eyes and nudged me in a comforting way.

It's an odd experience the first time you've lived enough life to look back and reflect on the moments that led to where you are now. The tiny clues along the way that determined the course of events, and the things you chose to see, chose not to see, or were too blind to perceive at the time.

I walked out of the math classroom with exactly two things on my mind. My selfish, burning desire to gossip with my friend, and my longing to forget about puking on Drew and win his heart with my charm and wit. I didn't know at the time that I was already making one of the biggest mistakes of my life.

. . .

I took a deep breath before entering the science classroom. I needed to get my shit together if I was going to act like a normal human being around Drew for the next hour. To my surprise, Drew was already inside, sitting in the same seat as the day before, with the seat next to him open. Lots of other seats were vacant, and I was faced with the impossible decision of sitting shamelessly next to Drew or casually picking somewhere else to sit.

After an awkward couple of seconds, Drew looked up at me and smiled like we were friends. Were we friends now? I started to walk in his direction until I noticed his backpack sitting on the chair next to him. He was obviously saving it for someone, or probably just trying to deter *me*, specifically, from sitting there. I shuffled past quickly and sat at the table behind him, just as he lifted his bag off the seat.

"I saved your seat, Annie." He smiled at me again.

I let out an awkward chuckle as my face blossomed with heat. I tried to let my long hair hang down in front of my neck and cheeks so that the whole world couldn't see how red and blotchy Drew's attention had made me. Damn my white, freckly skin. But thank God for long hair that doubles as privacy curtains.

We didn't have time to talk before Mr. Sanders started explaining that the person currently sharing a table with us was going to be our lab partner for the semester.

"Because we will be studying human anatomy and physiology this semester, there will be some touching involved between you and your lab partner. If anyone has any problem touching the person you're sitting next to, say so now, or don't come complain' to me later."

Several students whistled, some groaned, and a couple of students exchanged knowing glances and switched seats. I avoided eye contact with Drew just in case I caught him looking disappointed.

"You good with me touching you, Annie?" Drew said quietly. To my surprise, his tone was humble, and I couldn't detect even a hint of sarcasm.

For someone so beautiful, it was surprising to me that he would even think to ask if I, awkward Annie, would be okay if he, demi-god Drew, touched his body to mine. As far as I was concerned, this situation was a dream come true.

"Yep, all good over here," I said, then realized I should probably be asking the same thing. "Are you good with me touching…you?" I accidentally glanced up at his face as I asked him.

He smirked and looked down at his desk. "Yes, Annie, please touch me anytime you want."

I snorted in surprise at his response to me. There was no denying that Drew was flirting with me. He laughed a little in response and my heart melted into a sparkly little puddle. I raised my eyebrows and looked around, convinced that somebody must be filming this, and that at any moment a clown was going to cartwheel into the room followed by an elephant and George Clooney and any number of things as shocking and unreasonable as Drew verbalizing his desire for me to touch him.

No such anomalies appeared.

Our main task of the day was to take each other's temperature, blood pressure, and pulse, then record it and compare. We had the old-fashioned thermometers that had probably been in the science room since the 1980s, and I was grateful when Mr. Sanders handed out some anti-bacterial wipes, so we didn't have to spit-share with every student that had ever passed through there. I thoroughly wiped down the thermometer and popped it under my tongue, waiting for the little red line to stop and relieve me of the awkward position my mouth was in. Drew pulled it out of my mouth and wrote my temperature on his paper.

"Congratulations! 98.6. Pretty perfect." He smiled. So did I. Then he popped the thermometer right in his mouth without even wiping it down after me.

I didn't want to gross him out, so I didn't mention it. But part of me was starting to think he really wouldn't mind, anyway. And the thought of that gave me butterflies.

I checked his temperature, which was 98.9. Hot and lovely. We each had the blood pressure of champions (or just teenagers) and I found myself relaxing and chatting freely with this guy who I realized I didn't actually know that much about. I was starting to understand why he was so popular. I always chalked it up to his good looks and charm, but he seemed to be more than that. He was funny and kind, and he seemed genuinely interested in what I had to say. He was confident, but he also had a strong sense of humility that was intoxicating. His energy was like a warm light. And I was a big, desperate, lust-drunk moth.

Drew reached out and grabbed my hand and flipped it over, so my wrist was up. He held my hand in his hand as he put his other two fingers along my wrist to feel my pulse. I tried to keep my breathing steady as I watched Drew watch the second hand on the wall clock while he counted my heartbeats. I was grateful to have a naturally slow resting heart rate so that when he counted it, he wouldn't know how elevated it actually was for me. The touch of his skin on my skin was like an electric shock, and I could feel heat building up in parts of my body that I don't care to mention. I was so aware of his skin touching mine, that it was all I could do not to hyperventilate.

The minute was up, and Drew let me go.

"70 beats per minute. Not bad, Annie girl."

39

It was my turn to count his pulse and I wasn't confident that I would be able to focus on it. He handed his wrist over to me, and I realized how warm and golden his skin looked compared to how cold and white mine was. His hand was easily one and a half times the size of mine, with perfectly shaped nails and not a blemish to be seen.

I found his pulse and looked up at the clock. I started counting, knowing that I only needed to count for fifteen seconds, then multiply times four to get his BPM, but since he held me for a minute, I figured I would return the gesture. After I took a mental note of his pulse at 15 seconds, I chanced a glance at Drew's face, which was staring intently at mine. When our eyes met, I gave him a small smile, and his pulse quickened dramatically. I held his wrist, and we looked at each other for another few seconds before I remembered where I was and dropped his hand and noted a made-up number on my paper.

"So, what was my heart rate, then?" he asked.

"73," I lied. "But your pulse was jumping all over the place, so it was hard to get an accurate read," I smirked at him, and he scrunched his nose playfully.

"Well maybe if you didn't look at me with those big blue eyes, my heart wouldn't be trying to fly away with me. Next time, just avert your gaze and I'll think of lasagna, and we won't have this problem."

The bell rang before I could think of a response to that.

"See you tomorrow, Annie girl."

I walked straight out of the classroom, out of the school, and into my car, where I spent my entire lunch hour trying to process what had just happened to me. I couldn't wipe the smile off my face, and I let the butterflies flow freely and happily through my belly.

My overwhelming feelings of insecurity and embarrassment were starting to morph into a new kind of discomfort. I felt a twinge of fear that I might be quickly developing feelings for Drew that were deeper than the surface-level crush on a hottie. My heart was opening in a way I wasn't prepared for. With every minute that passed, I was being sucked tighter into Drew's orbit, which I welcomed eagerly and blindly.

SIX

I WAS STILL giddy when I walked into my last class of the day. It was my first art class of the year, and although I was terrible at art, I did enjoy the whimsical atmosphere, the big windows, and the no homework.

Normally, the room was set up with large wooden tables and metal stools in rows, but I was surprised to see the tables shoved aside and a string of easels arranged in a semicircle around a cylindrical concrete stool in the middle of the room. My curiosity was piqued, and I couldn't help but fear for anyone who was going to have to witness the abomination that was my drawing skills. During my science date with Drew—*was it a date? It was definitely a date*—he told me he had math last period, so at least I didn't have to worry about scaring him off so soon after earning some of his attention. My art was simply not fit for public consumption, but it was between that or Industrial Technology (better known as wood shop), and I felt that my chances of graduating high school with all of my fingers intact were better in art.

Ms. Young walked in—a flurry of frizzy hair and drapey florals and delight. She let us know how grateful she was to be walking alongside us on this sacred journey of life, and she made a point to honor the light in each of us with a quick *namaste*. Over the top? Yes. Did I hate it? Yes. But then again, 'namaste' trumps 'memorize these names and dates' any day of the week. And it's difficult to hate too hard on a little organic, hippie love.

"I had a detailed plan for our curriculum this semester, but last night, at 11:11 p.m., inspiration struck. It occurred to me that we spend so much time attached to our technological devices, that we don't really *see* each other anymore. So, I threw my plan in the trash and let my creative energy flow, and I came up with a new plan. I call it, *SEEN*."

Ms. Young looked at each of us, one at a time, directly in our eyes for an uncomfortable amount of time before proceeding.

"Each week, one of you will take a turn on the stool, posing for the rest of the class to draw. We will be working on all kinds of technical skills like proportion, perspective, shading, etc. etc. etc., but more importantly, we will be working on seeing each other with open minds and open hearts." She clapped her hands together, eagerly, like she'd told us we had just won the lottery. "So, who wants to volunteer to be our first model?"

As much as sitting in front of my peers for them to stare at for hours sounded like my worst nightmare, it…well, yeah, it was just my worst nightmare. Art class was starting to look much less fun. Just as absolutely nobody raised their hand to volunteer, the door opened, and Shea McAteer strode into the class and sat in the empty seat closest to the exit.

"Shea McAteer! So lovely to see you. Namaste. Our first volunteer has arrived." She smiled at him, and he looked around, obviously clueless as to what he had just accidentally signed up for by being late to class.

"Come. Sit here." Ms. Young patted the stool in the center of the room.

I could see Shea's features shift slightly as it occurred to him whom our drawing subject was going to be. He said nothing and took a seat on the stool and pulled out his phone, probably so he could have something else to focus his attention on while he sat in the middle of the room being scrutinized from every angle.

"Ope! No phones in class. We are working on *seeing* each other, and so I'll be asking you all to keep your devices tucked away while we are sharing this space together."

A couple of students groaned and some snickered as Shea handed his phone over to Ms. Young, who had one hand stretched out to take it, and one hand mussing around with Shea's hair to arrange it just so. I could see the moment she noticed the bruise on Shea's left cheekbone—she said nothing, but she flipped a wavy section of hair over to cover some of it.

I felt a pang of guilt as I looked at him sitting there. Maybe for not saying something to someone…maybe for not asking him if he was okay…maybe for seeing the incident in the first place. Did I do the right thing? Should I have done more? Was I even capable of more? Whatever the cause of my complex feelings, I could tell that looking at Shea for the next week was not going to feel easy.

Ms. Young asked Shea to pick a person to "connect with" as he sat there being eyeballed by the class, clearly with the intent of breaking down our collective emotional barriers or deep-seated generational traumas or some other such nonsense.

Turns out, none of those things are nonsense, but 17-year-old me hadn't lived enough to know that yet.

Shea scanned the room, making brief eye contact with everyone, and blinking right past where I was sitting.

Did he see me? Did he avoid me on purpose? Am I an obsessive lunatic for even noticing the blink?

Shea settled for staring right out the window just behind me, his eyes locked with no one's in particular, in favor of the treetops swaying outside.

"Have you locked your gaze on someone, Shea?" Ms. Young pressed.

"I'm connecting with myself," Shea stated matter-of-factly, with not a hint of sarcasm in his voice.

"Oh, I *love* that! Connecting with our authentic selves is perhaps the most important of all. Points to you for pushing creative boundaries."

The boy next to me snorted as he suppressed a laugh. I had to admit I was a little impressed at how effortlessly Shea had beaten Ms. Young at her own game of arbitrary mental gymnastics. In mere seconds he had her convinced that he was really going to be spending the week staring out the window and 'connecting with himself' and not daydreaming about video games and pizza, or whatever it is reclusive teenage boys are into.

I realized how strange it was that I didn't know more about Shea. For as small of a town as we shared, and for as close as we lived to each other (relatively speaking), I rarely ever saw him. We were both born and raised in our adjacent houses, and when we were little, we used to find each other and play together in the fields and trees between our two properties. When I really thought hard about it, I could remember Shea's brown eyes and rosy cheeks and blue knit hat that he wore when we built snow forts together. I could also remember the shape of his dirty, tanned hands as he cradled a frog in them that he had found in the creek behind his house. I remembered how he was so excited to show me and how I screamed and ran away from him.

45

But when Shea's mom died, he stopped coming out to play, and I was too shy to go over there and knock on his door. I wasn't brave enough to ask for friendship, and I certainly wasn't brave enough to speak to someone who was sad. Time passed and we grew up and forgot about each other. And it seemed like Shea forgot about the world too. As far as I knew, we all shared the same acquaintances, but Shea didn't have any real friends. He spent most of his time with his dad, who was never very friendly, and who I could now see was even worse than I thought.

I brought my thoughts back to the present moment and decided not to dwell on questions I would probably never have answers to. I would process my thoughts later in my journal, at my desk, in the solitude of my room. Because what else could I really do?

I looked at the paper in front of me with full confidence that I was going to completely strip it of its dignity as soon as my pencil touched it.

Heads are circles, right? I'll just start with a circle right here...and...oh my god how have I already fucked this up?

Ms. Young walked around the room offering pointers. When I could feel her hovering behind me, I looked up at her with an apology on my face.

"How's it going over here, Annie?" she asked sweetly.

"Umm...as you can see by my...can you call this a circle? Umm...I'm really not an artist, Ms. Young." I let out the awkward chuckle that people release when they are equal parts embarrassed and resigned to their own shortcomings. You know the one.

"Pish posh. Art is an expression of your soul! You can't do it wrong. That being said...it helps if you actually *look* at your subject."

I was caught off guard, realizing that I hadn't actually looked at Shea the whole time I had been faffing about trying to draw a person on my paper and dredging up fragments of memories from a far-gone place in time.

"Look at Shea as if he were made of various shapes. You might say his head is an oval. Then observe how that oval shape looks in relation to the triangle of his torso. Sketch out the shapes as you see them, and as they relate to one another, and from there, a human figure will emerge on your page."

I looked up at Shea, trying to visualize him objectively. I couldn't deny the triangle torso. His shoulders were broad compared to his waist, but he was leaning forward with his feet on a smaller stool and his elbows were on his knees with his hands resting one on top of the other, which made him look casual and effortless. I lifted my eyes up to his face, which was still looking out the window behind me, and I noticed the squareness of his jaw and how it tapered ever so slightly to a defined chin that had a little dip right in the middle of it. Shea's eyes were warm, dark brown with dark lashes that girls would murder their besties to have, and his eyebrows were straight and slightly furrowed. He didn't look mean, but he didn't exactly scream 'come talk to me' either.

My eyes fell on his cheek where an angry red bruise was peeking out behind his hair. I couldn't help but wonder what his ribs looked like. You know, since he got beat up, and definitely not because I was finding Shea attractive. I imagined Drew sitting up there next to Shea, and how different they were, like night and day,

47

but both really freaking hot. Drew definitely took the cake in the looks department, though. *Obviously. Right?*

The bell rang, and my paper was blank since I had erased my first sorry attempt at a drawing. We started shuffling toward the exit, and I heard Ms. Young ask Shea to stay back for a minute. I didn't glance back, but I had a feeling I knew what she was going to ask about. I let myself get caught in the swarm of students who ushered me out the door.

SEVEN

I WAS RELIEVED to see Becca leaning up against my locker, waiting for me so we could walk out of school together. Today she was in a mini skirt and a white tank top, and I chuckled to myself as I watched her scowl at a junior boy who ogled her as he passed by. When her eyes landed on me, she gave me a half smile, and it warmed my heart to be in the comforting space of my person again. We hadn't really had a chance to connect since we spent the day together at the beach, and I felt like if I didn't offload all my news on her immediately, I would burst into flames.

I nudged her out of the way of my locker, and she gave me an exaggerated eye roll like I was rudely interrupting her 'looking cool sesh.' Technically, I was, always, but she would never have actually believed that herself, even though I reminded her of our differences all the time.

She shoved me back, opened my locker, grabbed my backpack, and handed it to me with a wink. I'm pretty sure an unsuspecting nerd somewhere behind me actually fainted when he saw Becca's wink, but that was pretty standard in those days.

"You have no idea how glad I am to see you. I have so much to tell you it's insane. You will NOT guess who was blatantly flirting with me today. Like, prepare to freak out." I started dumping on Becca immediately, but before I could continue, she held up a finger to silence me.

"Okay. I can't wait to hear. But I also know that we will be standing here for the next seven hours if you start talking before we actually make a move in any direction. So, before you keep going, let's hop in your car—I want to stop by the sports shop."

"Why on earth do you want to go to the sports shop?" I was stopped short by her casual suggestion of going to a place that was decidedly not fun to hang out in. The sports shop smelled like gunpowder and fish. I waited for her to explain herself.

"Do you think Ricky will give me a job there if I ask nicely?" My dad's name was Eric Paulson, and normal people called him Eric or Mr. Paulson, but Becca had been calling him Ricky since she was five. My dad started calling her Becky in return, which should have annoyed her but didn't. It was just one of those things.

Becca gave me an overly sweet smile, which made me blink in confusion. She hadn't mentioned wanting a job before today, but I was happy to support her. It was just...the sports shop? Really? I knew my dad needed some extra help because he had been asking me to work there some days after school, but honestly, the stale smell of minnows, the guns, and the hunting and fishing gear... just wasn't for me. And I didn't think it was really for Becca either. But far be it for me to tell her what to like.

"I mean, yeah, my dad loves you and I know he needs help. We can go ask him and see if he thinks you can hack it." I gave her a teasing pat on the back, and she rolled her eyes at me and smiled as we walked side by side out to my car.

Once we were safely on our way in the direction of the sports shop, Becca gave me the green light to start talking. I told her about Drew, and his perfect hands, and his comment about my eyes, and his heartbeat, and how nice he was.

I could hear the elevated pitch of my voice and my quick breathing as I dumped all my excited energy out on my friend. As I spoke, Becca looked out her window and said nothing, but I wasn't really making space for comment, so I appreciated her giving me ample freedom to vent. We pulled up outside the sports shop, and she opened the door and got out of the car before I had time to mention the Shea thing. And I realized that I was okay with keeping it my secret for now. He wasn't my business anyway, and despite my usual inclination to gossip with Becca, I didn't feel the desire to gossip about Shea burning as hot as I had the day before. I let it go.

"Becky! To what do I owe the pleasure?" Dad shouted from behind the circular counter in the center of the shop.

"Hi to you too, Dad," I said in a mock-offended voice. He smiled at me and gave me a wink that said, 'you know you're always my number one,' and I got that comforting feeling you get when you know how much you're loved.

"I was just wondering if you could use any help around the shop. I could use some money, and you know how passionate I am about hunting, fishing, and the outdoors in general." Becca smiled at my dad, laying her charm on thick.

I was still really confused by this request and her adamance about my dad's shop, but Becca was a complicated person, and I was in the habit of taking her however she came.

"I mean, I'd be happy to have you, Beck, but are you sure you wouldn't rather get a job at the coffee shop or the clothing store or literally anywhere other than here?" Dad gestured to the fish tanks and the boot rack and looked back at Becca like she clearly hadn't thought her life choices through very hard.

Becca walked over to the open tank of minnows in the back, grabbed a plastic bag, dunked it in the water filling it with the tiny fish and tying it off before plopping it down on the counter right in front of my dad.

"Can I have the job or not, Ricky?" Becca tilted her head to the side as she asked. She was getting fiery now. People had a hard time saying no to Becca when she really wanted something, and as a diehard people pleaser, it was a curious delight to watch.

"You can start tomorrow after school." My dad let out a light laugh like he couldn't really believe this was how things were panning out, and he grabbed a green fishing shirt from the rack and tossed it over to Becca. She snatched the hideous shirt out of the air, and I couldn't help but notice how the green matched her eyes perfectly.

Of *course,* Becca would be able to make even a boxy fishing shirt look amazing. If I hadn't already loved her so much, I would have hated her. Then again, a little feeling was blossoming inside me that maybe I wasn't as plain and unappealing as I had always imagined myself to be. Maybe I hadn't been giving myself enough credit. After all, Drew Matthews seemed to think I was pretty interesting. The most popular guy in school basically told me I made his heart flutter. I didn't plan to model boxy fishing shirts anytime soon, but I was starting to think I was one step closer to becoming the person I had always dreamed of being.

EIGHT

FRIDAY WAS YET another delightful science class with Drew, and I was starting to gain confidence in my standing with him. I half-wondered if maybe he was just flirty all the time with any girl, but even if that were the case, I wasn't about to burst my own bubble so soon after it was inflated. Every once in a while, he would give me a casual nudge or write a funny note to me while the teacher was talking, and every time he engaged, my insides lit up, and I felt like I was floating.

As we were getting up to leave class, Drew gently elbowed my shoulder (an action that a confident person like Drew does on a whim, and I would have had to mentally weigh the pros and cons of doing first).

"You're a lot cooler than I thought you were," he said, and my heart lifted and sank in the space of a millisecond. "I mean...not that I didn't think you were cool before. You're just really fun to talk to, and I guess I always thought you were more shy or something."

I actually wasn't especially shy—maybe just not super confident? But I did tend to be hyper-self-aware when Drew was nearby, which meant I was usually stiff and quiet around him. No wonder he thought I was uncool.

"Thanks?" I said and shrugged. I'm still not sure what the appropriate response is when someone is surprised you aren't as shy or bitchy or weird as they expected.

Drew slapped his forehead with his hand. "I'm sorry, I say stupid things sometimes. I'll try again. You're cool, Annie. See you

53

next week." His humility was so cute. I couldn't believe that he could have possibly been embarrassed. I was the one who did embarrassing things, not him. I smiled.

"See you next week, Drew. You're cool too." I felt calm and alight, proud of how cool I played that conversation, and feeling like my dreams had a real chance at coming true. Plus, it was nice to know that Drew might actually be as human as me.

. . .

Later that day, in art, Shea showed up with his hair tied up in a man bun. I hadn't really spent any length of time contemplating man buns before I saw one on Shea, but I had to admit it was hot, which was confusing because he wasn't supposed to be the object of my desires. Drew was. Every moment I spent with him further confirmed it. Shea just made me curious, like a red balloon floating in the sky. Where did it come from? How long has it been there? Why is it so pretty? Can I touch it?

Apparently, though, it's possible to think two guys are attractive at the same time. With his hair back away from his face, I could see Shea's angular cheekbones and strong neck muscles, which made me wonder why I hadn't noticed him before. And why every other girl in school hadn't seemed to notice him, either. Maybe I was missing something. Or maybe Shea liked being invisible—it definitely seemed that way. He wasn't involved in any sports or activities, and I couldn't really put my finger on who his friends were, if he had any at all.

He sat still in his pose, and I peeked at him dutifully. At the end of class, I still hadn't drawn anything decipherable, but I was definitely developing a strong mental image of Shea. No harm in that, right?

...

The weekend passed by quietly, which was good because I needed some space to process my week. I found that I was more aware than ever of how close Shea's house was to mine, and therefore, how close Shea was to me. It's not like we were going to hang out or anything, but I did find myself wandering around near the property line and stopping down by the lake just in case we might accidentally cross paths. We didn't, because Shea obviously wasn't a psycho stalker like me, and definitely not as desperate or pathetic, but I wasn't going to let myself fall too far down that self-deprecating rabbit hole. I just set the thoughts aside and told myself a comforting story about how I just needed extra fresh air.

It was the precipice between summer and fall, and Sunday afternoon was fresh and perfect. The mosquitoes were mostly gone, and the horseflies had disappeared too, back to whatever hell hole they burst forth from every June. I grabbed a quilt from our overflowing basket of blankets and walked far enough away from my house to be alone. I spread my blanket out across the crisping grass so I could lie down and enjoy reading outside in the sun, not knowing whether or not I would have another opportunity to do so for the next seven to nine months. Winter always seemed to come too soon and stay for too long.

I lay on my back and lifted my shirt up so that I could soak up as much precious vitamin D through the eager white flesh of my stomach as I could. I held my book up above my head, using it to block the sun, and getting distracted when my arms started to tingle and ache. I draped the open book over my face and dropped my arms to the side in defeat. I let myself drift off.

"How did your baking turn out?" Shea's voice wafted over to me from some unknown distance away. I tugged my shirt back down and flipped onto my stomach, the book sliding off my face into a crestfallen pile next to me. I scanned the horizon and saw Shea about twenty feet away where his property merged with mine. He was standing with his hands in his pockets and his hair tossed to the side. I had the creeping feeling that he could see right through me. After all, I had parked myself particularly close to his yard. Was I hoping he would see me? Probably secretly subconsciously, yes.

"What baking?" I asked because I was unprepared for this conversation and also stupid.

"I don't know...the baking you needed so many eggs for," Shea said casually.

So, he *did* see me that day. Did he know that I saw what happened to him? If he did, he wasn't giving it away.

"Yes! *Yes.* Turned out great. Thank you. We made brownies. And a cake. And a pie. Just a lot of baking we did." I blabbered on like an idiot, but Shea let it slide.

"Glad to hear it," he said and flashed a smirk before walking back up toward his house, leaving me to drive myself crazy with confusing feelings, questions, and physical sensations.

I opened Instagram and searched for Drew's page. No new posts, but I scrolled through his photos anyway, remembering how good his attention made me feel. In a surge of recklessness, I typed him a message and clicked send.

ME: *Hey* :)

He viewed the message almost immediately.

DREW: *Hey* ;)

My heart fluttered as I let Shea fade away and put Drew back in his rightful place in the forefront of my mind.

...

The next week, school was humming. Student Council had decorated for homecoming, which was still a few weeks away, but it was kind of a big deal in our town, and we wasted no time preparing for it. There would be an early afternoon football game in which Drew would be starring, and after the game, there would be a dance at the high school gym. In a small town where not a lot happens, these events are everything. The sight of our black and gold school colors draped through the halls made me feel a pure and innocent sort of excitement, and also a wave of nostalgia knowing that this would be my last homecoming as a student at Concord High School.

I wasn't sure if anyone would ask me to the dance—I obviously hoped that Drew would—but even if he didn't, I was still planning to go with Becca and any of our other friends that didn't get dates. I knew Becca would get several offers, and I also knew she would shut them all down unless one of them was a hot girl, but as far as I knew at the time, Becca was the only 'out' lesbian within a forty-mile radius.

I had just sat down to lunch in the cafeteria after a dull science class (Drew wasn't there, so obviously there was no reason to be interested). However, I was still riding a high from a riveting English class that morning with my beloved, Mr. Gregory.

We had read "The Yellow Wallpaper" and discussed it at length, and I couldn't help but walk away feeling extra motivated to shout, "fuck the patriarchy!" which I definitely wasn't going to do, but I was pumped up all the same. I was still basking in the feminist burn when, out of nowhere, "Marry You" by Bruno Mars started playing over the intercom.

Twelve senior football players emerged, each in a tux, dancing to the music in a choreographed routine. Drew was right in the middle, and when I made eye contact with him, he smiled and winked at me. *What the actual fuck?!* Was Drew about to ask me to the homecoming dance with this grand, teen-movie-scene gesture?

I turned beet red as anxiety and anticipation ripped through me. I was literally seeing stars watching Drew dance with his teammates, and I couldn't believe that I was about to experience the kind of thing you tell your future grandchildren about.

All at once, the group of dancing football players surrounded the long table where all the cheerleaders and not-otherwise-specified hot girls were sitting together smiling and clapping. As the song came to a close, each player knelt down and grabbed the hand of one of the girls, held out a flower, and said, "Will you be my date to homecoming?"

There were flashes and applause as the photographer from the local paper, who had obviously been invited to document this wholesome event, snapped some photos. Phones were lifted in the air recording the whole thing for social media, probably so that my soul could be crushed over and over again on the internet.

As I watched Drew kneeling there in front of Stella, the prettiest, blondest, white-toothiest cheerleader of them all, my heart dropped down as far as it could go without me actually dying.

Death might have been preferable, though. I felt so stupid and so embarrassed for even thinking that Drew might be into me, let alone ask me to be his homecoming date. I felt tears welling up in my eyes, but I refused to sit there and cry in front of everyone because that would be a whole other level of shame and embarrassment. I left my tray where it was and headed out to my car, but this time, instead of butterflies, I felt nothing but shame and shallow breathing.

Becca came out to my car a few minutes later and knocked on my window. I leaned over and unlocked her door, and she sat down next to me in the passenger's seat. She didn't say anything, but she didn't need to. I let myself cry and be silently comforted by my best friend.

"Drew isn't worth your tears. You are a queen, and he's just another guy who isn't deserving of you." I cried harder. Becca was patient. "Should we skip the rest of the day and go eat ice cream until our faces freeze off? We've never let heartbreak get in the way of dessert before, and I don't think we should start now." Becca always knew how to cheer me up, no matter how far I fell.

I wiped my nose on my sleeve because I was a gross person, and I was elbow deep in self-pity anyway.

"Yes, please."

We went to Dairy Queen, ordered two extra-large chocolate shakes, and drank them until my tears of shame and disappointment became tears of laughter.

NINE

BECCA HAD MADE me feel better, but I still couldn't sleep that night. I was consumed by thoughts of how stupid I had been. I replayed the videos of the homecoming proposals on social media over and over again just to punish myself. I kept my eyes glued on Drew as he knelt down in front of Stella on repeat. Eventually, my phone died, which was definitely for the best, except then I was plunged into the unforgiving darkness and silence of my room. My thoughts had nowhere to go but around and around in my head.

I remembered a time when I was in first grade. In the mornings before school started, all the students would gather together in the gym before being herded off to our respective classrooms. This was a particularly nerve-wracking time of day for me, as there were no assigned seats, and any time Becca wasn't there, I would be forced to join another group or risk sitting alone, which was my worst nightmare at that age.

One morning, I came to school with one of my favorite pencils taped to a note that said, "I like you. Do you like me too?" I had made it for Drew in my bedroom the night before, but there was no way I would have been brave enough to actually give it to him. I watched him as he sat goofing off with his group of friends against a far wall, and I showed Becca my note. Before I could protest, she slid it across the floor to Drew.

My body ached with panic and hope that maybe he would tell me he liked me too. I watched as he read the note, and then snapped the pencil in half and laughed with his friends. Knowing what I know now, I can recognize that we were both so little, and he was probably embarrassed too. But I couldn't help but remember how that moment made me feel and start to feel the exact same way all over again: like an embarrassed little kid. Like a loser. Like someone who was never quite as pretty or as good or as likable as other people. Always the sidekick, never the leading lady. A person with an identity built around fear, insecurity, and self-limiting beliefs. I was a bookworm, average in looks and personality, and destined to do more dreaming than living—avoiding rejection at all costs.

Getting my hopes up about Drew only to watch them crumble around me was more than my delicate heart could take.

The anxiety overwhelmed me, and I decided to go outside, to be anywhere but lying down in bed with my thoughts. I stepped out onto the front porch, and the fresh air on my face made me feel slightly more grounded. The stars were out, and normally they were a comforting sight, but that night they just reminded me of how small and insignificant I was.

I listened to the night noise—crickets chirping loudly and the occasional frog groaning along, but I quickly noticed that there was another sound floating around behind all of that. Someone was playing music. It was past midnight at this point, but my curiosity got the best of me, and I tiptoed toward the sound, already knowing who it must be coming from. If I could just get to the grove of trees, I could peek around and see what Shea was doing up so late without him noticing me.

I came up behind the thick trunk of a giant oak tree at the edge of the grove on Shea's side. I pressed my hands hard into the bark so it hurt a little bit, and then did the same with my forehead, like if I pushed hard enough, I would just become part of the tree, and I could be done feeling feelings altogether. I was close enough to hear the music clearly now. It sounded like acoustic guitar and a soft tenor humming along to a sleepy tune. The sound was soothing, and I let it wash over me for a minute before building up the courage to peek around the tree to watch Shea.

My heart pounded as I made my move and inched my head around to look. The garage door was open and there was a small lantern glowing on the ground inside. I couldn't see Shea, but I could tell by the shadow falling on the floor that he was sitting just inside the open garage door. I chanced a step to the next tree along, and took one more peek around, this time seeing the musician's face. It wasn't Shea. It was his dad, John.

I quickly snapped back behind the safety of the tree and leaned my back against its trunk in shock. There was a stark difference between the man I had seen wiping his son's blood off his knuckles the other day and the one I now heard singing a lonesome, late-night lullaby in his garage. It just didn't compute.

"Come on Dad, it's time for you to get to bed." Shea's voice carried the words over to me on the breeze. The music trailed off, and I heard some gentle shuffling but didn't dare look back in case the McAteers saw me spying on them. I waited a few minutes before abandoning my post, and when I felt safe to go, I scampered back to my house. I climbed into my bed and lay there with my eyes wide open, relieved to have something to contemplate other than my own pathetic heartbreak.

. . .

I wasn't exactly sure how science class was going to go after I completely misread the signals, I thought I had been getting from Drew, but I was determined to keep my guard up. I also needed to avoid any sudden movements that might lead to blushing or crying or some combination of both. Drew obviously wasn't interested in me, and I would not be making the mistake of thinking otherwise again. And I certainly wouldn't be indulging in my Drew fantasy, which was clearly straight out of la-la-land. Once was enough for that particular brand of bullshit.

I was relieved to arrive first to class, so I didn't have to be the one to sit down next to him. I scrolled through my phone, trying to look casual and not like my brain was currently a dumpster fire, which it absolutely was. Drew walked in. He was still chatting with Jordan and Miles, two other guys from his team until he finally broke away from them and came to sit down at our desk.

"Hey Annie girl, how was your weekend? Sorry, I missed you yesterday—the team had a thing going on…"

Why was he calling me 'Annie girl' like I was someone significant when clearly I wasn't? The mixed messages were killing me. Like, I could totally buy being in the friend zone, but if that were the case, why would he say my eyes made his heart flutter? *Who the hell talks like that if they're not interested in you?*

"Yeah, I saw you guys in the auditorium. Those were some…dance moves, for sure." I mumbled but tried to hide my disappointment with an unnatural little uptick in my tone of voice at the end of the sentence.

"Yeah, you've definitely got me beat in the dance moves department." Drew smiled, and I was confused yet again. He was clearly referring to the night at the beach, but it didn't feel like he was making fun of me, even though I would have assumed that would have been the case considering that my inebriated dancing led directly to falling and vomiting and shame. *Ugh.*

63

Before I could say anything, Drew slid a note across the table to me.

"Please don't open this right now because, honestly, I'm nervous as hell and feel pretty stupid right now. Just…read this later, okay?" Drew's baby blues were looking into mine earnestly.

I simply nodded because if anyone was the fool it was me, and I was afraid that whatever was in that note was something that was going to mislead and hurt me. I had to admit, though, that this day had taken a turn that I hadn't expected, and my curiosity was piqued. After all, I couldn't exactly fall lower than I had the day before, crying into a milkshake over an Adonis I barely knew not asking me to homecoming like I always dreamed he would. I pocketed the note and decided to read it when I got home. Or maybe when I got in my car. Or maybe sooner. But definitely not right after class. I would not be playing the desperate loser again.

I walked out of science class and headed straight to the bathroom to read the note. Apparently, I was kidding myself about playing it cool. Oh well.

Annie,

Sorry for the cryptic note. I've been trying to think of what to say since last week, and I keep fucking it up. So here goes.
I know we don't know each other like at all. I'm sure you think I'm just a stupid jock, and maybe that's true.

BUT…I think you're cute. I have for a while, but we never really crossed paths inside school or out. I guess I sort of live in a bubble. And I think you're smart, and I can't really figure out what's going on in your head, but I'm into it. I wanted to take a chance and ask

64

you to homecoming, but the boys wanted to do the cheerleader thing, and I wasn't sure if it would be weird to ask you or not, so I just didn't. But I did want to.

All that said, maybe I'll see you there? And if you're up for it, maybe I could convince you to dance with me? I'm sure you'll be there with another date, but I'll be keeping an eye out for you and crossing my fingers for a dance with the prettiest girl in Concord.

Drew

I walked into the cafeteria and sat down next to Becca, who was sitting alone, eating nothing, and looking like she couldn't give two shits about anything. *Must be nice.*

I slapped the note down on the table in front of her and stared her down like some kind of possessed freak. She said nothing as she slowly reached for the note, not breaking eye contact with me until it was completely unfolded, at which point she slowly looked down and read it.

"What. The actual. *Fuck*," she said under her breath as she glared down at the paper.

"I know, right? Like here I thought he was some kind of player, and it turns out he's liked me for a while and just didn't know how to say so. Promise me you'll dress frumpy at homecoming, so I don't look like a total dweeb next to you." I babbled on, giddy once again as the truth of the situation washed over me. Becca interrupted me.

"I'm not going to homecoming, Annie."

For a second I thought I was hearing her wrong.

"What do you mean? It's our senior year. *Of course* you're going! You love dancing. And fun. And me. We can pre-game together. You have to go with me!"

I felt a desperate lump enter my throat as she sat there and shook her head. This wasn't like Becca, and I couldn't understand why she would want to ditch me during such a special event that she knew I was looking forward to.

"Annie, I'm sorry, I just don't feel like going. I'm just not into it this year. I want you to go, though! You deserve to have an amazing time. Just maybe not with Drew, because I'm not entirely convinced that he's not a total douche. And a coward. Honestly, you can do better. Do you not remember our ice cream date yesterday? And how sad it was?"

I was totally caught off guard by Becca's decision not to go, and I was a little surprised that she wasn't happier for me about Drew. I mean, yes, Becca was protective of me, and she also spent several hours wiping my tears away the day before over the same guy, but I didn't understand how she couldn't see the great misunderstanding that had occurred and how things were trending now. Something about Becca was off, and a good friend would have asked more questions, but I was selfish, and I didn't.

I decided not to hash things out further, partly because I was irritated that Becca wasn't wholeheartedly team Drew—a fact I simply couldn't wrap my head around—and also because our friends Sydney and Charlotte had just sat down at our table and started chatting away about their homecoming dresses and potential dates.

"I'll probably be flying solo this year, so if one of you wants to be my Princess Charming, then I'm here for it," I said, laughing sarcastically, but really meaning it. I wanted wing women.

Becca stayed quiet as the rest of us clucked on about hairspray and rhinestones like hens in a hen house who were too oblivious to know we were trapped, while a fox was lurking right outside.

TEN

I WAS IN such a daze from my morning that I forgot to pay attention in art class. Almost. I mean, I did notice that our model this week happened to be Stella's best friend Kamila, who just happened to shimmer with silky black hair and lush, natural beauty. I was less concerned with looking at her than I was knowing that Shea would also be studying her. I couldn't help but think that the two of them would make a beautiful pair, and it would probably not take him long to be completely entranced by her. Not that I cared. Except for some reason, I did care. *Am I insane? Probably.*

I glanced over at Shea several times as he worked on his drawing. He was relaxed in his seat, unlike most of the other students who were either stabbing each other with pencils or sweating out a combination of lust and stress as they tried to illustrate the divine creature on the stool. I gave her a nice square head, some extra bushy brows, and some out-of-proportion ears, because, after all, I couldn't help it that I was a terrible artist.

While I worked on my illustration, I let my mind wander. Drew's note, Becca's weird response to the attention he was paying me, and the confusing feelings I was having about the situation with my surprisingly handsome, but mysterious neighbor, were making my head spin. I felt like I was expanding in so many directions. Life was more exciting than it had ever been. And normally more activity would have led to more journaling, but I just found myself tossing and turning instead. I was on a rollercoaster with no brakes, and I hadn't taken the time to fasten my seatbelt.

I couldn't shake the feeling that something was up with Becca. She loved to party. Her decision not to attend homecoming didn't sit right with me. I could forgive her for needing time to warm up to Drew, but I couldn't forgive her for abandoning me on one of the most exciting nights of our life thus far.

I chanced one more glance at Shea and wondered if he was planning to go to homecoming. *Probably not.* It didn't seem like his thing. But Becca...it *was* her thing. I decided to stop by the sports shop after school to see if I could convince her to stop being weird and agree to come with me. The night just wouldn't be as fun without my person.

. . .

I arrived at the shop just a few minutes after Becca got there, but she was already in her workwear and standing behind the counter snapping her gum. She grinned at me, and I galloped over to her in an exaggerated happy run. Seeing her always felt good, even if I had just seen her mere minutes before at school, and even if, for some mysterious reason, she wasn't ready for me to marry Drew like tomorrow.

"Beck! I missed you!" I laughed as she rolled her eyes in mock exasperation.

"Come to smell the fish?" Becca said, and I wrinkled my nose. Despite my rural upbringing and the many hours I had spent in the shop, I never got used to the smell.

"Just wanted to spend time with my one and only," I said, as I leaned up against the counter and batted my eyelashes at her.

I handed Becca the Diet Coke I had picked up from the gas station on my way over. Caffeine was Becca's love language, and I

69

figured I needed all the help I could get if I was going to convince the most stubborn person I knew to change her mind about something.

The little bell above the front door chimed and a few bearded guys walked in, and their booming voices consumed the space. Becca and I rolled our eyes at each other—Becca had a particular hatred for unnecessarily macho men (another reason it was weird that she wanted to work at the sports shop, but I digress). I tapped my foot and waited for them to leave so I could talk to Becca in peace.

The little doorbell chimed again. This time it was someone more interesting -- Shea. I turned around quickly to face Becca so that he couldn't see my face turn red. Becca gave me a look that said, 'I'm definitely going to ask you about this later,' and I just shook my head and took a breath. I thought of Drew, and remembered that Shea wasn't my business, and I felt my face begin to cool.

"Hi," Shea said in a soft voice behind me, "can you guys tell me where to find the rope, please? Also, the duct tape." I turned around to see Shea waiting expectantly and the three other men in the store approaching the counter with an assortment of shotgun shells and Slim Jims. Becca cleared her throat.

"Annie, can you show Shea where to find rope and duct tape, please? I need to take care of these guys."

I nodded, and Shea followed me as I led the way to the items.

"Rope and duct tape? You aren't trying to murder someone, are you?" I blurted out. A stupid thing to say to someone whose dad does the things I saw John McAteer do. *Oh my god. Why, Annie? Why?*

Shea chuckled. "How did you know? I'm actually accepting volunteers to be my victims. You interested?" I looked up at his face and his expression was cheeky and sweet—a look I hadn't seen on him before. My shoulders relaxed at his obvious sarcasm. I forgot to feel like an idiot. I rolled my eyes playfully at Shea and handed him a roll of silver tape.

His fingers brushed mine as he grabbed it and my heart pounded so hard, I was sure he could hear it. I turned on my heel and walked quickly to where the rope was hanging so that he wouldn't notice my blush.

"What's a pretty little thing like you doing working here?" I heard a booming voice coming from the front of the store. I looked between the aisles to see Becca shoving things into bags, clearly trying to finish the bearded men's transactions as quickly as possible. I looked for the rope Shea needed, but I was distracted by the sound of the men laughing and commenting on Becca's hair and her figure. My dad was in the back office, but I wished he was out front. Nobody would talk to Becca like that with my dad around.

I found the rope and grabbed it off the wall, but when I turned around to hand it to Shea, he wasn't there. My eyes trailed over to the group of guys, and there he was, standing a few inches taller than the rest of them, somehow looking stronger and fiercer than he had a second ago when he was bantering with me.

I didn't hear what he said to them, but it was enough for them to take their obtrusive laughter outside. I walked over to the register and set the rope on the counter.

"It's on me," Becca said handing Shea his items. She gave him a half smile, which was more than I had ever seen her give any man, other than my dad.

Shea set forty dollars on the counter and left the store without another word.

The store was quiet again, but after seeing Shea, I forgot to ask Becca anything about herself, or why she didn't want to come to homecoming. Instead, I looked at my phone to see three missed calls and a text from my mom.

MOM: *Rosie's out of pull-ups. Can you grab some on your way home? And pick up some milk too. Please. Thanks.*

I went home having cleared up nothing with Becca. I instead ended up having a warm feeling about Shea after seeing him stand up for her. If my heart hadn't already been tentatively taken by a certain blonde prince, I might have gone for the dark knight instead. But my dreams with Drew were coming true, and I could envision the story of my life unfolding in the way I always dreamed it would—and I was determined to stay the course.

ELEVEN

THE WEEKS LEADING up to homecoming passed smoothly, and I had a chance to thank Drew for his note and get my shit together emotionally. I was grateful to have a prescribed amount of time with him each day so that my residual feelings of shame and disappointment could blow over steadily. Drew was confusing, but he was still a prize I dreamed of winning, and now that I knew there might be something there, I kicked down the walls I had been building around my heart and allowed a connection to build. If I was being totally honest with myself, proving Becca wrong about Drew would feel pretty good, too. I was confident he was *it*.

I left Drew hanging on purpose by not mentioning his proposal of a dance together because I had to leave *some* cards on the table, but obviously dancing with Drew was going to be my main objective for the night. We continued getting to know each other a little more each day, and the tension between us was building steadily. He was a relentless flirt, and I soaked it in like stale bread in water.

I learned that Drew's dad was a lawyer (which I let him think I didn't already know, even though I did), and his mom used to be a model, which didn't surprise me at all. He had an older brother that was 27, so he had been alone at home with his parents for a long time. Since my sister was only two and I had been an only child for most of my life, we actually found a lot of common ground to tread on. Our relationship also started to spread outside of the confines of the science room. We exchanged phone numbers, and it became the norm that we would text throughout the day—mostly just little things and the beginnings of inside jokes—but it still made my heart flutter every time my phone vibrated, and his name popped up on my screen.

Drew and I were steadily becoming something, and I could suddenly see the hazy shape of the future I had always dreamed of emerging. I had no idea at the time how wrong I was, or how much pain I was in for.

But before I knew it, homecoming had arrived, and I was beyond ready to have my moment.

. . .

The space between September and October in Minnesota sets the soul on fire. The brief, shimmering weeks of blue skies, golden leaves, crisp air, and anticipation of things to come used to make me feel more alive than anything else ever had. Being a country girl, I noticed the wild and subtle changes day-to-day and made an extra effort to spend time outside, among the yellowing grasses and the almost too-sweet smell of decaying leaves. The cold breeze would wash the burning summer heat from my skin, and I could finally swim around in my sweaters, drink my chai, light my candles, and bask in any other cozy delights that were available at the local drugstore.

Homecoming day was picturesque and perfect, except for the fact that Becca wouldn't budge on her decision not to participate. She had been busy working lately and seemed to be spending more time doing homework than she ever had before. I missed her.

We won the football game in the afternoon (which I attended with Sydney and Charlotte), after which my dad went to spend the rest of the evening at the local bar with his friends (a tradition), and

I went home to get ready for the dance. My mom and Rosie were there, and I made sure to spend a few minutes smooching Rosie's sweet cheeks before heading up to my room to start my physical transformation, which I hoped would seal the deal with Drew.

I trotted up to my room, trying not to focus on how much I wanted Becca with me, and instead focusing on how excited I was to finally wear the dress I bought last spring at the Mall of America, specifically for this occasion. I normally went for wearing neutral colors because I was painfully aware of the strange copper tone of my hair and how easily it clashed with other colors. But when I saw the silky red dress in the shop window, shining from a true red to some cool, dark undertones, it just sang to me. It was expensive, which is why I was shocked when my mom told me to try it on and didn't even question the price. It fit my delicate frame perfectly.

I combed and sectioned my hair and put some big, loose curls through it, then gave it a light spray and shook it out with my fingers. Some girls went all-out and got updos at the salon, but I actually liked the look and feel of my long hair flowing down my back. The dry autumn air meant I didn't have to deal with frizz, so I was good to go after my ten-minute touch up. I tried to keep my makeup fresh because my light skin meant that heavy makeup didn't really suit me. I applied a little extra mascara and topped off my look with bright red lips to match my dress.

I slipped on my dress and heels and stood in front of my full-length mirror. I felt pretty. The sun was just starting to set, and it was filtering through the window behind me and casting a golden glow around me. For the first time, maybe ever, I felt worthy of being admired. My full lips popped with color, and my hair flowed in honeyed waves around my face. I didn't recognize the person in

75

the mirror. She was bold and fearless. She was the main character in her own life. I wanted to get to know her better. My stomach took a happy tumble when I imagined walking into the dance and being seen by Drew. I had a feeling that this night might be the night that everything changed. And I was right, but not in the way I expected.

My mom was putting Rosie to sleep in her room, and I slipped quietly past her door so I wouldn't wake her up. Anyone with kids in their lives knows the sanctity of bedtime and would rather take their chances jumping off a cliff than wake a sleeping baby. I headed out to my car, and sat down slowly and carefully, lest I rip a hole in my dress and ruin my senior homecoming before it even began. I turned the ignition and…nothing.

My car was old and bottom-of-the-range, but she was trusty, and I had literally never had a problem with her. I turned the ignition again, and nothing. Again. *Well, shit.* I went inside just as my mom was coming out of Rosie's room.

"Oh, honey, you look so beautiful," she cooed, and I could see a twinkle of tears in her eyes. She reached for her phone to snap a photo of me, but I interrupted her.

"Thank you, Mom. And like, not to ruin your moment or anything, but my car won't start. Can I take yours?"

She looked a little miffed that I was rushing this special exchange, but she didn't fight me on it.

"Dad has my car at the bar right now, so just his truck is here."

My dad's truck was a stick shift, which I didn't know how to drive, so that wasn't helpful at all. I was trying to stay calm, but I was starting to feel the familiar sense of panic that had seemed to be accompanying me more days than not lately. This was not how things were supposed to go. The sun was going down and I was going to be late, or maybe not get there at all if I couldn't get ahold of anyone to drive all the way out here and pick me up. I called Becca. No answer. I called Sydney and Charlotte. Nothing. I'm sure they were busy getting ready, or maybe they were already there dancing and having the time of their lives. *Mother-FUCKER!*

My mom was calm because any rational person could see that this was a molehill and not a mountain of a problem. But I was young and not yet capable of rational thought, so I started to panic. I wasn't going to make it to homecoming. I wasn't going to dance with Drew. I was going to miss my moment. Mom could see me spiraling, but she knew better than to tell me to calm down. Telling someone to calm down never produces the desired results. She gave me a reasonable solution, instead.

"Why don't you go see if Shea is home and maybe he can drive you? Here." She started rummaging around in her purse, coming out with a twenty-dollar bill. "You can give him this."

I really didn't want to go begging Shea for a ride, because we were definitely more acquaintances than friends, and I wasn't prepared to spend fifteen to twenty minutes alone in an enclosed space with him, especially considering all the things I didn't know if he knew that I knew about his home life. Plus, my physical attraction to Shea was undeniable at this point, and tonight was supposed to be all about my moment with Drew. I was imagining a gross car and awkward conversation and severe avoidance of certain topics like baking and abuse and spying on your neighbors in the middle of the night. And probably some low-key sexual tension that I didn't want to acknowledge—you know, because of Drew. It wasn't ideal.

I rolled my eyes and stuck out my hand to accept the twenty. I wasn't going to let this little hiccup stop me from a magical evening. I started to trade my heels for some sandals, but before I could, I heard my mom clear her throat. I looked up at her and saw her holding her phone up requesting another photo before I left. She still had the twinkle in her eye of a proud mom who was saying goodbye to her baby and hello to a young woman. Her look softened me. It made me slow down. I posed for a photo on our front patio and then turned the phone around to take a selfie with my mom. We were starting to look so much alike. It made me smile.

Mom waved me goodbye as I walked across the field and through the trees and I enjoyed a sentimental minute. But as I approached the McAteer house, it occurred to me that John might answer the door, and a shiver went up my spine. I still didn't know what to make of him. All I knew was what I had seen, and that was pretty confusing. And scary. I stepped up onto their porch, knocked three times, and took a few steps back, just in case a dragon emerged.

Thirty seconds or so passed, and I thought no one was coming to the door, so I turned around and started walking back to my house, where I planned to shamefully beg my mom to wake up her sleeping two-year-old and drive me to the dance.

"Annie?" I turned to see Shea walking around the side of his house. He was in jeans and a white t-shirt and striding toward me slowly. *How does he always manage to look so effortless and handsome?*

I realized while I was eyeing him up that he was waiting for me to speak and probably also explain why I was standing in his yard in an evening gown.

"Hi, Shea...I'm so sorry to bother you, I don't know if you knew that it was homecoming tonight, and I was about to go to the dance by myself—I mean, not by myself totally, I'm going to meet my friends there, but like I was going to drive myself, except my car won't start, which is totally weird because my car ALWAYS starts, except for apparently not when I'm trying to go somewhere I really need, I mean *want* to go."

While I was blabbering on and not actually getting to the point, Shea continued walking toward me until he was standing just a few feet away from me.

"Would you like a ride?" he asked with his eyebrows raised, and a hint of a smirk on his lips. He was taller than I had remembered.

"Yes, please." I smiled back. This was easier than I thought it was going to be.

"Just a sec, I'll go grab my keys." Shea strode over to his front door and came out a minute later. There was something else in his hand, and just before he opened the car door for me, he opened his palm to reveal a white orchid blossom. He grabbed my wrist and attached the blossom to it with a piece of white string, which he tied off in a neat bow.

"There," he said, matter-of-factly. "You're ready."

Shea opened the door for me, and I climbed into the car, which was spotless, by the way. I took a deep breath as he walked around the front of the car and I tried to wrap my head around the fact that Shea kept orchids in his house, and that he just casually tied one around my wrist like that was a thing boys did even when their mom wasn't there choreographing the whole thing. It might have been the sweetest gesture anyone had ever bestowed on me. I felt warm inside, but I wasn't blushing. I just felt good.

Shea got in the car and started it, and I realized I had never actually been this close to him before, except for that time in the sports shop when everything smelled like minnows. Shea smelled like pine trees and earth, and his car smelled clean—I could tell it was meticulously maintained.

"Thanks so much for doing this, Shea, I really appreciate it. I hope I'm not interrupting something super important right now. I swear my car *always* starts. I don't know what happened."

"That's the thing about cars, they always start until that one time they don't." He smirked, and so did I because he was right.

"So…your car is actually really clean," I said.

"Actually?" He looked over at me like he was offended that I would assume otherwise.

"I mean, it's just that that one day down at the dock, you said you were jumping in the lake—and I quote—'to get the smell off' after cleaning your car, so I just imagined something a little bit dirtier than this, that's all." I realized I was probably digging myself a hole here, but this car ride was going to last a maximum of fifteen minutes, and as long as he dropped me off within a few miles of the high school, I would get myself there regardless.

Shea didn't say anything, but he had a huge smile on his face, and I couldn't help but take the bait.

"What are you smiling about?"

"Oh nothing…just remembering the last time you were in my car," he said, casually.

I frowned, confused. "I think you're confused, Shea, I think I would remember if I had been in your car before."

"Would you?" He looked over at me with his eyebrows raised.

"Definitely," I said, staring into his dark eyes so he knew I was serious. For someone with such hard features, he certainly had soft eyes. I didn't want to look away.

"So...just curious," he mused as he broke our eye contact and looked back at the road, "who took you home after the party at the beach?"

Flames ignited in my cheeks as it all came together in my mind. I hadn't noticed Shea at the party, but he must have been around somewhere, and he must have been the one to take me home after I puked on Drew, which means...I probably puked in Shea's car too. Hence the car clean-out the next day. *Oh my god, this is mortifying.*

"I am *so* sorry, Shea. That is so embarrassing. Why didn't you tell me? I could have paid for a car detail! Or cleaned it out myself. I cannot believe this, I'm so embarrassed right now," I said, too loudly and with fervor.

Shea just laughed and glanced over at me. "To be honest, I didn't know if you remembered it or not, and if you did remember, I didn't want to go making you feel worse about it, and if you didn't remember, which clearly you did not, I didn't see the point in making you feel bad. Turns out I just did that anyway, so I'm sorry I brought it up."

He looked back at the road, and I glanced at him, and for some reason, my shame had already faded. I felt safe in Shea's company. It was nice. I looked down at the flower on my wrist and then back up at Shea, and I realized I didn't know anything about him at all, but I was starting to really want to. And I couldn't help but imagine how gorgeous he would look in a tux.

"So…" I started, his kind gestures making me less afraid to pry, "what do you do for fun? I don't see you out very much."

Shea cocked his head to the side like he hadn't really ever contemplated fun before.

"I like to read. And listen to music. And draw. I draw a lot." His response put me oddly at ease. Because other than the drawing, I liked those things too. It had never felt safe before to discuss books with my peers because I didn't want them to think I was boring. I often pretended to like things I didn't, like sports and big parties, so that I would seem cool to other people. I dove into the conversation headfirst.

"What have you read lately? I love to read. And I love to write. Although I haven't been making as much time for it lately as I probably should—you know, since it helps keep me sane. And lately, I have been feeling anything but sane, and I'm just now realizing that not writing enough is probably the reason I'm crazy…" I carried on, probably too much, but Shea seemed to enjoy listening to me talk, and I enjoyed watching him enjoy something. He looked so handsome when he smiled.

Shea told me about his current reads, and I made notes in my phone so I wouldn't forget his recommendations. I felt like the authentic version of myself was filling her baby lungs with fresh air, and I was giddy with the shameless release of her. The minutes passed too quickly like they always do when a soul is flowing freely.

We pulled up in front of the high school, and I looked out at the girls and guys flocking together in their finest, all looking unnaturally orange and sparkly. The sight of the social jungle gave me a flutter of anxiety, but I shoved it down. I was relieved when I saw Sydney and Charlotte in their pink and blue gowns standing by a tree out front waiting for me. Even though I wasn't a little girl in elementary school anymore, I was still afraid of sitting alone. My security blankets were in place, and I was ready to tackle the night of my dreams.

I looked back over at Shea who gave me a quick smirk before putting the car in park and getting out to open my door on the passenger side. He didn't need to do that, but he did, and it was nice. He opened the door and held out a strong, tanned hand to me, which I took, and felt a spark of electricity shoot through my body at his touch. I waved at my friends who were looking at me like I had three heads, and I said a quiet 'thank you' to Shea. I tried to give him the twenty, but he refused it.

"Have a great time, Annie. You look beautiful."

I walked toward my friends with heat in my core and my head spinning with desires and questions. Shea was not what I expected at all.

TWELVE

AFTER EXPLAINING THE car situation, I linked arms with my girls, and we set out to have a perfect night. Apparently, they had done some pre-gaming together, which I had completely forgotten to do, so I was pleased when I saw that the naïve parents on the homecoming committee had booked Steve the bartender to serve beverages. I sidled up to the drinks table, feeling bare and much less persuasive without Becca by my side, and asked Steve what was on the menu.

"Just punch tonight, honey…sorry," he said with a wink. When he handed me the plastic cup, I expected half of it to be vodka, and I was disappointed to take a sip and find out that it was, in fact, just punch. It was pretty good punch, to be fair, but still.

"Hey, where's your friend tonight?"

I pretended I couldn't hear him because of the loud music, but really, I was just trying to avoid a longer than necessary conversation with the old dude in an out-of-season Hawaiian shirt. As I was backing away from Steve with my hand pointing to my ear and silently mouthing 'sorry,' I bumped into a wall behind me. And then the wall spoke.

"Hey, gorgeous. I saw you come in. You look amazing tonight."

I turned around and I was looking right at Drew's chest. When I raised my eyes to meet his, I was transported into some kind of surreal *Great Gatsby* moment. His blue eyes were twinkling with pleasure and confidence, his smile was wide and bright, and his hair was styled into a perfect blonde quiff. His cologne preceded him in a gentle cloud of carefully curated maleness.

"Um, hi there...you look amazing tonight too," I said, because he did.

Just then Stella sidled up beside Drew and grabbed his arm. She had a golden dress on that made her look statuesque and perfect. The two of them looked like they had walked right out of a magazine together and just happened to end up at a school dance in Concord, Minnesota with the rest of us.

"I want to dance with my date! Let's go!" She tugged on his arm, and he relented, giving me one last smirk before the two of them disappeared amongst the pulsating bodies on the dance floor.

I was actually kind of relieved to see them go because I wasn't really ready for my Drew moment yet. I was still settling into my surroundings, and I wanted a minute to take it all in and adapt myself to the mood of the room. I glided over to my friends, attempting as much grace as I could muster and standing up straighter, as naturally happens when you are dressed solely for the purpose of being on display.

I looked around and admired the twinkling lights, the streamers, and the balloons. The decorations were simple and humble but so were most of the people in attendance. I looked around at the students, most of whom I had grown up with, and I watched as they shined, or simmered, or laughed, or cried, or did whatever it was that they did, and I knew that no matter what, tonight was a good night.

Charlotte pulled me out of my daze and on to the dance floor just as an obscure song with loud bass reverberated through the air. I felt stiff at first without any liquid courage, but for some inexplicable reason, I felt more confident than I had in a long time, and after a few minutes I threw my arms up and let myself move freely. We danced for several songs, while Sydney and Charlotte each took turns dancing with some of the boys. Then the lights around us changed color to pink, and a modern cover of "Can't Help Falling in Love with You" came on. Some couples stayed out on the dance floor, and some meandered off to go get some punch, or possibly do some drugs in the bathroom.

Charlotte bowed dramatically in front of me and said, in an exaggerated low voice, "May I please have this dance, my lady?"

I laughed and reached out my hand to her, just as another voice behind me said, "My apologies, sir, but she's already promised this dance to me."

I swung around to find Drew looking at me expectantly for the second time that night. This time, I was thoroughly warmed up and prepared to play the game. Charlotte threw a wink at me and skipped off to the punch bowl while Drew grabbed my hand and pulled me in tight. I tossed my arms around his neck and looked up at him, watching as he trailed his gaze down to my red lips.

"Red suits you, Annie."

"Thank you. I was worried it would clash with my hair."
I lifted a hand to toss my hair behind my shoulder in a dramatic way that would let Drew know that I was aware that boys didn't notice or care about such things.

"Oh, absolutely not," he said, brushing the tips of his fingers lightly through the strands of hair at the side of my face. "You look like a goddess."

I actually laughed out loud at that comment. If I had been drinking something, I would have spewed it all over his face. I couldn't even count the number of times I had mentally referred to Drew as a 'god,' and to hear him throw the sentiment in my direction actually made me snort in disbelief.

Drew was looking into my face with a serious expression, clearly concerned that he had offended me, and I instantly felt terrible for laughing at him after he said something so nice.

"I'm sorry, Drew, it's just…to be honest, I've never really thought of myself as someone who would be 'in your league' so to speak…so to hear to you say that, just…" Apparently three perfectly placed compliments from Drew over the course of the evening was enough to give me the courage to be a new level of vulnerable with him.

"Oh no, you're right Annie, you are definitely way out of my league," he interrupted before I could finish.

"No! No, no. I mean *you* are out of *my* league! Just look at yourself!" My eyes widened in surprise that he genuinely seemed to think it was the other way around, and he also seemed to be completely okay with that.

"How about we just agree to play on the same team," he said with a smirk.

"I'd like that." I smiled back at him.

The song came to an end and the bass picked back up, and I was expecting Drew to let go of me, our divine moment having passed. Instead, he just gave me a cheeky look and started dancing faster and I just danced along with him until his date and my friends came to drag us away from each other a few songs later.

The teen romance script was playing out beautifully— everything felt so right. I couldn't have imagined the horrors that were playing out somewhere behind the scenes.

THIRTEEN

HOMECOMING NIGHT TURNED out to be just as magical as I had hoped it would be. As midnight approached, people started filtering out of the gym, and I picked up my phone just as a text came in from my mom.

MOM: *Hope you've had a great night, pumpkin. Dad's home and I'm on my way to pick you up. Be there in 15. X*

My feet were killing me, and my back was aching from standing up straighter than usual for so long. I had accomplished my mission—a perfect dance with Drew—it was time to go, and I wasn't going to fight it. I told my friends my mom was on her way, gave them some tight hugs, and went outside to get some fresh air while I waited.

The stark contrast of the noisy gym and the still night outside reawakened my senses, which had been numbed by music, flashing lights, and hormones. The cool air washed over me, and I sat on one of the benches in the grass out front, finally allowing myself to slouch. I reached down and took off my shoes, and wiggled the soreness from my toes, dreaming of a hot bath and some Ben & Jerry's when I got home. Or maybe just bed.

I didn't hear Drew come out of the building, but I could feel his eyes on me before he sat down on the bench next to me. That familiar tingle shot up my spine at his proximity to me, especially since I was no longer in the humid daze of the gym.

"Hey," he said, softly.

"Hey," I replied.

"Did you have a good time tonight?" He wasn't looking at me, but I could feel the heat coming off of him as his shoulder brushed mine.

"I did. Did you?"

"Yes," he said, still looking out toward the street.

"What was your favorite part?" I asked, guessing what he might say, and hoping I was right.

"This."

Drew reached up and slid his fingers through my hair and kissed me. My insides bloomed and my heart fluttered in surprise. His lips were so soft, and his hand was so sure, pulling me in toward him and claiming me as the object of his affection. It was so unexpected and so delicious. No one had ever kissed me like that before, and suddenly I felt my insecurity blossom into something new and something powerful. Experience.

Too soon the kiss was over, which, once I came to, I realized was good because my mom was going to be pulling up any second. As Drew pulled away from me, he looked earnestly into my eyes, and I could see so much truth in them. Drew liked me. And he wanted me to like him. I could tell by the way his eyes kept trailing from my eyes to my mouth that he hungered for more of me, and I felt the same way when I looked at him. It wasn't the night for that, but maybe soon it would be. The thought of doing more with Drew was almost more than I could take.

I glanced out to the street and saw my mom's sedan creep slowly along the side of the road and come to a stop.

"My mom is here. I'll see you on Monday?" I stood up and stuck my hand out to shake Drew's, unsure of what the protocol was after a surprise first kiss with a lifelong crush, knowing that this wasn't it, but it also wouldn't be the first time my knee-jerk reaction made me look like an idiot. And it wouldn't be the last.

Drew lifted my hand to his lips and kissed it. He smiled up at me and said, "It's a date."

I picked up my shoes that I had discarded on the ground and flashed an unapologetic smile at Drew, who I noticed had a little bit of my red lipstick on his mouth. I attempted a sexy saunter to my mom's car, but it was all I could do not to click my heels and high five the moon.

I got in the car and put on my seatbelt and my mom asked me the usual questions about how the dance was, if I had fun, who was there, how the punch tasted, etc. If she saw anything happen between me and Drew, she didn't let on about it. But something about her voice sounded off. Like she was weary but trying to cover it up with pleasantries. I was too tired and consumed with my own feelings to ask her about hers.

"So, who was that handsome boy you were sitting with on the bench when I pulled up?" So, she *did* see us.

"Oh, that was just Drew."

"Drew Matthews?"

"Yes, he's my lab partner in science class."

"Hmm…and he's also the boy you've had a crush on since Kindergarten, right?" She looked over at me with a knowing glance, and I knew that there was no point in beating around the bush, even if I wasn't really ready to talk about what was going on with him yet.

"Yes…that too, Mom. Thank you for pointing it out," I mumbled grumpily, because let's face it, teenage girls are mean to their mothers for no reason. They just are. And I was no exception.

"I won't mention anything about it, Annie…don't worry. Although I have to say, he *is* pretty handsome, and his mom is delightful."

So, my mom was Team Drew, then. Noted.

I didn't say anything and for a few minutes we just rode in silence while I processed the miracle that had just occurred.

My mom broke the silence. "Annie, before we get home…there's something I have to tell you."

My face started to tingle with anxiety because I knew that whatever she was going to say next wasn't going to be good. I had known something wasn't right as soon as I had gotten in the car, even if I had been choosing to ignore the weird energy. I began to mentally brace myself for whatever it was that was about the break that delicate barrier between the not-knowing and the knowing. My mom looked at me and back at the road and then back to me again. She sighed.

"John McAteer is dead, Annie."

Just as she said the words, I could see the flashing blue lights in the distance, promising sorrow and danger.

My head started to spin. "Oh my god, *what?* What happened?" A million thoughts and theories were flying through my head, along with the realization that Shea was now an orphan. The memory of handing him duct tape and rope also crossed my mind, but I shooed it away. The sparkling romance of my evening was suddenly swallowed up by shock and fear.

"Annie, this is going to be hard to hear, but you need to hear it. Shea came home and found him hanging in the stairwell. The police have taken Shea in for questioning, and to sort out what's going to happen to him now that both parents are deceased. Your dad went over and spoke to the police and offered to take Shea in until he could figure things out, but the police didn't think that would be in our best interests right now." My stomach dropped and my eyes widened.

"I'm sorry…what? They've taken him in for *questioning*? Why would they do that? Shea needs a hug, not an interrogation." I didn't even know anything about the situation yet, but for some reason, I was already fighting for Shea.

My mom was trying to stay calm, but I could tell that she was shaken up and trying to make sense of things herself.

"Annie…it's just…your dad had the same questions, and the police said they couldn't tell us much, but they did indicate that there were some…questionable bruises and lacerations on John's body that could indicate foul play."

My jaw dropped. I had witnessed John beating up Shea. I had seen how brutal he could be. I also saw Shea reluctant to fight back. And then I saw Shea taking care of his dad just days later. It was clear to me that there was a misunderstanding, and suddenly I deeply regretted not telling someone about the abuse I witnessed when it happened. Maybe then, the police would understand that Shea would never hurt his father. Or if he did, it would have been in self-defense.

But how could I start talking now? And would it even matter? And what if Shea actually *did* murder his father and tried to make it look like suicide? Could the sweet boy who drove me to the dance really have come home and murdered his own dad just minutes later?

I didn't think so, but I had been wrong before. A lot. I suddenly had no confidence in my own judgement of character.

The orchid Shea gave me was still on my wrist. It was wilted now. When we got home, I skipped the bath and went to my room. Without thinking, I took a heavy book down from my shelf and pressed the orchid between the pages to dry. I'm not sure why I did that. I think maybe a part of me didn't want to forget how Shea made me feel that afternoon. Special. *Myself.* Even though I was convinced that Drew was my future, there was something about Shea I wasn't ready to let go of. I went to bed, hoping that wherever he was, he was okay. And that I was right about him being a good person.

I turned off my thoughts and decided to leave my questions and judgements and sadness and joy and fear and fantasies and memories and deep-rooted confusion for another day. I cried a little—my feelings too overwhelming to process properly—and then I slept.

FOURTEEN

I WOKE BEFORE dawn in a cold sweat. In my dream, I was on a Ferris wheel by myself, looking out over the ocean. I was gazing at the watercolor skies and cotton candy clouds, when suddenly, I looked over and Drew appeared next to me. He didn't speak, but he reached for my hand, and a warm sense of happiness and peace washed over me. I closed my eyes and lay my head on his shoulder, and when I opened my eyes again, Shea was sitting in the seat across from us with a blank look on his face. We circled up to the top of the ride, and the Ferris wheel stopped. Drew didn't seem to notice Shea, he just kept smiling at me and pointing to the view. When I looked back at Shea, he was covered in blood. He stood up and jumped off the Ferris wheel, his body slamming into the rocks below. I screamed and reached for him. I looked back for Drew, but he had disappeared. I was alone, again, and terrified.

When, at last, I opened my eyes, it took me several minutes to realize where I was and shake the shock from my system. I walked over to my window; it looked cold outside with a slight touch of frost on the brown grass. I pulled on a thick sweater and slid out the back door into the weak, gray light of early morning. The air cut into my still-damp cheeks and neck as I walked my well-worn path down to the lake. My dream had spooked me, and I wanted to face the day with what I felt in my heart was true—that Shea wasn't a murderer—but...what if I was wrong?

I was halfway to the dock before the panic set in and my bravery faltered. I knew that Shea wouldn't be down at the dock this early in the morning, but what if he was? What if I *was* wrong about him, and the goodness I saw at the sports shop with Becca, and with his dad, and the kindness he showed me the day before was all some elaborate act? Somehow the fresh air and daylight put the logical part of my brain in the driver's seat, and I realized that I wasn't ready for the possibility of bumping into Shea yet.

I didn't even know if he was home or if he was still in police custody, but I realized that I wasn't ready to find out right then, in that way. What if he never came home? What if he was shipped off to foster care somewhere? I wasn't sure I could bear that. Although there was fear in my heart, I also had seeds of affection and curiosity living there. I just couldn't imagine never seeing Shea again, as confused as that made me about everything—even my feelings for Drew.

When I went back inside the house, my dad was awake, sitting with a cup of coffee at the breakfast table, staring into space and lost in thought. I wondered what he saw last night when he went over the check on the McAteers. Did he see John? What did Shea look like? I was burning with questions, but I knew from experience that it was always better to let Dad process before interrogating him. I didn't say anything, but I poured myself a glass of orange juice and sat next to him at the table.

We sat in silence for a few minutes, and it occurred to me that Dad was normally heading out to do his weekly inventory at the sports shop at this time. He didn't seem like he was in a hurry to move, which shouldn't have felt unsettling, but it did.

"Are you heading to the shop today, Dad?" I broke the silence in a shy voice.

"Not today. Becca offered to do the inventory and I could use some time to think anyway."

His tone wasn't as sad as his facial expression had led me to expect it would be. He sounded...focused.

I found myself needing to know what he was thinking, but unsure how to dig it out of him without him shutting the conversation down. "It must be a lot to process," I offered, "you know...everything you probably saw."

My statement hung in the air between us for a few minutes.

"Annie, I want to believe the best in people. I really do. It's who I am. But I got a glimpse of John last night after..." His throat caught on the last few words, and he coughed the emotion back down to where it had bubbled up from. He started again. "After they took him down. And he was in rough shape, Annie. Something happened to that man more than what he may have done to himself. It just has me thinking about you and your mom and your sister and what the right thing to do is here." He finally looked at me, and for the first time maybe ever, I saw fear in his eyes.

"Do about what, Dad?" I said, mostly understanding, but wanting him to say it out loud. He looked down at his hands wrapped around the mug he hadn't moved since I sat down.

"What to do about Shea. He lives next door. I want to think he's a good boy, but I honestly can't say I know that much about him—I'm ashamed of that. I feel like I should have done more for them after his mom...after Emily died. The fact that you were alone in a car with him last night...the fact that something could have happened to you...it's just more than I can think about without losing my mind."

He looked away and the little waves in his coffee told me his hand was trembling. And that he hadn't actually drunk any coffee the entire time he had been sitting there.

I didn't know when, how, or with whom I should share what I knew about Shea and his situation, but I was beginning to feel like this was information my dad needed to have if Shea was going to have a fighting chance in the court of public opinion. Who knew where he was right now or if he was being treated fairly? The idea of Shea hurting someone just didn't add up to me. But if he didn't do it, then who did?

The McAteers kept to themselves. I couldn't imagine someone being out to get either of them. Nothing about this made any sense.

"Dad, there's something I think I need to tell you, and I hope you're not mad that I didn't tell you sooner…it's just…I didn't know that something like this was going to happen." I felt my throat closing as emotion surfaced. Dad's eyes met mine and I saw the endless well of love and patience he had for me. I let a tear fall but kept my composure.

"Of course you didn't, sweetie. You can tell me anything, anytime you're ready." My dad was so gentle with me. I don't think I ever fully appreciated what a gift that was until that morning.

"So…the other week…" I found myself struggling to get the words out. I didn't realize how much this had been weighing on my subconscious until it was time to spit it out. "I sort of saw John punch Shea. Like…hard. In the stomach and the face. Shea didn't fight back. But he had an angry bruise on his cheek for a week. After I saw it…please don't be mad…but I drove over there and honked my horn to interrupt John. I just wanted to distract him. I just wanted him to stop. I asked John for some eggs and left. Also…"

I let out a big sigh because I didn't want him to know that I had snuck over there in the middle of the night to spy, but given the circumstances, it was relevant information.

"Please, don't be mad. I heard some music the other night and it was coming from the McAteer place, so I went closer and heard John playing guitar, and I stopped to listen for a minute and then Shea came out and took his dad to bed, which is kind of weird, right? Like one second he's getting beat up and the next he's basically tucking his dad in bed? I don't know…just…from what I've seen I can't imagine Shea hurting anyone, especially not his dad. And he stood up for Becca at the shop one time when some guys were making her uncomfortable. And he was so sweet with me last night too. He even gave me a flower. I mean…I don't know. It just doesn't add up."

I finally stopped rambling and looked up at my dad, expecting to see shock, anger, or disappointment in his eyes. I didn't. He reached out across the table and squeezed my hand.

"Thank you for telling me, Annie. That makes me feel so much better. And maybe like I don't have to stop seeing the good in people just yet…" He shook his head from side to side. "And thank you for telling me about Becca at the shop—I clearly need to do a better job of protecting her there. We can't have that happening. It's unacceptable."

Dad stood up with a renewed sense of purpose. "You make me so proud, sweetie. I hope this all gets sorted out quickly. For everyone's sake."

Rosie started babbling in her room and Dad moved to get her up for the day. Before he reached the stairs, he turned back to me. "Annie, you're a lucky girl that you haven't had much experience with grief yet. But you should know that grief does strange things to people. I watched John grieve his wife for so many years. Shea grieved her too. They did it together, in their own way. It looks different to everyone. I hope it waits a long, long time before it reaches you, but when it does…just be gentle with yourself."

The depth and sincerity of his words made my breath catch in my throat. When I finally let it go, tears came with it. I didn't know what else to do, so I just started making Rosie breakfast. When she came running over to me in her bunny jammies, I let her little light wash over me and gleaned all the goodness I could from her. I silently wished the same goodness for Shea.

I went up to my room and spent several hours writing, just writing anything and everything in my mind, stream of consciousness style into my journal. I filled it up to the last page and set it on the shelf next to the book with the orchid inside. I had resolved nothing, but I felt a little lighter all the same.

FIFTEEN

ON MONDAY MORNING, I still didn't know if Shea had returned home or not. His car was there, because the police had driven him to the station, and I had no way of knowing if they had brought him back home or off to somewhere else. I wasn't looking forward to school because I knew that the hallways and classrooms would be a rancid symphony of hearsay, speculation, and misinformation about the McAteers. I needed more time to figure out my own opinions about the situation before being thrown into the whirlwind of gossip, which would more than likely be directed at me since I was Shea's only real neighbor.

The day before, I had noticed an influx of traffic on our normally quiet road, as curious locals drove past to partake in the melancholy or look out for signs of a ghost or a murderer on the loose. It's odd how people generally do whatever they can to avoid experiencing tragedy, but when it befalls someone else, those same people—even the 'good' ones—would spend their last dollar to buy front row tickets to the show.

As expected, when I walked into school, I could feel extra sets of eyes on me. Avery Munson, who wasn't my friend in the slightest, maneuvered his way into my space.

"Hey, Annie…do you know what happened to Shea's dad? Is it true Shea murdered him? I heard he shot him in the head. So sad…" He wore a concerned look on his face that was attempting to say 'the McAteers are in my thoughts and prayers,' but really just said 'I'm here for the gossip and nothing else.'

"I wasn't there, so I really can't speak to what happened. But yes, it's super sad." I kept walking at a brisk pace, just trying to make it to my locker so I could get to math class and sit by Becca in peace for the next hour. Becca and I had texted a little on Sunday about what happened, but I hadn't told her about the complicated feelings I was having about Shea yet. She didn't ask how homecoming was, and I was still a little annoyed that she had decided not to come, so I didn't offer up any unsolicited information. I knew we'd get to the dirty details at some point—we always did.

When I arrived at my locker, Drew was there. He looked like a charming Ralph Lauren model in his crew neck sweatshirt. There was a strange dissonance between the tragedy that had been consuming my thoughts over the last thirty-six hours and the unaffected person standing in front of me. Like, how could the rest of the world be easy and breezy when someone's life was falling apart just up the road?

"Hey gorgeous," he said, smiling. And then he carefully shifted his expression to one of concern—he was good at that, I noticed. He furrowed his eyebrows together, casting his blue eyes into an even deeper shade of beautiful.

"I heard about what happened…are you okay?" He raised his eyebrows slightly, right on cue.

Well, this was new. Drew was seeking me out at school now. And definitely thinking about me on the weekends. If the kiss was as good for him as it was for me, then I could understand why things were trending this way. And I definitely wasn't mad about it. Seeing Drew's smile and his twinkling eyes made me feel lighter than I had a minute ago when Avery was stalking me and digging

101

for dirt. Like maybe it was okay to be okay when other people weren't. Like maybe Drew was the only one I should be focused on. I ignored the fact that his attention still didn't feel completely real or rational.

"I'm fine, thanks for asking. I'm more worried for Shea than anything. I hope he's okay and somebody is taking care of him." *Why do I feel like that person should be me?*

A nearly imperceptible flash of jealousy crossed Drew's face. I had a habit of reading into things, so I could have been wrong, but for a second I thought I felt tension from Drew at the mention of my concern for Shea. I selfishly like the idea of Drew feeling possessive of me. Maybe soon things would become official, and I could die a happy woman. As if life worked like that.

The bell rang and I realized that while I was stuck in my trance with Drew, most of the students had disappeared into their classrooms and I was late. Drew reached down and gave me a peck on the cheek.

"See you in class later, babe."

Babe? Okay. I accept.

I tried to slip into Miss Jones's class without being noticed, but she had already started her lesson and the door was creakier than expected. She was cool and didn't say anything, but the silence that surrounded me as I made my way to my seat still brought heat to my cheeks. I stared at Miss Jones with her creamy, dark complexion and felt jealous that her face wouldn't automatically turn crimson at any inkling of embarrassment or insecurity. Not that it seemed like she was the type to be easily embarrassed, like me. She had a cool air of confidence and authority. She was understated and relatable, but also unattainable in her maturity and elegance. *Note to self—be more like Miss Jones.*

I looked over at the other person I wished I was more like. Becca. She gave me a look that said, 'Where were you?' and when I mouthed 'Drew' to her, she just rolled her eyes at me. I took note of Becca's outfit out of habit, and now that the weather was getting colder, she had opted for an oversized sweater and leggings. The sweater completely swallowed her up, but with her hair in a casual bun and a fresh face, she looked effortless and mature. Before I could question her new, understated look, I glanced down and saw the leather boots with six-inch heels she was wearing, and I laughed at myself for thinking Becca's fashion sense would be changing any time soon. *Still a badass. Note to self—get some of those sexy boots.*

The morning came and went without incident. Drew and I didn't get a chance to talk much during science because Mr. Sanders was lecturing. He was the type of teacher who liked the sound of his own voice. Fair enough, but I did mourn the loss of my time to chat with Drew. That being said, there was something about sitting so close to each other in silence. I could feel the heat building between us as I imagined all sorts of private things and wondered if Drew was thinking along the same lines. Every once in a while, he would brush his pinky finger against mine and send a throb right down to my core, and I imagined what it would be like to feel that sensation in other places.

"I'm hosting a party at my house on Friday. Will you come?" He looked at me hopefully just as the bell rang and we all started shifting up and out of our seats.

"Yeah, sure! I'd love to." I gave him a closed lip smile that I was hoping would read 'seductive,' but probably didn't. I texted

Becca immediately so that she wouldn't have a chance to secure other plans and ditch me again. This party was a huge win, and I needed my wing-woman by my side. Plus, between everything going on and Becca's new job, we hadn't been connecting as much lately and I was feeling her absence. Something was different about her, and I needed to find out what it was.

ME: *Becca!! Drew invited me to a party at his house on Saturday, and I need you there so we can have fun together but also because I might need someone to scoop me off the floor after Drew's smile melts me into a puddle.*

She took no time to reply.

BECCA: *I'll be there with bells on. And when I say 'bells,' I mean I'll be wearing bell bottoms that could rival Jimi Hendrix.*

She finished the text with a fire emoji, a bell emoji, and a zombie, just for good measure. I did a miniature happy dance and thanked the discolored ceiling tiles above me for the grace I was just bestowed.

When art class arrived, my day took a turn, but only because it was Monday again, which meant a new person was going to be our model, and that person was apparently me. I knew this week was coming and I'd had time to mentally prepare for it, but it didn't make me loathe the process any less. Kamila, on the other hand, seemed disappointed to be descending from her throne, where she had obviously enjoyed the extra attention paid to her and her flowing hair. If I were her, I would have probably felt the same way.

Some portraits of Kamila had turned out better than others, but none were worse than mine. When Kamila saw it, she actually snorted as she laughed, and Ms. Young had to remind her and the rest of the class that all art is worthy by virtue of simply existing. That made Kamila laugh even harder, and I couldn't blame her. I started laughing too, and pretty soon the whole class was gathered around laughing at my pathetic attempt at a portrait. Even though the laughter was at my expense, it actually helped break the ice and make me feel a little calmer as I took my seat on the stool in the center of the room. I mean, the whole class had already laughed at me. How much worse could it possibly get?

It turns out, posing for the class was actually boring as hell. My back ached, and I couldn't believe I would be doing this for another four days. As I sat there, my mind drifted from planning my outfit for Drew's party, to Shea's empty seat screaming at me to ponder him some more. I tried not to, but his absence was acute, and my feelings surrounding him were so complicated and so unresolved. As I drove home from school, I couldn't help but feel the pressure in my chest building the closer I got to our little corner of the world where nothing used to happen, but apparently now, scary things did.

I couldn't help but chance a glance over to the McAteer property as I slowly drove past and turned into my own driveway. The garage door had been closed this morning, but it was open now. I guessed that meant Shea was home.

They say our bodies can't tell the difference between excitement, anticipation, and anxiety, which explains why my heart pounded, my breathing quickened, and I felt like I wanted to run and hide, and also why I smiled at the same time.

SIXTEEN

SHEA WASN'T AT school for the rest of the week, and by Friday, the rumors and theories surrounding the McAteers had died down from a roar to a buzz. Apparently, I had shrugged enough people off that I was no longer in danger of being interrogated between classes, and besides my own burning questions eating away at me, I was left to live my life normally again. Relatively speaking.

Drew's party wasn't set to start until 9:00 p.m., which felt pretty late to me, but then again, I hadn't been to that many parties and I would need to get used to staying up later than 10:00 p.m. if I was going to hack it in the college social scene. I planned to pick Becca up at her house sometime after dinner so that we could show up to the party together. Also, she was generally good for a free style consultation on an as-needed basis, which was more often needed than not. She was taller than me, and boob-ier, but she tended to wear her clothes so tight that when I borrowed them, they usually fit me as they were probably originally intended.

My family was pretty basic and traditional, built on a strong midwestern foundation of niceness and togetherness. Hence, dinner was at 6:00 p.m. every night, and while attendance wasn't mandatory, it was highly encouraged. I don't want to use the words 'guilt trip,' but I'm also not going to say I was never made to feel bad for skipping family dinner. We were typical Minnesotans, which meant dinner was usually some version of 'hot dish' (casserole, to the rest of the world), with the occasional Taco

Tuesday just to spice things up. Not that any spices were actually involved in any way, shape, or form.

This particular night was Tator-Tot Hotdish. My least favorite of the hot dishes, but with the saving grace of the crispy tator-tots on top to provide some relief from the stodgy mixed vegetables and under-seasoned ground beef in the middle. We usually had some homemade bread on the side, and I often wondered why my mom spent so much time making it, but now realize it was probably to entice everyone around the table regardless of what was on the menu. Barring allergy restrictions, no human being has ever said no to a hot slice of fresh baked bread with a slab of butter on it. I'm still convinced that's what heaven is made of. If you disagree, you're wrong.

We sat around the table together and went through our routine of sharing what we were grateful for, and I said, "Rosie," because whenever I said her name she giggled and said 'Wosie' back to me and it never failed to make me smile. My dad said he was grateful for his family (a classic), and Mom said she was grateful for how much time we had had together, "because time is never guaranteed."

I could tell what was on her mind as she said it, because underneath the routines and the hot dishes and the warm bread, we were all thinking about the house next door and the sadness that lived there. It was impossible not to. When we were finished, my mom put the leftover hot dish in a Tupperware container, along with the rest of the bread and several cookies from the cupboard.

"I'm going to bring this over to Shea. I'll be back in a few minutes," she said. Why hadn't I thought of that before? When someone died, it was customary to bring the family food. Had anyone brought Shea anything? He was still a teenager and all alone. What had taken us so long to reach out to him, besides our own selfishness and fear?

"Let me take it over," I shouted in her direction before she could close the front door behind her. She looked back at me curiously and I thought my dad was going to protest, but he just gazed at me with a look of trust in his eyes, and I appreciated it even though it was clearly only there by sheer force of will. I felt consumed by blind bravery as my mom handed me the container, and I made my way to Shea. It was the right thing to do.

I knocked on Shea's door and panicked, suddenly unsure of what I was going to say when he answered. It took a few minutes before the door opened, the entirety of which time I spent frozen in space, unable to think, plan or move in any direction.

When the door opened, I remained stuck, but this time because I was staring straight into Shea's dark eyes, the ones that I hadn't been able to get out of my mind ever since homecoming night, and probably before that if I was really being honest with myself. He was dressed in his usual white t-shirt, but instead of jeans he was wearing gray sweatpants and his hair was messy like he hadn't given it a thought all week, which, of course he hadn't. I realized too late that I was supposed to be the one to say something first since I was the one that came knocking, but Shea was the one who bridged the gap.

"Hi, Annie." He didn't sound surprised or annoyed, he just sounded...tired.

"Hi, Shea...I'm sorry for bothering you, and I'm sorry about your dad, and I'm just sorry in general," I started, flailing in the abyss of the space between us, feeling like an idiot with no tools in my toolbelt for this particular job.

I now know that it's hard for people who have never grieved to comfort someone who is grieving. It's almost impossible to soothe away the darkness if you've never known the darkness, and at this point in my life, the darkness and I hadn't officially met yet.

"You have nothing to be sorry for. Is that for me?" he asked, gesturing to the Tupperware container in my hands.

"Oh my gosh, yes! This is for you. Mom made Tator-Tot Hotdish, which I know is, like, nobody's favorite, but I hope you like me. I mean, it. I hope you like the hot dish." My face turned bright red, and I shifted my hair to the front of my neck out of habit. This was an awful encounter, and I was regretting my offer to take the food over. My mom would have been over and back by now, and probably would have actually made Shea feel better, like moms do.

I got the urge to ditch the situation entirely, so I quickly handed over the food and I turned back toward my house. As I was walking away, Shea's soft voice carried after me.

"Thank you for dinner, Annie. I do like Tator-Tot Hotdish. And you."

I stopped in my tracks and turned around to look at him, but by the time I did, he was already closing the door.

...

I pulled up to Becca's house an hour later, wearing a half-assed attempt at a cool outfit, and planning to lean heavily on Becca to make me look cooler than I actually was. Her house was right in town, in a neighborhood that was built in the 1980's. The houses on her street were inconsistently maintained, and while some were occupied by old people who had been trimming their grass using a measuring tape and a pair of scissors for the last twenty plus years, other properties needed a fresh coat of paint and some serious weed killer. Becca's house was of the latter variety.

There was a dog food factory in Concord that employed a big chunk of the town's population, and Becca's dad, Jim, worked shifts there. Becca's mom, Sandy, worked nights at the local bar, and Jim usually spent any time that he wasn't at work at said bar, wearing out the same stool and fighting with Sandy about lord knows what. Becca had basically been fending for herself since well before she was legally allowed to stay home alone. It was part of why she was so fearless and independent. But she was also so much more than her lackluster (and sometimes abusive) home life. Becca was going to do things in this world, and I couldn't wait to watch her steamroll over any sniveling assholes that tried to stand in her way.

I let myself in without knocking, because at this point it was standard practice for us, and she knew I was coming. Her parents weren't home because they never were, and I was glad about that. They liked me, I think, but they made me uncomfortable. I wasn't used to being around adults who smoked in the house and punctuated each sentence with several swear words and opinions with no solid basis in fact.

When Becca was home alone, the linoleum floors and sagging sofa and cheap knick-knacks sang to a different tune entirely. It wasn't a dingy, loveless home when we occupied it alone. It was a retro bachelorette pad, and we were just passing through to put on our lipstick before we launched into stardom.

"I'm here, B!" I shouted down the dark hallway that led to her room. Her door was closed so I knocked before I swung the door open.

"You have *got* to be kidding me, Annie." Becca looked over at me from her perch on her bed with a look that was half disgust and whole love. I looked down at my outfit.

"What?" I stuck out my arms and one of my legs in a pose that said, 'Ta-da! I'm pathetic, please fix me.' Becca rolled her eyes and pointed to her closet. This was always the fun part. I was glad to see Becca in her element, preparing to go out for the night. It made me think maybe she was totally fine, I was reading too far into things, and she was just too cool for homecoming dances and preppy people like Drew. Our lives were so different; it wasn't uncommon for her to say and do things that I didn't always understand. It was part of what drew me to her in the first place. Her depth and mystery and experience, which far exceeded my own.

I decided to let shit go. I was so self-absorbed that at the time, I thought I was doing her a favor by moving on without a fight. I now know that this was just another bullet point on my growing list of wrong choices.

Becca stood up and walked over to peruse her closet with me, and I was stopped in my tracks at how amazing she looked. As promised, she was wearing dark red velvet bell bottoms, white boots, and a KISS t-shirt that she had cut up herself. Her dark hair was down and slightly messy, and her eyes were lined seamlessly in black. She looked like she belonged in New York City or at Woodstock or literally anywhere but here. She was too good for

111

Concord and too good for me, but for some reason she didn't seem to believe me when I insisted on it.

"So…you know I love you, Annie. I do. But leggings and a cardigan are not your friends tonight. You definitely over cardigan-ize in general—let's work on that." Becca took my cardigan off and I rolled my eyes in fake annoyance and let her do her thing.

I remembered the first time Becca ever dressed me—it was sometime in fourth grade, and she put me in a pair of cheetah print leggings and styled my hair in a messy bun. I walked around school feeling a mixture of cool and too visible, like at any point, someone was going to call me out for dressing outside of my character's assigned boundaries. Nobody did, and by the end of the day, I felt like my sense of self had expanded an inch in every direction.

Becca rummaged around and then finally tossed me several items to put on. I picked up the black plaid skirt which looked way too short, especially for fall, but before I could protest, she handed me some black tights. I put them on and tucked the oversized sweater she gave me into the skirt, and then finished with some black leather lace up boots that came up just around my ankles. Becca arranged the top half of my hair into a ponytail and teased it out, so it looked casual but pretty. She gave me a smokey eye but didn't overdo it.

I looked in the mirror and felt powerful. I felt like myself, but like a version of myself that I wasn't confident enough—yet—to explore on my own. Becca didn't try to make me into her. She made me into a badass version of me, and I was suddenly ready to go to this party and give Drew a run for his money. Becca was a true gift in my life, and I suddenly felt guilty for being mad at her over such stupid things. Becca nodded in approval at her

112

handiwork, and I hugged her tight for a long time, as long as it took for me to feel her body relax and her tough girl guard go down. As long as it took for me to feel connected to her, and for her to feel loved. I needed Becca. And I knew that Becca needed me, too.

SEVENTEEN

IT'S IN MY nature to feel stressed about being late. As a general rule, if I'm not ten to fifteen minutes early, I panic. Lord help you if you're driving in front of me while I'm on my way anywhere, and scheduled to arrive right on time. I sometimes imagine the stress flowing out of me in big waves and making everyone in my general vicinity feel exactly what a terrible person they are for daring to be on the same path as me while I drive to my destination with several minutes to spare.

That being said, I was grateful to Becca for holding my horses, and not allowing me to arrive at Drew's party at 8:45, or even at 9:00 p.m.

"Desperate people show up to parties early, Annie. Are you a desperate person or a cool person?" She looked over at me with a mixture of exasperation and amusement on her face, as I sat up straight on the edge of her living room couch and bounced my knee up and down (a habit I have yet to rein in).

"Is that a trick question?" I asked her seriously. Because we both knew exactly how desperate I was for Drew and also how not cool I was. But she seemed to want me to think the opposite was true. *Silly Becca.*

My feelings for Shea were starting to spill over into places they weren't welcome, like there, on Becca's couch, as I prepared to go to Drew's house for the night. I remembered the sound of Shea's voice saying he liked me. I couldn't stop replaying it in my mind. My feelings made me feel guilty, like I was cheating on a boyfriend I didn't have yet. Being around Shea felt so different

114

from being around Drew, who made me feel so…different. Like the red-headed version of Stella that I always dreamed of becoming. But Shea had this way of making me feel exactly like the person I already was—but like a more visible version, who wasn't in a hurry to change.

Maybe I don't really need to change?

I wasn't worried about impressing Shea, and it softened me. But I wasn't going to let his smoldering, *seeing* brown eyes slow me down from playing my part in the fairytale I was living in. An invitation to Drew's party was everything, especially after the kiss we shared, and I couldn't wait to be in his space again. Maybe Shea was just some kind of divine test of my will. I had never failed a test before, and I wasn't about to start—not when my dreams were on the line.

Too much thinking, not enough driving.

Finally, at 9:17, Becca stood up and said, "Welp! I think my couch has had enough punishment for tonight. Let's go."

Relief and anticipation flowed through my veins in equal measure. This night was a blank canvas, and I was ready to create something magical with it. Metaphorically speaking because we all should know by this point that I'm a blank canvas's worst nightmare.

We hopped into my car. I couldn't rely on a ride home, and I wouldn't be asking my parents to come get me at a (hopefully) very late hour, so I planned to stay mostly sober and drive home after the party. Worst—but actually best—case scenario, I could always stay at Becca's house. I wasn't going to put expectations or limits on this night. Some nights just aren't for that. But after the last party I attended, and how it ended up in vomit and shame, I wasn't especially eager to try my hand at alcohol again anyway.

We pulled up to Drew's house at 9:22 p.m. Drew also lived in town, but his house could have been on a different planet entirely for how dissimilar it was to Becca's. He lived on Boxelder Street, in one of the oldest neighborhoods in town, where the original houses were built in the very early 1900s and boasted a combination of stately charm and modern updates. All the homes on Boxelder Street were two stories with mature trees and creeping vines and stained-glass accent windows. Drew's house was the largest on his street and was apparently the original home of the town's founder, Abel Concord. In a larger city, Drew's house probably wouldn't even stand out. But in Concord, it was one of the jewels of the town, and in my opinion, well suited to the flawless family that lived in it.

I parked up the street and Becca and I made our way down the dark sidewalk toward the Matthews home and stepped into the light spilling out onto the lawn from inside. I could hear music floating past me and my heart started to race in anticipation of crossing the threshold. I reached up to knock on the door, but Becca pulled my hand down and opened the door, and let herself in. When the door opened, a wave of sound extended around me, and I stepped into it and let it envelop me.

I had only ever seen Drew's house from the outside, and the inside was so beautiful, it took my breath away. There was a large entryway with a staircase going right up the middle to the second floor. To the left, there was a large formal sitting room, where people were hanging out and talking. To the right, there was a formal dining room, where drinks and snacks were lined up, and

116

several football players and other girls from my class were flirting with each other and pouring drinks in excess. That room was definitely going to get messy fast.

More people started coming in through the door behind us, so we shifted ourselves through the sitting room and around to the large living room at the back of the house, where a fire was burning in the fireplace and music was playing from somewhere inside the beautiful hardwood built-in cabinets. I was immediately drawn to an emerald-green sofa next to the fireplace that was unoccupied and perfect for two people to sit and get their bearings. Not that Becca needed to sit and get her bearings, but I certainly did. I pulled her over to the couch and sat down, taking a full breath for maybe the first time since we walked in the door.

Becca didn't sit down with me. Instead, she said she was going to go get us some drinks and walked back toward the dining room. I felt naked without her, but I also felt naked without a drink in my hand, and all this nakedness was just more than I was prepared to handle.

I took out my phone and pretended to text someone because in today's world, it's basically socially unacceptable to exist anywhere without actively talking to someone or reading something important on a small screen. I tapped away at my screen and took a mental note of who was in the room around me. Jordan and Miles were bobbing around like drunk puppies on the other side of the room, and Kamila was sitting on the arm of a chair next to Teagan, who was casually touching her knee as much as he could get away with, which appeared to be a lot. There were clusters of attention-seeking girls talking loudly and flipping their hair and adjusting their bras in an attempt to snag the attention of the drunk puppies, and my guess was that they were succeeding. It's hard to look away from jiggling cleavage no matter who you are or what you're into.

I was starting to wonder where Drew was since I hadn't seen him yet. Becca came back with two plastic cups of cheap beer, and I took a swig, ready to feel it work its magic on my inhibition, my previous hesitations to not drink forgotten. Just then, I locked eyes with Charlotte and Sydney who were just walking in and looked ready to party. Charlotte was wearing hot pink jeans and a white graphic t-shirt that said 'GOOD VIBES' in big, oversized letters. Her joy and her confidence always made me smile. Sydney had a purple cowgirl hat on for some reason, and I didn't question it. That was just her. They were both high achievers in school, like me, but they were also incredibly fun, not like me. Becca and I stood up and greeted the other half of our group of four, and we stood in a circle chatting, but I was only half listening as I continually scanned the house for Drew. He was the only real reason I was there, after all.

My heart fluttered as I saw him walking down the stairs, and then it dropped as I watched Stella following close behind him. Really close. I could guess what they were doing up there together, and once again, I was struck by the reality that Drew probably didn't care about me as much as I thought he did, and I burned with the shame of getting caught up in this absurd crush yet again. Why was he kissing me and dancing with me and writing me notes if he was still messing around with Stella? What made me think I could honestly compete with her in the first place?

I stepped away from my friends and sat back down on the green sofa, deflated, and contemplating my exit strategy. Becca needed a fun night out—I could tell. And I was her ride. But I didn't want to be there anymore, feeling like the complete joke that I was.

"You made it!" Drew emerged, meandering through the bodies, his face lighting up as he made his way to the couch. He sat down next to me as if there was nothing wrong with that, and I guess there technically wasn't, but I was crestfallen all the same.

"Your house is beautiful, thanks for inviting me," I said, unsure of where to take this conversation. This night was not going to be what I imagined, and I wasn't planning to stay long.

"It's more beautiful now that you're sitting in it." Drew smiled at me, and I watched the light from the fire dance across his face. My initial reaction was to roll my eyes at his compliment considering what I had just witnessed, but I managed to keep a straight face. I just looked at him for a moment, and despite myself, my gut told me that he was sincere. Was I just terrible at reading people? Was I just seeing what I wanted to see? His eyes twinkled at me, and after a beat, when I didn't respond, he looked away, almost sheepishly.

The music was growing louder, and I could feel Becca's eyes on me. When I looked back up at her she quickly threw back a shot and headed to the front room to dance with our other friends—the fun ones who were there for her while I was continuing to fumble around like a possum in a trash can.

"Sorry, Drew, this party is really nice, but I think I should go…" I wasn't ready to have a conversation about feelings with him, and I also didn't want to be in his house anymore.

"Is there a chance I can convince you to stay a little longer? I was hoping we could maybe find a place where we could talk. I mean, you don't have to stay, but I was hoping you would."

Despite my uncertainties, I found myself wanting to take a chance and hear him out. Drew's blue eyes looked dark and magnetic and kind, and I couldn't help myself wanting to believe that he really liked me, even though I had plenty of evidence to suggest that I was being played. I wanted this fairytale so badly. And I wanted it with a guy like Drew. I softened my posture and nodded at him.

"There's a room upstairs where we can sit and talk. Will you come with me?"

"Sure." I smiled weakly, and Drew grabbed my hand to guide me through the party and up the stairs. His hand was strong, but surprisingly soft, too. The beer I had was making me feel uncharacteristically relaxed and confident, but not so much that I wasn't still buzzing with a cocktail of anticipation, desire, and fear of rejection.

We walked up the stairs and I let my hand glide along the solid wood railing and wondered who was watching us and thinking we were going upstairs to do more than just talk. Were we? I had no idea what my expectations were, but a part of me didn't mind the thought of people seeing us together. Even if I was possibly making a fool of myself.

Drew took a left at the top of the stairs and led me down a hallway, and through a door on the right that led to what I guessed was a library or study of some sort. There were bookshelves and soft chairs and a big window that faced the backyard but was covered in vines, which must have crawled up the side of the house. There were several old family photos on the bookshelf, and I took a moment to study them. Old photos have always fascinated me.

"Is this your dad?" There was a photo from sometime in the 80's or 90's of Shep Matthews and another young man about the same age. They were in swim trunks and had the same winning smiles that Drew did.

"Yeah, that's Dad," Drew said, shifting from side to side in an odd sort of way that made me feel rushed.

"Who is this guy with him?" I asked. He looked so familiar, and it was frustrating to me that I couldn't place him. I imagined he had to be a relative and I was just picking up on genetic similarities, but Drew just shrugged in response and gestured to the couch. It seemed weird to me that he wouldn't know, but I let it go.

The night was cloudy, but the yard lights cast a fragmented glow across the floor. A desk lamp was on, and we sat on a small sofa near the window.

I was surprised at how relaxed I felt in that moment. Like I already knew I would be disappointed, so I didn't have hopes to crush, but at the same time, a carnal part of me still craved his body, and his gaze on me made my head spin. I pulled my legs up onto the couch and crossed them, facing him like I would do if I were talking to a friend. Which I couldn't be sure if I was in that moment. It surprised me when Drew did the same.

"Do you always sit crisscross-applesauce when you chat with your friends?" I teased.

"Crisscross-applesauce? Do you always use playground lingo while looking so kissable? Because it's really blurring some lines for me right now," he threw back at me with a smirk.

One point Drew, zero points Annie.

"Do you always flirt with multiple girls at once? Because it's really blurring some lines for me right now, too." I didn't know

121

where that came from. I mean, I *did,* but it wasn't like me to be so forthcoming. Anyway, it was out, and I couldn't take it back.

Drew looked at me with confusion on his face, and a little bit of hurt feelings, too.

"I…don't think so? I'm not sure what you mean." He looked genuine and I was confused. He was either a great actor or I was completely misreading the signs.

I took a deep breath and looked out the window because I couldn't look at Drew and still form complete sentences right then.

"I mean, it's okay if you don't like me, or like if you kind of like me but you aren't sure if you want to date me or be seen with me or whatever. But you took Stella to homecoming and then spent most of the time dancing with me. And then you kissed me. And the kiss was great for me. And maybe it wasn't great for you, and maybe that's what you took me up here to tell me, I don't know. But I saw you and Stella come down the stairs together earlier so please don't try to tell me that you and she aren't together or hooking up at least. I'm just…I've had a crush on you for a long time. And as much as I want to kiss you again, I don't want to keep doing it if you're seeing someone else too. Obviously. And if you don't like me at all and this is all some big prank, then if you could please just be honest and have your laugh so I can move on, that would be really nice of you. I mean, not nice, but better than waiting."

I sighed at the end of my rant, feeling a hair lighter for telling the truth, before feeling the unmistakable weight of a dream that just died. The charade was officially over. I looked back at Drew, and he had a mixture of sadness and amusement on his face.

"Annie…"

I waited a minute for him to speak, and it felt like an eternity. I almost got up to leave, but before I could, Drew started talking.

"I'm not sure why you think that me showing an interest in you would be insincere. I really hope I haven't given you the impression that I'm a diabolical sociopath, but it seems like that's the case and that doesn't make me feel super great. And I'm also not sure why you think that I'm some kind of amazing, untouchable person, but I couldn't be more honored or pleased about it." He smiled at me as he said the last part, and his look was boyish and cute. Then he continued.

"Stella and I have some history…I wouldn't lie to you about that, but you're right—I haven't exactly been clear about my relationship with her either. I promise you that what you saw tonight isn't what you think. We have some things going on right now…but they don't have to do with anything of a romantic nature. We just needed to talk tonight. That's all. I promise." I believed him. I desperately wanted to know what they 'needed' to talk about so badly, but I also didn't have a right to ask. Especially after I just basically accused him of being a manipulative jerk in his own home.

"Would it be okay if I held your hand for the rest of what I have to say?" He looked at me earnestly and I nodded, suddenly feeling like I wanted the space between us to shrink as much as it seemed like he did. He grabbed my hand for the second time that night and pulled it over to rest on his knee with his hand resting gently on top of mine.

Flames shot up my arms and made my throat constrict. I might have drooled if I wasn't so focused on keeping my shit together.

"Annie…I like you. Honestly, I hate science, and it's the best part of my day because I get to sit next to you. I know that night at the beach didn't end how you wanted it to, but that whole night I couldn't take my eyes off of you. When you fell over, it was hilarious, and also cute, and also gave me an excuse to touch you. Which sounds really fucking creepy, but I'm sitting crisscross-applesauce, so I feel like radical honesty is in order."

I actually laughed out loud at that as I let his words wash over me.

"So, I wanted you to come here tonight because I wanted to ask if you would be my girlfriend. If you say no, it's okay. I understand that I might have already fucked this whole thing up. But I hope you give me a chance, because I like you a lot, and I'm dying to spend more time kissing you."

I couldn't even form words to respond. Drew waited for a minute and then lifted his hand off of mine, obviously feeling like a 'no' was coming. I left my hand on his knee. Then I leaned into him and kissed him softly. His lips were soft, and I could feel him smiling as I moved my mouth over his and savored him for a moment. A moment that didn't feel real but was.

"Okay, Drew Matthews, I'll be your girlfriend," I said the words I had dreamed of saying since I was in elementary school. I couldn't believe this was really happening.

Drew and I stayed there for a little longer, kissing each other and enjoying a quiet space that was free from secrets and assumptions. When we, at last, decided to rejoin the party, Drew held out his hand to pull me up off of the couch and gave me a squeeze.

"I love this sexy outfit you have on. Can I see it again sometime?"

"Thank you," I said, striking an exaggerated pose. "Becca styled me. If I ever say, do, or wear anything cool, you can safely assume it's because of her."

An unusual look flashed across Drew's face, but before I could decipher it, it was gone.

"So…what do you think Becca will think of us dating? Do you…think she'll be cool with it?" It was an odd question, but too many sparks were flying for me to think about it.

"Normally I would say something like 'I don't need my friends' permission on who I can date,' but in all honesty, Becca's like my other half, so it's a fair question," I laughed, teasing him. He let out a tight laugh in response. "Don't worry about Becca, she just wants me to be happy, and I'm happy. She'll be totally into it." I reassured him and he looked relieved.

Becca and I were always together, and dating could definitely complicate BFF relationships sometimes. But she loved me, and she knew this was what I wanted. I couldn't wait to get downstairs and spill the beans so we could jump up and down together and squeal like pre-teens at a boyband concert.

As we walked down the stairs, Drew said, "You live like right next door to Shea McAteer, right? Do you think he did it? That guy is sketchy as hell, so I wouldn't be surprised if he did. But I don't like the idea of you living so close to him if he's as cold-blooded as people say he is."

For some reason, I instinctively felt defensive. Nobody really knew Shea, so how could they think they knew anything about the situation? But then again, I didn't actually know anything either. Not really.

"Shea doesn't seem so bad to me. I'm not worried about it. Who knows? He might end up in foster care or something anyway." I tried to brush the conversation off, desperate to bask in my moment and not think of the ghosts next door.

"Well, I can tell you for sure that foster care isn't going to happen. That's why the whole thing is extra sketchy. My dad has connections at the police department, and he told me that homecoming night was apparently Shea's 18th birthday. So, his dad just suddenly decides to kill himself on his son's birthday? Or did Shea wait to make his move until he could legally keep the house and live there alone? Not trying to throw shade on the guy, but I definitely won't be going over there to hang out anytime soon, and I hope you stay clear of him if you can because I care about you." Drew squeezed my hand and smiled a saccharine smile.

I appreciated that Drew had some pretty fair opinions on the matter, but I couldn't shake the nagging desire to defend Shea. I was shocked to know that the night Shea gave me a ride to homecoming was actually his birthday. Why hadn't he mentioned it? I suppose I hadn't really given him a chance to, but it did seem like sort of a big thing not to celebrate or even mention. And Drew was right—why would Shea's dad choose that day of all days to kill himself? He seemed like a mean guy, but I knew that there was some love in him too, and I just couldn't see why he would make that choice.

Maybe nothing is ever clear in love, or in death.

EIGHTEEN

BY THE TIME I found my friends again, they were in the dining room, which could only mean one thing. They were all sloppy drunk. Charlotte and Becca were pawing at each other while they talked, like cats in slow motion. And Sydney was sitting on someone's lap and dipping her head back too far every time she laughed.

Being a sober person at a drunk party is 10% amusing and 90% irritating as hell. The humor of watching your friends act like idiots lasts for a few measly seconds before you try to have a conversation with them or make a move in any direction and find that it's like herding large toddlers. Suddenly you become responsible for their safety and well-being, and they basically do everything they can to make that difficult for you. I supposed that I was willing to pay my dues to the universe for the gift it gave me that night in the form of my dream boyfriend.

I watched Becca as she took a step back and fell right on her ass. She started laughing like I'd never seen her laugh and then, out of nowhere, she burst into tears. Before anyone could get their phone out and record Becca crying uncontrollably on the floor, I ran over and lifted her under her arms and led her out to my car. It was definitely time to go home.

Becca didn't usually lose control like this. She drank frequently, but in modest amounts, unlike her parents whose blood alcohol level was probably over the legal limit for driving more often than not. It surprised me to see Becca unable to walk straight, and it surprised me, even more, to see her overcome by her emotions. I thought maybe someone had slipped her something. In which case, I was definitely going to get her to bed ASAP and stay with her awhile to make sure she was okay.

I got her home, in pajamas, and in bed. I wiped her makeup off with a makeup wipe and put a glass of water on her nightstand. I wasn't going to spend the night, but I wasn't going to leave her right away either. I texted Drew to let him know that I had to take Becca home and that I'd see him later that weekend. He responded: DREW: *Okay, babe. Text me when you get home safe.* <3

I won't say that Drew calling me 'babe' felt like the most natural thing in the world. No one had ever called me that before, and it was an odd feeling to have someone suddenly transition from an acquaintance to someone who called me pet names and cared about my safety. A simple little label did all that. It felt good, but also weird, and a little unreal. It would take some getting used to.

Becca was sound asleep and breathing (I checked three times to make sure), so I got in my car and drove the long, dark miles to my house. I normally listened to music in the car, but that night I needed silence. I let the events of the previous hours hum along to the sound of my tires on the road as I processed my new girlfriend status. I moved alone through the dark until I approached my driveway, and my bubble of silence was interrupted by the sound of my blinker clicking. My parents had left the porch light on for me, and I turned it off before I tiptoed up to my room. I fell asleep quickly, but not before I texted Drew to tell him that I made it home safe.

...

Saturday morning, I slept in, and when I got downstairs, the rest of the family was already done with breakfast. Rosie was watching Sesame Street while Mom folded towels. I wasn't ready to eat yet, so I sat down next to Rosie just as my dad picked up the basket of warm, unfolded towels and dumped them on us. Warmth and comfort soaked right through my skin and into my soul, and Rosie's giggles were the sparkle on top. Life was good that morning. I was safe and loved. I didn't appreciate it as much as I should have.

"So, how was the party last night?" I knew this conversation would be coming. Mom wasn't going to ask me directly what happened with Drew, but I'm sure she had a hunch that something might be going on between us after our cozy little moment on homecoming night and now a party at his house.

"It was good. Charlotte and Sydney were there. And lots of other people. Have you ever been inside the Matthews house before? It's amazing." I tried to keep the conversation neutral. I wasn't ready to tell her that Drew was my boyfriend. It wasn't a secret, but I needed more time to feel it out and make sure I wasn't dreaming before I started spreading the news.

"So, how was Drew?" I could tell that she was intentionally not looking at me and just looking at the clothes she was folding, probably trying not to spook me out of giving her details.

"Umm…he was good I guess, but I didn't really get to stay too long because Becca got tired, and I had to take her home. We just hung out at her place for a while and then I came here."

Technically this wasn't a lie, but it wasn't exactly the truth either. I didn't like lying to my mom, but I had a feeling that saying

'I don't feel like talking about it right now' wouldn't send the right message, and she would end up worrying about me unnecessarily.

My dad, who was reading the newspaper on the other side of the room, chimed in. "Have you noticed anything different about Becca lately?"

His question surprised me—I didn't know why he would ask me that out of the blue.

"I mean…no…she was pretty tired last night, but other than that, she's just Becca. Why do you ask?"

"No reason, just making sure she's not overworked at the shop or anything. Becky does a lot for her parents, and I hope she's not spread too thin."

It seemed like there was something my dad was skating around, but I wasn't going to push the issue. I remember feeling a sudden pang of guilt for not paying as much attention to Becca as I normally did because I was so busy focusing on myself, and the stupid things I thought were problems. Looking back, I wish I would have just been honest with my dad. Something did feel off with Becca. She didn't go to homecoming. She got super drunk at Drew's party. She got a job at the sports shop of all places, and I felt like when we talked, she was distracted most of the time. She was never as happy for me as I expected her to be.

I try not to beat myself up too much about all the times I could have stepped up and been a better friend but didn't. I simply didn't know then what I know now.

I texted her:

ME: *Hey B, just making sure you're alive and well this morning. If you aren't dead, then you should come over to my house and hang out this afternoon. Stay for dinner.*

Three dots showed up and then disappeared.

BECCA: *Alive. Not well. Technically I meet the requirement of "not dead" — so I'll see you later. There's no fucking Advil in this house. Be there soonish.*

I was relieved that she was coming over. We needed this. We hadn't spent quality time together that wasn't all about me in a shameful amount of time. I went upstairs and showered, and a smile pulled at my lips as I imagined how excited Becca would be for me when I told her that Drew asked me to be his girlfriend. I made a mental note to ask about her, too, and not just talk about myself the whole time.

A couple of hours later Becca arrived, looking rough. Her face was puffy, and she had on an oversized t-shirt that sat on her big boobs like bed sheets falling off a shelf. Her hair was up in a messy bun, and for once, she didn't look sexy and put together. She actually looked younger. Like a tired kid, instead of a teen vixen modeling leather pants on top of a motorcycle.

Becca showing up in this vulnerable state reminded me of our middle school days when we were on the edge of puberty and hadn't discovered makeup yet. She would come over for sleepovers several times a week with fear in her eyes and hunger in her tummy. My parents would go pick her up any time she called, and they made her visits special every time with snacks and movies and homecooked meals. At the time, I thought they did it all to spoil me by letting me have my friend over whenever I wanted. Now, looking back, I see that they were rescuing a scared girl from a sad situation.

Becca took one look at me and ran to the guest bathroom to throw up. I made her a turkey sandwich with some plain potato chips on the side. She normally dipped them in ranch, but I skipped it because I figured less was more given the circumstances. I set it out on the table with a glass of water, a glass of orange juice, and a mug of coffee all in a row. Her nausea this morning may have been self-imposed, but I still didn't like my best friend feeling like shit, and I was ready to pamper her accordingly.

Becca came out of the bathroom and sat down and tossed a potato chip in her mouth. She took a sip of coffee, and then she burst into tears, except this time, she did it completely sober. I picked up her coffee mug and hooked my arm through hers and walked her up to my bedroom where we could talk privately, and she could cry for as long as she wanted to.

"Okay, Bec, I'm listening. Tell me what's going on."

Becca didn't say anything. She just sat down on the side of my bed and then slid herself all the way to the floor, so she was sitting with her back against my mattress. I sat down next to her and reached for her hand, patiently waiting for her to speak.

"I'm tired, Annie. I'm just so…so…tired. I'm tired." She started sobbing again and I held her hand while she did it.

I crawled over to my nightstand and handed her the whole box of tissues so she could tuck into it liberally, which she did. I knew why she was tired. She basically did life alone. She was responsible for so much, including keeping up the appearance of a being a badass bitch who had her shit together. She was all of those

132

things, but it was a lot of pressure on a girl with no real support. I assumed this was the reason she was upset. That she had just reached a breaking point. I should have asked more questions, but I didn't. I just assumed I knew everything.

"If you want to talk, I'm listening." That was all I said. It wasn't enough.

Becca looked me in the eyes for a long time.

"No, I think I just needed to have a cry. I'm over it now. Can we talk about you instead?" she said finally.

I sighed and gave Becca a long look that meant I would be following up with her more later, whether she liked it or not. She raised her eyebrows at me, and I rolled my eyes at her, relenting. I *was* excited to tell her about Drew, anyway. Plus, I thought maybe the news would cheer her up. Most friends say they are 'so happy for you,' but they really aren't. Or if they are, they exaggerate their feelings to look like nice people. But I knew in my soul that seeing me happy brought Becca joy. I knew it because I felt the same way when I saw her winning in life, and our connection was as divine and true as they come. And anyway, Becca was a lesbian. She definitely wasn't interested in Drew, so I didn't have to worry about possible jealousy like I inevitably would when the girls at school found out about us on Monday.

"Well…so…you and I obviously didn't really get to talk last night—I brought you home and you fell asleep right away. I was dying to tell you…but, it's big, so I wanted to wait until you could fully freak out with me."

"Spit it out already, Annie!" Becca seemed to be perking up a tiny bit already, with the potential of exciting news on the horizon.

"Drew asked me to be his girlfriend and I said yes." I looked at her with wide, happy eyes, ready for her to jump up and hug me or squeal with delight.

I had a hard time hiding my disappointment when Becca just gave me a half smile and said, "I'm happy for you."

"I know you're hungover and tired, but why don't you seem as excited for me as I thought you would be? Like, no pressure, but I was expecting some confetti to burst out of your bra or something."

Becca rolled her eyes at me, because I was obnoxious, and I knew it.

"First of all, I'm not wearing a bra. And also, I *am* happy for you. And I know how excited you are. Drew seems really nice, and I know how much this feels like a dream come true for you."

"…But???" I looked at her with raised eyebrows, asking for truths I didn't actually want to hear.

"But…if I'm being completely honest, I just don't think that he's good enough for you, Annie."

I was dumbfounded. Becca had officially lost her mind. This situation with her was clearly more serious than I had originally thought.

"What?! If he's not good enough for me, then I have no idea who possibly could be. He's perfect. He's sweet and gorgeous and charming and smart…I honestly can't imagine someone better for me than Drew. I've kissed him several times now and my mouth is pretty sure he's good enough for me too." I'm not sure who I was trying to convince, Becca or myself. My defenses were high. Becca just sighed.

134

"It's not that he isn't all of those things, Annie…it's just…there's something about him that I don't like. Like he's insincere. And underneath all the bravado, I don't think he's really very brave at all."

"Insincere? *Bravado?* What does that even mean? Because he's good-looking and popular, there's no way he could seriously be interested in *me*? Believe me, Becca, I don't need you to remind me how much better he is than me. Even if you are trying to frame it like I'm the one that's too good for him." I started tearing up as my insecurities bubbled up to the surface.

I had carried my labels and limitations around like suitcases full of cockroaches for so many years, and after last night, I thought I had finally dropped them along the roadside. When Becca suggested that Drew might be playing me (whether or not that's what she actually meant, that's what a heard), suddenly the heavy bags were back in my hands and the cockroaches were climbing out of them and weaving their way up my arms.

"Annie, you know that's not what I mean."

I didn't know that's not what she meant.

"I'm sorry. I really am happy for you. Drew is a seriously lucky guy. He has excellent taste in girls if I do say so myself." Becca threw me a wink, and I let my guard down.

I couldn't be mad at her. She was just tired and protective of me and my feelings. She loved me and I loved her, and that meant giving her the benefit of the doubt, even if my own insecurities wanted to tell me a different story.

I threw a pillow at her and made her groan in pain from the hangover headache that she was still nursing. She climbed up onto my bed and pulled out her phone so we could watch cat videos on YouTube and set aside dealing with our feelings for another day.

We were still kids, after all. Weren't we?

NINETEEN

BECCA AND I sat in my room and snacked for the rest of the afternoon. We weren't even hungry by the time my mom called us down for dinner, but we went down anyway. It was lasagna night, and some of the emotional heaviness from earlier had dissipated, leaving more room in our bodies for carbs.

After dinner, Mom went over to the fridge and took out a whole second lasagna covered in tin foil, and I had a feeling I knew who it was intended for.

"Do you girls want to walk this over to Shea or should I?" she asked. Before I could respond, Becca jumped in.

"We'll do it! Thanks, Mrs. Paulson!" Becca jumped in before I could even decide if I wanted to go over there again, especially after Drew's apprehensions had sunken in a bit. I had lost all faith in my ability to read people lately, so I wasn't overly keen on stopping by Shea's house.

Becca grabbed the lasagna and grabbed me, and we headed out the door.

"Why so eager to bring the lasagna, Becca?" I asked as we walked across the field and into the grove.

"I'm dying of curiosity, aren't you? Let's go investigate!" Becca always did enjoy a murder mystery and had a much higher tolerance for gruesome happenings than I did. As much as I liked seeing her energized by something, it irritated me that she saw Shea, in the same way, everyone else seemed to—like a sad spectacle.

137

"I'm not sure how much investigating we'll be able to do between handing over a lasagna and walking back home," I said, hoping she wasn't going to push this particular button tonight. Not only did I want her to leave Shea alone, but I also had a feeling if she saw me around him, she would be able to see right through me and my secret attraction to him. I had managed to keep her off my trail after he made me blush at the sports shop, but I didn't think I could get away with it twice. Speaking about my feelings out loud to my friend would make them real, and I wanted to avoid that at all costs. I was someone's girlfriend now.

"Watch me," she replied with a glint in her eye. *Oh, for fuck's sake.*

Becca knocked on Shea's door, and I could feel the excitement coming off of her in tidal waves. She lived for an adrenaline rush, and I really just wanted to go home, bask in the glow of having a new boyfriend, and forget about the hot potential murderer next door.

Shea opened the door and his eyes shifted from me to Becca, and then back to me. He gave me a tiny smirk and a bomb went off in my chest. I tried to pour mental ice water on the heat that his presence sent through my core. It didn't work. I was already failing miserably at being a girlfriend. *I'm a horrible person.*

"Here," Becca said, handing Shea the lasagna. "We brought you dinner. Can we come in and hang out?"

Well, that was pretty fucking direct. I looked around and behind me, as if not looking at Shea would indicate that I wasn't a part of this plan to bombard him.

"Umm…sure?" Shea sounded confused but he didn't resist Becca as she smiled brightly and shimmied her way into his house.

I followed her meekly, feeling like we were definitely crossing a major line.

"So sorry about your dad…" Becca kept talking as she made herself at home. "I guess this house is all yours now, huh?"

I gave her a death stare. What the hell was she doing carelessly barging in here and asking these pointed questions?

"Thanks. Yeah, the house is mine, I guess. Not that I would have wanted it this way. But I suppose I'm glad it's paid off and I have a place to live while I figure out what I'm going to do with the rest of my life. Alone." Shea didn't sound mad, but he didn't sound happy either.

There was an awkward silence. This conversation was Becca's doing, and I wasn't going to help save her from it.

"Both my parents are alive, and I'm still doing life alone. Not saying that to diminish what you're going through, but maybe just to let you know that in some ways I can relate. To the aloneness."

Becca surprised me with her honesty and vulnerability in that moment. She didn't talk about her home life with anyone, not even me, really. Shea nodded at her understanding. And just like that, the tension in the air dissipated.

"Can I get you girls something to drink? Your options are pretty much limited to water, Gatorade, or…beer."

I had to think that the beer was left over from when his dad was alive in this house, and the thought of that gave me goosebumps. I couldn't imagine what it was like for Shea to be here alone after what happened, surrounded by memories and John's earthly possessions lingering around.

"Water is great, thanks. I'm A LOT hungover from Drew's party last night. We can't all be as responsible as Annie. If it

139

weren't for her, I'm pretty sure I would have ended up in a ditch somewhere." Becca shot me a look that was teasing and loving all wrapped up in one.

"Annie is certainly something," Shea added, giving me a look that wasn't far off the one Becca was giving me.

It occurred to me in that moment what a gorgeous couple the two of them would make if it weren't for the obvious problem with that scenario. Well, several problems. They were both tall and dark-haired, with the kind of features that made you stop and stare. Where Becca's eyes were green and seductive, Shea's eyes were warm and dark and inviting. Anytime either one of them looked at me, I felt like I was truly being seen. Both of them looking at me together made me feel twice as visible, which would have normally made me uncomfortable if it weren't for the strong sense of endearment swirling around me. These two people were happy that I existed, and when they looked at me, I felt it.

"Okay, back in a sec." Shea walked through the living room and into the kitchen, while Becca and I sat ourselves down on a brown leather couch.

I had only been inside the McAteer house a few times, and the last time was probably when I was seven or eight. From the little I could remember, not much had changed since then. The house had the same wood floors, simple furniture, and plain walls that it had had ten years prior. And the place was immaculate. Apparently, Shea kept a clean house as well as a clean car. It appeared that he was, indeed, either the perfect man or a serial killer.

From where I sat in the living room, I could see through the doorway into the kitchen, and in the window above the kitchen sink, I noticed the orchid plant that my blossom had originated

140

from. I smiled at the memory. Just then, my phone rang, and the name that popped up on my screen was Drew's. I decided to answer, but I wasn't going to sit there chatting with him in front of Shea, so I stepped out onto the front porch to take the call.

"Hey! How's it going?" My voice sounded so high-pitched and cheery it annoyed even me.

"Hey babe, I'm good. Just wanted to hear your voice. What are you up to?"

Starting off this relationship with a bald-faced lie wasn't great, but I couldn't exactly tell him that I was hanging out at Shea's house after he explicitly requested that I steer clear of him for my own safety. I was my own person and could make my own decisions, but I didn't think it would be sending the right message to tell him what I was really doing in that moment.

"I'm just hanging out at my house with Becca. We needed some girl time."

"Ahh...okay...so you're crisscross-applesaucing without me? That's cool, I guess..." I could hear the smile in his voice, and it made me smile. He was just too freaking cute for words.

"Yeah, I like to share the love...But I'm looking forward to the next time I get to do it with you."

"Do what, exactly?" Okay, now Drew was making me blush.

"I guess we'll see, won't we?" I said, smirking into my phone.

Drew laughed and it sounded like church bells. I said my goodbyes so that I could 'get back to Becca,' and hung up with a smile in my heart.

When I walked back into the house, I heard laughter. Becca and Shea were sitting in the living room talking and laughing together about something I must have missed while I was lurking outside on the phone. I sat down on the couch next to Becca and asked her to clue me in on the joke.

"Oh, just swapping drunk parent stories," Becca said, looking back to Shea and they both snorted and burst out laughing again.

This was a topic that I couldn't personally relate to, but I had never seen Shea laugh out loud before and it made the whole room light up around us. I'd never seen eyes so dark shine so bright. I found myself wanting to be near him. Wanting to look at him and touch him and know his secrets. He walked the line between danger and light, and I wanted to go there with him, wherever 'there' was.

Too bad I had a boyfriend now. Undressing someone with your eyes isn't the same as actually cheating, though, right?

We stayed for a while longer, talking like the three of us were old friends. It was strange how natural it felt, considering we had never actually spent any real length of time together. Shea and Becca were a natural fit, and, while I was trying my damnedest not to admit it to myself, there was a seed of jealousy sprouting as I watched them intermingle so seamlessly. Every time I interacted with Shea, I seemed to freeze up and make an ass of myself, and then bombshell Becca just goes and pushes her way into his house and probably into his heart as well. Did it matter that she wasn't interested in him sexually? There's no way he wouldn't be attracted to her. And maybe if she liked him enough, she would consider trying the boy thing again, and they would date.

And also, why the hell should I have even cared if that were the case? I had my dream guy, and Shea was available to anyone for the taking. If Becca decided she wanted broad, brown shoulders and smoldering eyes, I certainly wasn't in any position to tell her not to go for it.

Why the hell am I even thinking about this right now?

My intrusive thoughts were impeding my ability to flow with the conversation, so I chimed in with the bare minimum. Every once in a while, Shea would glance over at me, and every time our eyes met, a jolt of adrenaline coursed through my body and made my heart race. I tried not to be hyper-aware of my posture and facial expressions, but I couldn't help it. Being seen by Shea felt different than being seen by anyone else. I felt like he could somehow read my thoughts. Every time he looked into my eyes, I felt like I was naked. And an ever-growing part of me secretly wanted to be.

My phone vibrated in my back pocket, and I picked it up to see a text from my mom asking if we were okay. I replied.

ME: *Yes, just at Shea's house. Becca wanted to stop in and chat. Be back soon.*

"Who's texting you?" Becca asked, loudly.

"Just mom checking to make sure we are safe."

As soon as I said it, I felt stupid. I didn't want Shea to know that me or my parents were scared for my safety when I was around him. "We just told her we'd be back right away for a movie she rented," I added, hoping I could quickly cover up the little hole I had just started digging.

"No, I get it. You girls should get back." Shea's eyes landed on me. "Next time you bring me lasagna maybe you could stay and eat it with me. If you give me some warning, I could make you some dessert." Shea wasn't speaking to Becca now. He was looking right at me.

I couldn't help the smile that crept up onto my face, and when he smiled back the heat between my legs made me squirm in my seat.

"Watch yourself, Romeo—Annie's already taken." Becca tossed the comment into the air between us, and it lay there like a dead fish.

Fuck you, Becca. And also, fuck me.

Shea's expression didn't betray his feelings, but the lightness in his eyes darkened a shade.

"Guess I'll just eat my pumpkin pie alone for now," he said as we all stood up and walked toward the door. A sad part of me knew that there were few things in this world I would rather do than eat pie and talk about books alone with Shea, and in that particular moment, I couldn't think of any of them.

Shea opened the door for us, and I thanked him for letting us barge in on him. We stepped out onto the porch.

"Anytime. This was great," he said, and I could tell he meant it. Before Shea could close the door, Becca turned back to him.

"So, everyone's saying that you killed your dad. You seem like such a nice guy, and you won't get any judgment from me either way, but I just have to ask, is it true?"

Shea and I looked at Becca. The silence was suffocating, but Becca didn't seem to mind. Is this the reason we spent all this time here making friends? So that she could satiate her curiosity? I felt the need to defend Shea for the second time that weekend.

"Becca, of course he didn't. How could you even ask that?" I glared at her, hoping she would take the hint and drop it.

"No, Annie. It's a fair question. I guess I'd rather that people be direct with me than speculate."

I looked over at Shea, surprised at how calm he was considering what Becca just asked him.

"I did kill him. It was me."

TWENTY

I WAS STUNNED into silence. Becca wasn't.

"Holy shit, man. Really? Did you really just admit to murder right now? Why aren't you in jail?" She asked him directly without an ounce of trepidation.

"Your guess is as good as mine," Shea replied darkly. He wasn't looking at us anymore. His eyes were cast to the ground and his energy seemed to be snuffed out entirely.

"How do you know we won't go and tell the police what you just confessed to us?" Becca was genuinely curious. I was in shock.

"I don't know that. Actually, I hope you do go talk to the police. Although you wouldn't be telling them anything I didn't already tell them myself. I deserve to rot in prison. But I guess they want me to rot in this house instead."

I could tell Shea was done with this conversation. All the lightness that had radiated from him earlier had fizzled out and was replaced by a cold cloud of despair. Becca gave him a nod as he quietly thanked us for stopping by and closed the door.

Becca was full of thoughts and theories, and a part of me felt happy to see her glowing a bit after how drained she had been earlier. But I still couldn't focus on the words coming out of her mouth. I was too wrapped up in the complexity of my own emotions and the nagging feeling that there was so much more to this story, and so much more to Shea that I needed to discover before I could ever be at peace.

Shea was a murderer. Supposedly. My bet was on self-defense, but even still, that's pretty scary shit, and one thing I was sure about at this point was that I couldn't be sure of anything anymore. Was I a bad person for feeling attracted to Shea? If Shea was the murderer he claimed to be, why wasn't I more scared? Why couldn't I stop swooning every time I was around him when my heart belonged to someone else? Was I some kind of psychopath? My mind was spinning with cold-blooded scenarios and suddenly everything I thought I knew about the world came into question.

Becca and I crawled into my bed together and she fell asleep quickly, which made me happy, because she really, *really* needed to rest. I checked my phone and saw a 'goodnight' text from Drew, which should have made me smile, but tonight it just made me feel guilty and stupid.

I lay awake for hours before sleep finally rescued me from my spinning thoughts.

...

When I arrived at school on Monday, I didn't see Becca by our lockers, so I went straight to math class early. I was surprised to see Becca already in there, half sitting on Miss Jones's desk and chatting with her. Only Becca would have the balls to sit on a teacher's desk, even if the teacher was barely older than us.

"Hey, Annie," Miss Jones greeted me with a smile. She was the kind of teacher that it would be cool to be friends with, so I was pleased when she seemed happy to see me. Becca slid off her desk and she and I sat down in our usual seats.

"Miss Jones was just telling me about New York City," Becca said with stars in her eyes.

Neither one of us had ever had a chance to travel anywhere outside of the Midwest, and I could tell that Becca was dreaming of bigger places. As sad as it made me to think of Becca moving away from me, I knew that the big city was where she belonged. I was glad that she had a teacher who could give her hope for the sparkling future that she deserved.

"You'll get there someday, Becca. The world is your oyster."

"I'm definitely into oysters," Becca replied, and Miss Jones chuckled.

That seemed like a pretty suggestive comment for a teacher to laugh at, but then again, maybe Miss Jones was more human than a teacher. I was definitely getting that vibe, and I was into it. Obviously, Becca had spotted it right away and had built a friendship with her while I was too busy being boy crazy and worrying about myself. The rest of the students trickled in, and Miss Jones turned on her teacher voice, and we got to work learning various calculus concepts that I have yet to apply to my daily life in any way, shape, or form.

In English, Mr. Gregory handed out a creative writing assignment, and for the first time, maybe ever, I didn't even know how to begin to write. I wasn't ready to put words to the feelings going on in my body, and every time I tried to invent something unrelated to my current obsessions, I came up short. A poem about flowers became a poem about orchids. A poem about the sky became a poem about my first kiss with Drew under the stars. A poem about love became a poem about death. I erased and erased and erased until there was hardly any paper left to write on.

"Having some writer's block today, Annie?" Mr. Gregory's gentle voice floated over my shoulder.

"I am. It's just…" I wouldn't normally be this forthcoming with another person, but Mr. Gregory was special. I trusted him. "I just have some things on my mind, and I'm not ready to write about them. But I'm afraid they are currently taking up all the space I have in my brain right now, and they haven't left room for anything shareable."

"Hmm...well I know that you know that the best writing comes from the truth. And I also know that you know that writing is a great way to help you sort out complicated feelings."

I nodded in agreement, and he continued.

"That being said, it's not fair to expect a student to share their deepest feelings with me or anyone else if they don't want to, especially not a student as passionate or capable as you." He gave me a kind smile that made me feel like a valuable human being. "I hope you do write about what you're feeling, for your own sake, and I hope you don't share it with me unless you really want to. In lieu of this assignment, you can write me a short literary analysis on the reading of your choice, and we'll call it even."

I appreciated Mr. Gregory giving me grace. I'd miss him when I went to college. I spent the rest of the class time googling short stories to read and analyze, and it was a welcome mental break from the dizzy elephant stomping around in my head. By the end of class, I hadn't sorted out my feelings whatsoever, but I *was* ready to see Drew for the first time since we became official. I made a conscious effort to pack Shea away into a sturdy filing cabinet in the recesses of my mind, so I could make plenty of space for the guy who really mattered to me.

The bell rang and I joined the masses as we all transitioned between classrooms. Out of nowhere, music came over the loudspeakers, and the dull murmur of student conversation was replaced by silence as we all stopped and tried to decipher what was going on. I stopped and looked around, waiting for something to happen to someone else.

The second I recognized the song, my heart started pounding and heat crept up my neck. "Can't Help Falling in Love" played loud over the intercom, and the students around me parted as Drew came walking down the hallway with a bouquet of roses in his hands and a smile on his face that said, 'I know exactly how cute I'm being right now.' He remembered the song we danced to at homecoming, and now he was basically announcing to the whole school that we were an item. I started to wonder if the whole football player dance routine at homecoming was really the other guys' idea, or if Drew had a thing for public displays of affection.

I glanced around quickly just to make sure there weren't any photographers from the local newspaper around waiting to snap photos of this event too. It turns out no professional photographers were needed because several students had their phones out and were recording the whole thing. I blushed even harder. Being the center of attention wasn't my thing, but I couldn't deny that it felt pretty great to be seen getting doted on by Drew Matthews.

When Drew finally reached me, he handed me the flowers, which revealed a fitted white t-shirt that said, 'Annie's Boyfriend' across the chest. So incredibly cheesy. So incredibly unnecessary. So incredibly sweet.

"What is all this about?" I said, trying to keep my cool, but struggling.

"Just making sure everyone knows that you're mine." Drew winked and sent a flutter into my belly. "Also, after the whole Stella homecoming thing, I felt like I owed you your own personal moment in the spotlight." He beamed at me.

I didn't have the heart to tell him that all these people looking at me made me want to pee my pants with anxiety. I just reached up and kissed him on the cheek and he grabbed my hand so we could walk together to science class.

So, now everyone knew. Drew and I were officially together in the eyes of the public. As we walked to class, I saw some sophomore girls swooning and a group of Stella's friends snapping their gum and rolling their eyes. It made my stomach drop. Stella was nowhere to be seen, which was a relief. Even though, according to Drew, they were just friends, I couldn't stand the idea of being secretly hated by someone.

Most boys didn't seem to notice or care that Drew and I were holding hands, except for the few assholes who whistled or reached out to high five Drew. I knew deep down that they weren't congratulating him on snagging me, specifically, but rather, congratulating him on a successful public display and for getting what he wanted in life. I didn't have a problem with that, per se, and I was looking forward to the social benefits of being on Drew's arm.

But there was a part of me that housed a tiny bit of resentment for how much easier life was for some people by no real merit of their own. Spending time with Becca and Shea together made me realize that I belonged in that category too. I was ashamed of how much time I had spent feeling sorry for myself for this reason or that, while I had two living parents who loved me and a safe place to call home. Drew and I had both lived pretty uncomplicated lives and watching him receive endless adoration from his peers just didn't impress me the same way that it used to.

If anyone needed love right now, it was Shea. But nobody seemed to give a shit about whether or not he was okay. Did he murder someone? Apparently so. Was there more to the story? There had to be, or he'd be in prison right now. I decided in that moment that I would find out the whole truth. I didn't know his story, but if my interactions with him were any indication, he seemed to have a good heart, even if he didn't seem convinced of that himself.

Drew held my hand all the way to class. Just before we reached the door, I felt a cool energy nearby. I glanced around and made eye contact with Shea. I suddenly felt the urge to take my hand out of Drew's, but I didn't. Shea looked at the flowers I was carrying and then down at my fingers intertwined with Drew's and then back up at me and raised his eyebrows a fraction as it became clear who the boyfriend was that Becca had alluded to the other night. I gave Shea a half smile as Drew pulled me into the classroom. The moment was over in a second, but the imprint it left on my mood colored every interaction I had with Drew for the next hour. It was irritating how easily Shea escaped from the depths of my mind and made his way to the forefront of it.

My anxiety was building as art class approached. Since I had seen Shea in the hallway earlier, I knew he was back at school, and during the last conversation I had with him, he'd confessed to murder. I wanted more information, but school wasn't exactly the place to be talking about it. If he even wanted to talk to me again, that is. After Becca stormed in and drilled him about wounds that were obviously still extremely fresh, I wouldn't be surprised if Shea wanted to avoid me altogether. It's not like we were *really* friends, after all.

I arrived at art class first and chose an easel on the far side of the room. Every time another student walked through the door, I prayed that they would sit next to me so that Shea wouldn't have to since he tended to arrive late for some reason. The seats were about half filled when Shea walked in. I looked down at my phone avoiding eye contact as my heart pounded in my chest. I tapped furiously at my screen as Shea approached, and when he sat down next to me, I let out a big breath that I didn't realize I had been holding in my lungs.

"If you want me to sit somewhere else, I'll understand," Shea said quietly in the direction of the easel in front of him.

I looked up at him, but he wasn't looking at me. His jaw was tight and there was pain in his face. I couldn't imagine what coming back to school was like for him after what had happened. With everyone gossiping and nobody really caring about him, even if he really *was* the bad person claimed to be.

"You can stay, but you have to swear that you will not laugh at my drawing skills or lack thereof," I said, offering up a mock-serious face.

The sadness in Shea was like a magnet, drawing all of my loving energy to my surface. As wrong as it probably was, all I wanted to do when I was around him was make him smile. If I could just see his light shine for a second, I would be fulfilled. I was beginning to think there was something seriously wrong with me. It turns out I was just growing into my own gifts, but I didn't know myself well enough to recognize them yet.

"Unfortunately, I can make no such promises," he said. He looked over at me then, and when our eyes met it felt like my soul was leaving my body and reaching out desperately for his. It was like there was a deep, divine part of me that knew things I didn't. I found myself following her lead, against what the squeaky, seventeen-year-old voice in my head was telling me to do.

I took a sharp breath in again and his eyes twinkled. *Does he know how he makes me feel when he looks at me like that?*

"Okay, well then, I just won't draw anything so you can stay without breaking the terms of the agreement. The world will be better off with less of my art in it."

Shea laughed audibly, and tears pricked my eyes as the warmth inside my heart expanded around me. He was so handsome when he smiled. The fact that I had made it happen made me feel full to the brim. I never wanted to stop feeling that feeling.

Ms. Young announced that our next model would be Bennett Gray. Bennett was quiet, but not shy. He was just a nice person and had always been mature for his age, which meant he spent much less time acting like a fool than most boys our age, and more time doing things that were productive and helpful. He was nice-looking and kind, and I was glad to be looking at him instead of the likes of self-obsessed Kamila or douchey Jordan. I just hoped that Bennett wouldn't be offended when his portrait turned out to be a stick figure with glasses on. Then again, if there was anyone in our class who was capable of a kind comment about someone's work, it was Bennett. I made a mental note to draw a heart and a smiley face on the picture as a humble offering before letting him see it.

Shea started sketching, and I watched as an abstract form took shape and began to look like the figure sitting before us. I couldn't take my eyes off of his paper as I watched him scribble away like it was the most natural thing in the world. Shea's pencil stopped, and I snapped out of my trance to find him looking at me with curiosity.

"How's it going over there, Annie?" Shea asked, and I realized I hadn't even picked up my pencil. "You weren't serious about not drawing anything, right? Because I'd hate for you to fail art class just because I can't control my emotions around you."

I gave him an exaggerated eye roll. "Well, to be fair, if I would have known you were a professional artist, I definitely would have sent you far away from this corner of the room."

Shea drew a simple smiley face on the oval that was clearly going to be Bennett's head.

"Better?" Shea looked at me and smirked. It was so cute I think my heart stopped for a second.

"Yes. Now keep being shitty, or you're getting kicked to the curb," I teased.

"Done." Shea proceeded to draw little figures of aliens and balloons and curly Qs all over his paper. He drew silly little faces that made me laugh, and by the time class was over, my paper was empty, and his looked like a mashup of upscale graffiti and vintage comic book illustrations. Ms. Young walked by and shook her head at the two of us but didn't say anything. Maybe she was more human than a teacher, too.

My heart had officially doubled in size. It belonged to two people at once. And I didn't want to have to choose.

TWENTY-ONE

THE REST OF the week was both stressful and delightful. I looked forward to seeing Drew every day, but I was also secretly excited to see Shea every day, which made me feel a tiny bit naughty and a lot guilty. Halloween was coming up, and Drew suggested that we dress up together as zombies. It wouldn't have been my first pick, but I also knew that Becca would knock that costume out of the park for me, so I agreed.

Being with Drew was starting to feel less shocking and more normal. He had football practice after school, but we always met up after to sit on the swings at the park and talk. Drew was sweet to me, and when I was with him, I felt an uncomplicated kind of contentment. Sometimes we would park somewhere private and make out, which was a thrilling experience for me, as it was something I wasn't used to doing on a regular basis. I was getting to know his patterns and the things that turned him on and made me feel powerful. Being savored by Drew Matthews was simply delightful.

I also officially told my parents about Drew, because after Monday's display in the hallway at school, the whole town knew about us, and I didn't want to have to sneak around to see him. My parents were happy for me, and thankfully they gave me their trust and plenty of space to manage my relationship how I saw fit. I started missing family dinners, which felt wrong to me but also opened up a whole new world of what college life would be like next year if I could get my shit together and decide where I was going to go.

156

Drew's family being Drew's family, my parents didn't have any apprehensions about me dating him. My mom had always known about my lifelong crush on Drew, and therefore I'm sure my dad did too. I was socializing more, and I think it made my parents happy to see me having more fun. They didn't know how crazy or confused I felt, or that there was another guy consuming my thoughts and feelings—one who lived next door, and was mysterious, the center of town gossip, and pretty much the opposite of Drew, the golden boy of Concord. While I was happy my dad trusted Shea enough to let me visit him, I knew that actually *dating* him would be a different situation entirely—one that wouldn't fly over as smoothly as my relationship with Drew was.

. . .

It was late Friday night, and I was alone in my bedroom. I was mentally and emotionally maxed out from all the growing up I was doing, and I needed rest. I turned my phone on silent and asked the universe to take it easy on me and let me fall asleep quickly and peacefully. I had nothing planned for Saturday. Drew and his family were going to the twin cities for the weekend, Becca was working in the morning at the shop, and I really needed some downtime anyway. Maybe I would bundle Rosie up and take her for a walk in the afternoon.

At first, I thought the music was in my imagination, a product of my brain transitioning from wakefulness to REM sleep. I tossed and turned for several minutes before I opened my eyes and strained my ears to determine where the sound was coming from. The sound was definitely outside because there was no way my parents would play loud music at night and risk waking Rosie up. The rest of my family slept with noise machines on anyway, so that

157

they could stay as sane as people in their forties with a toddler could possibly manage.

I threw a slouchy sweater over my tank top and pajama shorts, slipped on some shoes, and stepped onto the front porch. I could hear the sound pulsing through the air, coming from Shea's house. *Is he having some kind of house party right now? Does he even have any friends to invite to a party?*

Either way, it was pretty obnoxious that his music was so loud that it carried all the way to my house and into my bedroom, especially at 11:30 p.m. As much as I liked Shea, I was having absolutely none of this. I filed it away in the mental folder I was building marked, 'Reasons I'm Not in Love with Shea.'

1. Murderer
2. I'm in love with Drew.
3. Loud music. Unacceptable.

I adopted my most self-righteous posture and walked quickly to Shea's house. It was cold outside, but my frustration kept me warm enough. Maybe I was spoiled living out in the country my whole life, but nothing annoyed me quite as much as late-night noise when I was trying to sleep. Maybe I'm the obnoxious one. I probably am. But I just can't cope with my sleep being disrupted for any reason whatsoever.

I shouldn't have to be storming over here right now like somebody's goddamn mother. Shea doesn't have a mother. I'm a monster for thinking that. I should be sleeping right now, but I'm not. UGHHHHH!

Shea's car was the only one parked outside. *So not a party then. Unless…maybe he has a girl over?* The thought of that made me panic, which was not fair or rational considering I was the one with a boyfriend. But feelings are rarely ever fair or rational, and definitely not always in our control, so I let myself have the preemptive jealous moment, just because.

I could see through the windows that there were a few lamps on. It wasn't bright inside, but Shea was clearly either awake or deaf. Now that I was standing right outside the door, I could hear the song that was playing. "Sweet Caroline" by Neil Diamond was blaring through the house, and I could hear Shea singing loudly to the music. He was perfectly in tune, and it was all I could do not to peek through the window and watch him. My annoyance was dissipating and being replaced by curiosity and that warmth that I always felt when Shea was nearby.

I waited for the song to finish, and then I knocked hard on the door. Half a beat later, Shea opened it, just as Freddy Mercury's voice started singing "Somebody to Love" from the speakers. Shea didn't say anything, but a smile spread wide across his face as he reached his hand out to me. I didn't even think before accepting it, and he pulled me into his house and shut the door behind us.

In a series of flashes through my mind, I saw a brown-eyed little boy grabbing my hand and pulling me through the fields between our houses. Then he was guiding me across the slippery river rocks down by the creek. His mittened hand was holding mine as we shuffled around on the frozen lake and then his fingers were wrapped tight around the rope as he pulled my pink plastic sled over drifts of snow. I was transported through the memories of our childhood, long forgotten, buried under years of distraction and distance and milestones. A friendship, and a deep knowing, that was stolen by tragedy and time. Suddenly I knew why it was so easy for me to trust him, and my heart opened even wider.

Once I was inside, Shea pulled me into his body and rocked us side to side with all the confidence of someone with nothing to lose. He could dance. He spun me around and laughter spilled out of me as he closed his eyes and exaggerated his movements while the music kept building.

I let him take me around the room with him. By the time the song was coming to a close, Shea was holding me tightly to his body and we were moving together in perfect synchronicity. His carelessness and capriciousness were exhilarating and endearing. He seemed younger. He seemed more alive. I didn't want the song to end. Apparently, he didn't either. When "Places We Won't Walk" by Bruno Major came on next, Shea just held me close and rocked me back and forth in a slow and steady sway.

Sunlight dances off the leaves
Birds of red color the trees
Flowers fill with buzzin' bees
In places we won't walk

I had always loved poignant music, and I was surprised that this obscure song (one that I played regularly) was on Shea's playlist. I surrendered myself to the moment and it felt good to let my guard down for once. I lay my head on Shea's chest and listened to his heart beating. I listened to the air moving through his lungs and felt the warmth of his body escaping through his black t-shirt.

Neon lights shine bold and bright
Buildings grow to dizzying heights
People come alive at night
In places we won't walk

Shea leaned his cheek against the top of my head. He held me close. His arms fit easily around my shoulders. I felt safe. I had no makeup on, no real clothes on, and who knows what state my hair was in, but it didn't even occur to me to think of any of those things. I don't think I'd ever spent a moment around Drew where I wasn't completely photo-shoot ready.

Children cry and laugh and play
Slowly hair will turn to gray
We will smile to end each day
In places we won't walk

Shea had opened the door to me. He smiled and danced with me. He held me close, and he moved with me. We still hadn't exchanged a single word, and yet, with each moment that passed, so much was being said. With each moment that passed, my heart was expanding and breaking at the same time. This was all wrong. But it was also one of the most real and beautiful things that had ever happened to me. Like a dream or a movie scene, but touchable. I let myself have it. I inhaled deeply and committed the moment to memory.

When the song was finished, Shea didn't let go right away. I was waiting for the next song to come on, but the only sound that remained was the sound of the breeze in the fields outside. We just stayed like that for a while.

Shea broke the silence.

"Thank you for the dance, Annie. You should probably go now." I took a step back and looked up at Shea's face. His cheeks were wet. His expression was dark but pleading. He looked tired. He looked broken. And he was asking me to leave.

"Do you really want me to leave?" I looked up at him, needing to know the truth for once, even if it was going to hurt.

Shea leaned down and kissed the middle of my forehead. I felt it all the way down in my knees.

"No," he whispered. "I never want you to leave. But I'm not good for you, Annie. I fucking hate it so much, but you deserve someone like Drew. Someone good. I can't undo what I've already done. And you deserve better. You deserve more than a shell of a person. You're so fucking bright, Annie. You're so bright and beautiful it hurts."

Shea's honesty was as raw as it was surprising. Until then, I hadn't really given much thought to how Shea felt about me—I was so worried about my own rapidly blossoming attraction to him. Now I could see the pain in his eyes as I watched him battle with himself, trying to push me away before I could get any closer. I didn't know what to say. I hugged him. His heart was pounding so hard that it was all I could hear. When it started to slow to a normal rhythm, I took a step back again.

"Shea…I think it's time that you tell me exactly what happened. I hardly know anything about you, but I do know that you aren't a monster. I don't think I've ever felt as safe with anyone as I do with you. Maybe I'm stupid. Maybe I've got it all wrong.

162

Maybe I'll end up in your freezer later tonight. But I'm willing to take that chance, because every bone in my body is telling me that you're good. And I want to know your story. I want to know you. And although I was hoping to get some solid sleep tonight, I think I'd like to stay and talk, if that's okay with you."

Shea sighed. He looked unsure, but I wasn't. Not anymore. I batted my eyelashes at him and gave him my most saccharine smile, so he knew I meant business.

"You're a piece of work, Annie." Shea shook his head and gave a half smile at my attempts at charming him into spilling his secrets. For a second my old friend self-doubt stepped in, and I felt stupid for being so open with Shea and for thinking that he liked me enough to give into my girlish attempt at seduction. When he finally relented, I felt brighter. Shea gestured to the couch before stalking off to the kitchen to get us some water and I sat down and made myself comfortable.

"By the way," I shouted over to him, "in future, if you could please control the volume of your music, that would be much appreciated by me, and every other living thing within a ten-mile radius."

Shea shot me a devious smile that told me he had no intention of respecting me or the surrounding wildlife any time soon. I shook my head at the audacity. For someone so haunted, he certainly had a playful streak that was delicious. I was desperate for more. I swatted away the thoughts of Drew that were buzzing around my head like mosquitoes reminding me of how *not* good I was being, and how much I was probably going to fuck up my own happy ending.

Shea returned from the kitchen with one glass of water and his presence felt heavy, like a mixture of suffocating sadness and a warm comforter.

"None for you?" I nodded at the glass as he handed it to me. "Not to, like, kill the vibe or anything, but you didn't slip anything in this, did you?" I teased trying to keep things as light as possible. I hoped he knew I was joking. I had a habit of saying stupid things in uncomfortable situations and this was no exception.

"I mean, besides the cyanide I added, it's just well water. I wouldn't worry about it too much." Shea cracked a smile and I swear the moon shined brighter in approval. He got my joke. He got me. I always felt like he got me. I relaxed in my seat.

Shea sat down on the bare wood floor in front of me. An odd choice, but I didn't question it. I crossed my legs and prepared myself to hear hard things. And real things. Maybe the first real, hard things I had ever heard from a person, not just from a made-up character in a book.

"Ready when you are Shea," I said hoping that the lightness with which I was approaching this conversation would make him feel more comfortable in opening up to me.

"I'll never be ready to tell you about me, Annie. About this house. The things that happened here…" He looked around and I followed his gaze. It was hard not to picture his dad hanging in the stairwell just a few paces away. Goosebumps rose on my arms, but I focused on keeping my breathing steady. I didn't want to do what I always tended to do and make this about me. Shea continued.

"I'll never be ready to say goodbye to that look in your eyes that I see when you look at me. That look that hopes maybe I'm not as bad as I keep assuring you I am. I'm selfish, and I don't want to lose that little...*big*...thing."

Shea paused and I waited. My heart was breaking for him, and terrified for him, but if I'm being honest, also for me. I wanted to know the truth, but I didn't. What if he said something that I couldn't reconcile with the feelings I was having for him?

"I also know that I'm pretty incapable of saying no to you, Annie. So, I'll tell you what you want to know if you're sure that's what you really want. And when you never want to speak to me again after tonight, then I'll just have to live with that. It's what I deserve."

I knew that if I wavered at all, this conversation would be over. I shook my head and held firm eye contact with him. "I honestly just want to listen, Shea. I just want to hear you. It's not because I'm curious. The way you make me feel when I'm around you...it would actually be easier not to know. But I feel like I should know who is eating my mom's lasagna." I kept a straight face but raised my eyebrows for comedic effect.

Shea let a small smile crack across his face, and I smiled too. I felt my soul reach out for his again, like it did days before in art class. The deep knowing. The older and wiser part of me that was fighting her way forth and making her case for Shea.

"So...just to be clear...how exactly do I make you feel when you're around me? I just feel like I need to know who is feeding me lasagna."

"Nope!" I shot him down but was delighted that he chose to partake in the banter. "We aren't talking about me. We are talking about you. You may proceed."

165

Shea shook his head and then rubbed his eyes with the palms of his hands. Any ounce of tiredness I had felt earlier in the evening had disappeared as a result of this strange turn of events and the adrenaline that went along with it. When Shea finally spoke, his voice was low and withdrawn. I hated feeling like I was causing him pain, but I also knew that I wouldn't be able to move on with my life unless some shit was explained to me.

"This is where the coffee table used to be."

"What?" I had no idea how that was relevant.

Shea continued, "There was a coffee table here since before I was born. My mom loved it. It had dark green metal legs with grapes carved onto them and a glass top. When I was a kid, I wasn't allowed to touch it because my mom couldn't keep up with wiping my dirty little handprints off of it. Not many things in this house were precious to her but the table was. And me and my dad were."

I nodded, and a lump threatened to form in my throat before he could even finish his story.

"My mom died. And ten years later I threw my dad through her glass table." My face started to tingle like it did when I was about to panic. I pictured Shea's little boy face in my mind again and the feeling passed.

"Oh my god, Shea, I'm so sorry...I'm sure it was an accident...I'm sure you didn't mean for it to kill him. I know he was...rough with you." I felt terrible for the weight of guilt he had been carrying around over what was most likely an accident and probably provoked by his father.

"Oh, no, that's not what killed him," he said, and sighed. "That was just something that happened."

I started to get the feeling I might be in over my head. But my desire to hear Shea's story and comfort him was stronger than my fear of reality. I took a deep breath and waited for more.

TWENTY-TWO

"I REMEMBER THE day my mom died. She had been sick for years, but I didn't really know it until the last few months of her life. I was too young to understand what was happening or how much my life would be changing. And Mom was such a happy person, even when she was tired, and she looked different, and she knew her life was being cut short.

It was harder for my dad. Unlike me, he knew what was coming. The love of his life was dying. Can you imagine that? I think everyone has their own way of dealing with cancer ripping their heart out. And in her last days, my dad just kind of withdrew from everyone and everything. I guess he just couldn't watch it happen. But I wanted my mom and I stayed by her side all day every day when I could."

Shea closed his eyes, and I stayed quiet. Minutes passed before Shea started speaking again. He was so still. I kept my eyes on him, so he knew I was listening. I waited. When Shea opened his mouth again the words came out quieter than before.

"It was a sunny morning when she died. I remember the light shining around her room and her smile as she held my hand. The home care nurse had stepped out, and it was just me and my mom together as she took her last breath. It's a strange thing to witness...you know...someone dying. Like the body that's left there isn't that person anymore. Like her body was there, but her soul became the light filtering through the window, and she felt happier that way, somehow. I didn't question where she had gone. I just knew she was the sunshine.

But I still cried. I don't remember how long the nurse let me sit there by my mom before I had to go to my room and let the adults take care of things. When my dad went in to see my mom, he cursed and threw a bedside lamp against the wall. I'd never felt so scared or so alone. But I also felt like somebody else in this world felt as angry and sad as I did, and somehow that made my sadness more bearable. My dad and I were robbed of our love and our light that day, and there's no way of escaping that emptiness. There's just nothing. Nothing at all."

Shea's body was slouched as he sat on the floor, his elbows resting on his knees and his head hanging down as he spoke. His words soaked into the things around us—the things that were touched by his mom years ago. Shea looked up and into my eyes and I saw his vulnerability there.

"But I did try," he continued. "The thing about kids is, they try to find joy. I was relentless—I looked for happiness everywhere. I built things, and colored things, and ran as fast as I could, and I did it all alone. My dad didn't have it in him to go out anymore, so we stayed in, unless he was at work, or I was at school. I made friends here and there, but Dad would never let me have friends over to the house or take me to see them, so that made friends hard to keep. Even you."

My heart lurched as Shea's story unfolded, and I realized the part I had played in his loneliness. I wanted to reach out for him, but I didn't want to interrupt the truth-telling. I kept my hands firmly in my lap, and a soft gaze firmly on Shea.

"Probably like most teenagers, I eventually stopped trying to find happiness, and I just settled into a pretty dull life. My dad developed a drinking habit, and the bigger I got, the rougher he got

169

with me. Eventually, I was bigger and stronger than him, but I just didn't have it in me to fight back. My dad was an asshole and a terrible father. He made my life shit. A part of me will always hate him for the way he left me the same day my mom did and never came back." I saw a muscle in Shea's neck twitch, and I felt the remnants of the tension that lived in his house not very long ago. I looked over at the stairwell again and pictured John's still body there. I squirmed in my seat and focused my attention back on Shea.

"But...I also knew that my mom took part of his soul with her when she went. I watched it go. I watched two whole people become two empty people before my very eyes. And as much as I hated my dad, I understood him too. I hated that my mom had to die more than I hated my dad's anger and grief about it. I let him hit me. Maybe sometimes it even felt a little bit good to feel something. To feel the pain that I was dragging around in my heart be beaten into my body." Shea's skin and bones were healed now. He looked so strong and so healthy, despite the bruises underneath—the kind of wounds that sometimes never go away.

"I got used to him punishing me. And I took care of him when he needed me to, and I kept the house clean. Because who else was going to do it? He didn't have anybody else, and neither did I. But I had something he didn't have, and that was some kind of hope for a future and some kind of desire to have a life that wasn't covered in beer cans and mold." Tears were forming in my eyes, but I didn't let them drop.

"You wouldn't know this, but homecoming night was actually my birthday. I did the same thing I usually do, which is nothing. But it felt different this year. I'm an adult now. For the first time in

170

my life, I have choices. I spent the whole day thinking about what I might like to do with my life after high school. Dad and I never talked about it. I honestly never really thought too much about it, because why would I? I read a lot, but I've never actually been anywhere but here. It's lame, I know. But it is what it is. I started thinking about traveling. Seeing the world. I've been thinking a lot about Alaska. I don't really know who I am yet, but I do know that I want to do things, like climb mountains and ease my way into populated areas. Or maybe just hike around the world by myself, forever.

I started to look forward to my life for the first time maybe ever. When you dropped by, I was actually in the backyard looking at maps like a little kid. I mean, I didn't have a magnifying glass or anything, but I might as well have." For the first time since Shea started telling his story, I saw a glimmer of hope in his eyes. He was sitting up taller now. He looked like a full-blown adult. One with experience and depth and strength. I guess he was—all of that.

"And then you were standing in my driveway. You were the most beautiful thing I'd ever seen. You were just standing there looking at me in that red dress with your hair like the leaves and your eyes like the sky, and I literally thought I was dreaming. The light was shining all around you and it's the most perfect thing I've ever seen, Annie. I'm sorry for saying all that, but you asked for honesty, and it is what it is. And honestly, I take that half-assed apology back. I'm not sorry. You're beautiful, Annie, and you deserve to hear it, even if it's from a piece of shit like me. If I were actually deserving of you, I'd…I'll stop. I know this isn't what you want to know."

171

My heart pounded at the sincerity and eloquence with which Shea described the way I made him feel. He was like a piece of poetry—thoughtfulness and emotion and enigma combined in a beautiful package. I don't think anyone other than Becca had ever been so transparent with me in my life, and even she had been confusing as hell lately. These were more words than I had ever heard Shea speak, and it was like he was a blank page being colored in before my very eyes. My heart was breaking for Shea and also filling up with affection for him. It was all I could do not to kiss him right there and then.

But I wanted him to keep talking too. I gave him what I hoped was an encouraging smile and said, "So far, none of this story is telling me anything except what a good person you are, Shea. I'm not sure how you plan to convince me otherwise." My intuition was so much wiser than I had ever given her credit for. Despite Shea's insistence to the contrary, I knew his heart was good, and I knew I was on the right path.

Shea lay all the way down on his back in the middle of the floor. I watched as he closed his eyes and opened his mouth to speak.

"Don't worry, I'll get there, trust me." I did trust him. I listened.

"Driving you to the dance was one of the highlights of my life. And I know how pathetic that sounds. I know how pathetic my life is, and how pathetic you probably think I am, even though you seem hell-bent on being nice to me, which I appreciate. But still. The good vibe I was feeling when I was dreaming about Alaska just grew by being around you. Even though I didn't get to actually dance with you."

"You danced with me tonight, though, didn't you?" I said and he smirked.

"Yes. That I did." His smile was precious. I had the strangest urge to lie on top of him.

"And you're a surprisingly good dancer," I replied.

"I'm surprisingly good at lots of things." Shea smiled with all his teeth showing, and I saw a whole new person appear.

I laughed at his cockiness. Except it wasn't cockiness when it came from him. It was something else. Something innocent and adult at the same time. Something honest and sweet and sexy too. Pretty much everything about him was sexy. Staring at him as he lay stretched out on the floor, scanning the triangle of his torso and his biceps flexing as he placed his hands behind his head... I didn't want to let it distract me from the weight of this conversation, but my body wasn't about to let me forget how much it wanted Shea.

We were both quiet for a minute. I broke the silence.

"So...what happened after you came home, then? You just...found your dad? I don't understand."

"No. I didn't just find him. I killed him. And as much as I don't want to tell you about it because I like you, I'm also hoping maybe you'll believe what I tell you so you can steer clear of me like you probably should."

My face tingled in anxious anticipation. Shea's words stung. I liked him too. We liked each other. Things were so fucking complicated, but he was easy to be around. I liked how I felt when he looked at me. And now that I knew how it felt to have him hold me close to his body, I couldn't imagine never feeling that again. But if what he said was true, that would change everything. I couldn't fall in love with a murderer. *What if I already am falling in love with him?* Looking back, I don't remember Drew crossing my mind at all. I was so present in the moment with Shea that the outside world didn't even occur to me.

When Shea spoke again, his voice was dark.

"When I got home, I walked into the house. And I wasn't expecting a 'happy birthday' or anything, except maybe I was. Maybe this year he could have acknowledged it. Maybe my dreaming and my being near you made my expectations rise above what was possible for my dad. Maybe I wanted something from him that I knew he couldn't give me, and I was mad when I didn't get it." He was speaking faster now, and my breath quickened to match his pace.

"I let it go. I didn't say anything. I just sat over there on that chair and started googling pictures of Alaska on my phone. But with every photo I looked at, I could feel resentment building. I was so tired of understanding him. I was so tired of caring for him and doting on him and letting him beat me up. I resented him for the childhood that I didn't get to have and the friends I didn't get to have and all the love that I didn't get to have. So, when he came into the living room drunk and started bitching about why I hadn't made dinner yet, I lost my mind. I completely lost my mind, Annie." Shea looked at me, and his gaze was intense. Still, it was hard for me to imagine Shea losing his mind. His energy was always so calm and comforting, even now, while talking about the hardest thing imaginable. It was hard to imagine his warm, brown eyes smoldering with hate instead of playfulness or desire.

"I told my dad that he could go fuck himself and that I wasn't taking any more of his bullshit. He came at me, but he was drunk and clumsy and I was stronger. I threw him through the table, like I said. He was bleeding all over the place and he lost consciousness for a minute. And you know what the scary thing was? I didn't want him to wake up. I felt…relieved. Like a weight was lifted. How fucking twisted is that?" Shea was still lying on the floor, but he sat up on his elbows as his story intensified.

"And then he opened his eyes. He stood up. I thought maybe he was going to come after me again, but he didn't. I said to him, 'Do you even know that it's my fucking birthday today, Dad?' He looked at me like a deer in headlights and then he started crying. Right there in front of me. Bleeding all over the floor and crying. And if I were a normal person, it might have made me sad. Or maybe even feel sorry for him and his shitty lot in life. But I only felt more anger. Anger that he got to cry, and I didn't. That he got to push me around and when I pushed back, he got to feel sorry for himself." Shea was sitting all the way up at this point, the memory of his anger pulsing through him and making his muscles twitch.

"He was a victim. Always a victim. A victim of circumstance. A victim of fucking fatherhood. And as he stood there and felt sorry for himself for forgetting my fucking birthday, I just couldn't hold back." Shea took a breath and lay back down on the floor. He rubbed his eyes with his fists. He paused for a minute, and I waited for the other shoe to finally drop.

"I told him the truth. That every day since Mom died, I prayed that we could go back in time, and it be him that died instead. I told him that he made my life miserable. That I would be happier if I never had to see his fucking face or smell his fucking whiskey again. I told him that my mom was the only person who ever loved me, and that he was a complete and utter waste of space and a dishonor to her memory. I told him I hated him, and that I wished he were dead."

I kept my gaze steadily on Shea, expecting the worst, but determined to hear him with as little judgement as possible. Tears were streaming down the sides of his face and his voice had shrunken to a tight whisper.

"I hit him over and over again. I just kept hitting him and telling him how much I hated him. He just stood there crying while I hit him over and over and over again. I couldn't stop. I just couldn't stop. Finally, he fell over into a pile on the floor. I thought he was actually dead this time. He didn't move. I had gotten all my anger out, but now the reality of the situation was hitting me, and I started to panic. I went outside and walked down to the lake to think. I was so scared, Annie."

He paused. I swallowed.

"But I also felt a little bit free too. And that is all kinds of fucked up. I know it is." Tears were forming in my eyes as I watched a real person relive a real situation that I could never imagine experiencing myself. I should have been scared of what Shea was telling me, but the deepest part of my soul just wanted to comfort him and heal him and love him like he deserved to be loved. I felt both like I was coming unhinged and coming into my true self at the same time.

"I went back inside maybe an hour later, and Dad was hanging right over there. Right in the stairwell. He was just gone." Shea was crying now. "And I knew that I was the one who put him there. Maybe I didn't literally hang him up, but I put him there. I told him to die. I told a sad and vulnerable man that the world would be better off without him. His own son told him he hated

176

him. The last thing I said to my own father was that I wished he were dead. He made my birthday wish come true. And I hate myself for it. I hate myself so much for it. I hate myself for letting myself hate someone so much that I would say those things. And do those things. And be that thing. The fact that I was even capable of all that tells me that I don't deserve happiness. Annie…I'm a murderer. Do you hear me now?"

Shea looked into my eyes pleadingly, asking me to believe him, but asking me to love him too, even though he didn't want to admit it.

I didn't say anything. What could I possibly say? 'I'm so sorry?' or 'It'll be okay?' Those were the things nice people said, right? But none of that felt right. Nothing felt like enough. Shea had said and done some brutal things. It scared me. But what scared me more was Shea living his whole life thinking that he deserved to be punished as if his whole childhood hadn't already been punishment enough. Shea beat the shit out of his father. But he didn't kill him, even if he did feel responsible. Obviously, the police felt the same way, which is why he was here and not in prison right now.

Shea wasn't a murderer.

But he was a very sad, very lonely, and very hurt little boy who didn't deserve the hand he was dealt in life.

Shea still wasn't looking at me. His eyes were closed tight like he didn't want to see what awaited him after his confession. The look on his face was chiseled with pain at reliving the events of his life and his father's death.

I knelt onto the floor next to him and curled up beside him. I placed my head on his shoulder and curled my arm up over his chest, lying my palm flat against his heart. I waited until the rhythm of his heart slowed down and his breathing steadied, and then I waited some more. I waited until the sun was threatening its ascent over the horizon, and then I slipped out the front door while Shea slept. But not before I put a blanket over him and kissed him on the forehead. I didn't want to abandon him, but I needed to get home, and Shea deserved as much peaceful sleep as he could get.

I was falling for Shea, and I knew it.

TWENTY-THREE

ON SATURDAY, I woke up to the sound of the doorbell. My room was strangely bright, and when I looked at my phone, I saw that it was already past noon. I was not in the habit of waking up at a time that didn't start with a seven or an eight at the latest, but apparently, I had needed the sleep. I was glad that it was Saturday and I had nothing planned, so I could stay in my room and sort my life out.

The night before with Shea had felt like a strange dream. It was like I was some kind of sleeping beauty, awoken by a dark prince who pulled me in and danced with me and told me dangerous secrets and bared his beautiful, tormented soul. I felt connected to Shea in a way I couldn't fully reason or comprehend. I was living a daytime fairytale with Drew, but something richer and deeper was brewing with Shea and my mind was spinning with the intensity of my feelings.

I got out of bed and made my way to my desk. I needed to do some writing to help clear my mind so I could function. Just as I settled into my journal and my favorite pen, I heard familiar voices from downstairs floating in through the empty space below my bedroom door. My stomach dropped as I realized that they belonged to my mom and...*Drew*.

I slammed my notebook shut and froze, completely unprepared to face reality, and unable to decide if I should try to look normal or play dead. *Isn't Drew supposed to be out of town right now? What kind of ambush is this? Does he know what I did last night? Everyone in Concord is about to find out what a cheating scumbag I am—I can't believe I've fucked up my life so much before it has even begun.*

179

I looked in the mirror and cursed myself and my puffy eyes and unbrushed teeth. I could *not* let Drew see me looking this disheveled in the goddamn afternoon, especially if anyone had noticed my absence last night and had questions about my whereabouts. *What if my mom heard me leave last night and thought I was with Drew and asked him about it when he came over?*

If I had had time to write, I would have processed all of these things before coming to wild conclusions, and I would have been able to face Drew with a plan in mind. But that wasn't the case today. I made my bed, brushed my hair, put some jeans and a t-shirt on, and popped some gum in my mouth that I always kept in my backpack for emergency purposes. I threw some mascara on my bare lashes and smiled at myself in the mirror as if practicing a happy face would make it more convincing when I whipped it out for Drew downstairs.

I took a deep breath and prepared to be normal. I opened my door to see my mom standing there, with her hand up, clearly about to knock.

"Good afternoon, sunshine. Glad you've decided to join the land of the living. Drew is downstairs waiting for you." Mom didn't seem curious or accusatory. That was a good sign. She actually seemed pleased, which confused me, since it didn't align with how I was feeling at all.

"Waiting for me? Why?" I looked at her with wide eyes, and she looked at me like she was questioning why I was acting crazy. I slapped my smiley face on.

"I think he wants to spend time with his girlfriend," she said with a wink, and I couldn't help but roll my eyes. I loved that my mom liked Drew, but she had no idea the shitstorm that was going on inside my brain and what a traitor her daughter was turning out to be.

I walked down the stairs to find Drew standing in the kitchen with pink flowers in his hands and a dashing smile on his perfect face.

"Ready for our date?" Drew said as if I should have known we had plans.

I forced a cute smile. "Umm...yes? What are you doing here? I thought you were going away this weekend with your parents." I looked over at my mom who was watching this transaction with delight in her eyes. I imagine reliving these moments through your children is one of life's treasures. If only she knew how complicated my feelings were in that moment.

"Well, as you can see, I'm not in Minneapolis...and I wanted to surprise you with a date. Are you up for it?"

There was no getting around the fact that Drew was dreamy. The more his eyes twinkled at me, the more I was sucked into his gravitational pull, and charmed by his attention, and soothed by his easy way of being. A sneaky smirk tugged at the corners of my mouth. The closer I was to Drew, the farther I was from Shea. Maybe it wouldn't be such a bad thing to spend the afternoon with my actual *boyfriend,* so I could enjoy all my dreams coming true instead of making things complicated for myself. I nodded at Drew, and he beamed at me and held out his arm for me to take it. I could have sworn I heard my mom release a tiny squeal of delight as I grabbed my bag from the hook by the door and stepped out into the afternoon with Drew.

Drew had some extra gym clothes in the front seat of his jeep, which he tossed into the back so I could sit down. Everyone knew

Drew's car because it had a bright yellow custom paint job. Riding in his car felt good, and also like everyone in town would see us together, which I both loved and hated. Sometimes a little anonymity feels good, especially when you aren't entirely sure who you are anymore.

As we pulled out of my driveway and onto the road, I flipped my hair back behind my shoulders and let myself soak in the moment. I didn't want to do it, but my body betrayed me, and my eyes scanned over to the right just enough for me to see Shea, sitting in his garage, watching as I rode away in Drew's car. I had never wanted to be invisible so badly.

"You're quiet today, Annie. Everything okay?" Drew was looking at me and I realized that I was, in fact, being completely weird. I let out a sigh and vowed not to ruin the rest of this day if I could help it. Maybe I'd ruin tomorrow, or the next day. But not today.

"You're right, I'm sorry. I'm just so surprised to see you, and I slept in super late, so I'm still sort of waking up. Super embarrassing, but school has me exhausted! I don't know what's wrong with me." I smiled and tried to make light of the situation. Drew looked relieved.

"Maybe if you didn't stay up so late writing essays that make the rest of us look bad in English class, you wouldn't be so tired," Drew said with a smirk. His teasing was cute.

"So sorry that the rest of you are slackers, but someone has to set the standard in life," I threw back at him and tossed in a wink for good measure.

Drew laughed and I'm pretty sure that somewhere, an angel gained its wings. Drew was like a golden statue in the autumn light, and I just wanted to stare at him and forget life for a while. Looking back, it's clear to me that putting on a mask was second nature. I had practiced it so much growing up. I was used to setting aside authenticity and exchanging it for something different— something that looked like me but felt like someone else; someone I imagined to be more appealing. When Drew was around, like an automatic reflex, I became the watered-down version of me. The version I thought I wanted to be before I discovered the well of power inside the person I really am.

We pulled up to Nita's Café, which was one of the only restaurants in town, but also one of the best I'd ever eaten at. Despite the humble offerings on the menu (burgers, fries, BLTs, shakes), everything was made from scratch and the place was never quiet. Drew opened the door for me, and we stepped into the dull roar of the Saturday lunch rush. Everyone knows that Nita's is first come, first serve, but several of Drew's friends worked there bussing tables and cooking, and when we walked in, there was already a table set aside for us by the front window.

As soon as we sat down, our server was at our table with two burgers, two sodas, and two pieces of chocolate pie. I looked over at Drew who just shrugged at me and smiled like he was as surprised as I was. I looked over toward the kitchen and saw Tyler sweating, smiling, and throwing us a thumbs-up like this was one of his life's biggest accomplishments thus far. I laughed and shook my head at him, finding him equal parts annoying and sweet. *So, this is how the other half lives. Popularity has decent perks.*

Drew picked up his burger and took a bite just as I reached for my fork and stuck it into the pie.

"Dessert first? Interesting…" Drew was chewing his burger and smiling, and it was impossible not to stare at his mouth.

"You only live once, right?" I said with a mouthful of pie.

I saw Drew glance around the restaurant and then back at me. It was a thing I had noticed him doing sometimes. At the time I thought he was just interested in people, but I now know that he was more likely checking to see how many people were looking at *him*. Drew and I were different in that way. He liked the attention. Some people do. It wasn't a bad quality necessarily, but it just wasn't for me. Every time he looked around, I felt disconnected from him. But when his sights were set on me, I felt like I had won first prize and it made me feel special.

I continued eating my pie, and we bantered back and forth about nothing in particular while I focused on trying not to feel like we were eating on stage under a spotlight. My phone buzzed, and I glanced down to see a text from Becca. Seeing her name on my phone grounded me.

BECCA: *I need you to help me with something. Can you come over right now please?*

My instinct was to get up and run to Becca's house. She wouldn't text me like that if she didn't actually really need me for something. But I felt like I owed it to Drew to stay and enjoy the surprise date he planned.

"What's up?" Drew was looking at me and I realized I had been studying my phone, unable to decide how to respond.

"Becca just texted me—she wants me to go help her with something right now and it sounds kind of urgent," I said, and sighed loudly, so he knew that I wasn't trying to ditch him. I secretly hoped he would tell me to go to her, or maybe suggest that we could go together, but he didn't.

"Oh man, really? It's a bummer you're already busy." Drew's response felt sort of callous to me. But he was right. I *was* busy. Becca would definitely be understanding of that. Nothing could be so emergent that I couldn't just catch up with her later that night. I was selfish and trying to please Drew and probably manage my own guilt about my feelings for Shea. I convinced myself that whatever she needed help with wasn't as urgent as my need to be on this superficial date. If she knew I was out with Drew, she would understand.

I slid over to Drew's side of the booth and held my phone up so we could take a selfie. I texted the picture to Becca.

ME: *Drew planned a surprise date for me :D :D :D – can I help you out tomorrow instead?? Luv u!!! xoxoxo*

I put my phone away and spent the rest of the afternoon eating, driving around, and kissing Drew. I felt like the more time I spent with Drew, the less my emotional transgressions with Shea counted against me. Drew numbed me and blinded me with his popularity and charisma—things that matter immensely to a teenager but not so much to someone more evolved. I was starting to know what feeling a true connection felt like when I was with Shea, but that didn't erase the years I had dreamed of these moments with Drew, and I selfishly wanted as much of them as I could get, even if deep down, I knew it wasn't right.

Choosing to spend that day in denial with Drew instead of in reality with Becca will always be one of my biggest regrets.

185

TWENTY-FOUR

IN MY DREAM, I was in my house all alone, wandering through the empty rooms, looking for something I couldn't find. I looked out my bedroom window and saw a tornado off in the distance. The tornado split into three. I smelled smoke and realized my house was on fire. Alarm bells were ringing and there was nowhere for me to go. I grabbed some photos and books from my shelf, desperately trying to pack anything special that I could carry in a bag, so it didn't burn in the fire. Shea's orchid fell onto the floor and the floor disappeared beneath me.

My eyes snapped open as I woke with a start, in a cold sweat, and panting. My phone was ringing next to my head. It was Becca. I looked at the time. 5:30 a.m. I missed the call. It started ringing again, and I answered right away.

"Becca?? What's wrong? Are you okay?" I said, still emerging back into reality.

The voice on the other end wasn't Becca's.

"Annie, this is Miss Jones. Becca is in the emergency room. Can you come?"

My heart pounded in my ears. I think I said, "Be right there," before I threw on a jacket over my pajamas and ran out to my car. It was a frosty morning. My breath formed clouds around me as I willed my car to start despite the cold. My mind was racing with horrifying scenarios as my breath caught in my throat, my eyes watered, and guilt ripped me apart from the inside out. It's terrifying how, in life, everything is fine until it's not. One minute you're eating pie with your boyfriend and the next minute, as far as you know, your best friend could be dying.

I skidded into the hospital parking lot, which was quiet that morning, as hospitals in small towns tend to be at that time of day. June Anderson was at the front desk, and I didn't have to say anything to her—she knew who I was there to see.

"This way, Annie. Becca has just been moved from the ER to the ICU."

I was too scared to ask the nurse what had happened, and I wasn't sure if she was allowed to tell me anyway. She led me through a sterile maze of fluorescent lights and shiny tile floors. The green-white hue and clinical smell were nauseating and unnatural for the time of day it was. Nothing good happened to people in that place at that hour. Nurse June turned left and pushed open a large wooden door that led into another hallway and showed me to the second door on the right.

I stepped cautiously into the room, not sure what I was about to see, but knowing that there was no place in the world I could possibly be other than there with Becca.

She was lying in bed under a white blanket, and her face was as pale as the bedding. Her eyes had dark circles under them, and she looked like a shell of herself. An automatic blood pressure cuff turned on and off, and there was a persistent beeping coming from a machine in the corner that was monitoring her pulse.

When Becca looked at me, she didn't smile. Her eyes were hollow. She looked broken. I came to her and grabbed her hand, which was like ice.

"Hi, Annie," she whispered.

As soon as she said my name, she looked away from me and started to cry. She cried for what felt like hours. I held her hand and willed her pain to be in my body instead. I so desperately wanted to take some of it away from her. Take it for her. When her tears started to slow, she looked back at me.

"Becca, what happened to you? I'm so sorry I wasn't there for you. Did somebody hurt you?"

Becca nodded at me but kept her lips tight together.

"Who hurt you, Becca?"

She didn't say anything. But I watched as she lifted her left hand and pointed to herself. She let out a sob and I crawled up into her bed and lay with her. I lay with her until eventually she fell asleep.

I texted my mom to tell her where I was, and that I was safe, but that I didn't have much information about what happened to Becca. The nurse came in and out a few times, and brought me some coffee and toast, and left some breakfast for Becca to eat when she woke up.

At 8:00 a.m. there was a gentle knock on the door, and Miss Jones came into the room with coffee of her own. I had been so shocked by the news this morning that I didn't even think to question why Miss Jones had been the one to call me. She gave me a half smile and sat down in the chair on the opposite side of the room. It was strange to see her in plain clothes, out of her natural habitat, and in this private and personal space. She looked so much younger somehow. Like one of us.

"Hey, Zoey," I heard Becca whisper. She was awake. *Zoey? How are they on a first-name basis?*

"Good morning, Becca. How are you feeling? Annie's here." Miss Jones looked over at me and smiled.

"Yes, I know," Becca smiled at me, and I smiled back. She was still in there somewhere, and tears pricked my eyes with relief.

"So…how was your date yesterday?" Becca asked as if everything was fine, and we weren't in the ICU with her. It was salt in the deep wound of my guilt.

"Becca, Drew is the furthest thing from my mind right now. I need to know if you're okay, and I need to be here for you, and I need to make it better, and I should have been there for you yesterday, and I need to…" I started crying and Becca got a hollow look in her eyes again as I watched her retreat back into herself.

Miss Jones led me out of the room and into the hallway, and I broke down completely. She was patient with me, and when I was finally able to compose myself, she pointed to a bench where we could sit down.

"Did Becca tell you what happened?" Miss Jones asked.

"No. I have no idea what's going on. All I know is I asked her if someone hurt her, and she pointed to herself. Did she try to hurt herself?" The thought of Becca trying to take her own life was more than I could handle. I desperately waited for different news to come from Zoey Jones's mouth, and the seconds between words felt like hours.

"I'm telling you this because you're Becca's best friend, and as far as I'm concerned, you're her only family. Her parents aren't here right now because they are drunk and don't even know what day it is." She shook her head, and I could see the pain she felt for Becca.

"Did you know that Becca was pregnant?" she asked.

My mouth hung open in shock. There was no way Becca could have been pregnant. Becca was not interested in men. Period. I shook my head.

189

"Becca tried to…get rid of the pregnancy by herself. She won't tell me how she became pregnant, but I'm guessing she was probably raped, considering who she is and who she loves, and the fact that she's keeping it such a secret. Becca's strong, and independent, and I don't think she wants anyone to see her as a victim, not even you, or me."

Miss Jones's eyes started to glisten with tears that she didn't let fall. "I just wish I would have known her plans sooner—I could have helped her do this thing safely. I thought she was going to choose adoption. I didn't realize…I should have known…"

I was stunned into silence. Becca had probably been raped, was pregnant, and had tried to terminate the pregnancy herself, and for some reason, Zoey Jones knew she was pregnant before I did? How had I missed so much? How had I not seen the signs? How had I been so self-centered that I didn't even see how much pain my best friend was in? Shame washed over me in tidal waves. I had failed as a friend. And suddenly, the things that felt big to me the day before now felt childish and stupid. No wonder Becca confided in Miss Jones before me. I was too innocent and ignorant to possibly understand what she was going through.

"Becca lost a lot of blood. But she's going to be okay. And so is the baby. Becca needs you right now, Annie, more than ever. And I'm going to be here for both of you as much as you need."

I looked at Miss Jones with a million questions circulating through my brain and sitting in the reality that Becca was going to be a mother.

"How…" I started, "When…how did you know she was pregnant? What is going on between you and Becca?"

Miss Jones gave me a half smile.

"Becca and I are friends. But it's not really my story to tell—I'll let her fill you in if and when she wants to."

I wasn't sure about Zoey Jones yet, but I had to admit that her adult presence here was a comfort, and her energy was kind and sincere. I swallowed down the ball of jealousy that was forming in my throat. I hadn't been there when it counted. Apparently, Miss Jones was. It was hard not to let my own self-hatred spill over onto her, but I vowed not to fail Becca ever again, and if Zoey Jones was important to her, then she was important to me too.

Feelings are rarely ever singular. In our hearts, we carry love and sadness, respect and shame, guilt and delight, passion and fear. All interwoven into a complex reality that shapes the stories of our lives. As I sat on the blue plastic bench in the hospital hallway, I felt everything and nothing. Suddenly, nothing in the world mattered to me but Becca and her baby. We would be in this together, and I wouldn't be distracted from what mattered again.

TWENTY-FIVE

I DIDN'T LEAVE Becca's side for the rest of the day. We didn't talk about anything. I just lay by her, and we watched innocuous videos on my phone. Sometimes Becca would sleep, and I would type journal entries into my notes, letting my heavy feelings live on the pages of my phone screen, so I could be calm and strong for Becca.

Becca didn't give me any details about what had happened to her. I knew Becca, and I knew that she wasn't going to talk to me until she was ready, and I had to be okay with that. I had all the information I needed for the moment, and I wouldn't be letting her down again. I felt my spirit rising up inside me the same way it did when I was with Shea the other night, telling me that I was a giver—a caretaker, a helper, and a lover of things that needed love. Despite how I had been feeling about myself lately, guilty for the feelings I had about two guys at once, and guilty for not paying attention to the changes happening in my best friend, my soul was telling me a new story. That I was loyal, and that I had an endless well of love to give. Becca's trauma broke my heart. But it showed me a new version of myself too. I was learning that I could trust my gut and that I could be there when it counted.

The nurse came in and told us that they wanted to keep Becca in for one more day just to monitor her and the baby. I learned that she was about ten weeks along, and since my mom had had a baby just a couple of years before and this was all fresh in my mind, I knew that Becca would be entering the second trimester pretty soon. Her body would start changing a lot. And while we still had a little time before the secret had to come out, there were a lot of things that Becca needed to figure out.

"I feel stupid even asking this, but do your parents know?" I asked her gently.

"No. Only Zoey knows. And you. My parents probably won't find out until I'm basically about to give birth and then they'll give me some bullshit about how stupid I am and how they raised me better than this. Which is funny, considering I raised myself, and I'm way too smart to have chosen this situation."

I could see hot anger creeping up in Becca's cheeks, and it would have been intimidating if it wasn't such a relief to see color in her face again.

"Do you want me to ask my parents if you can stay with us for a while? Just while you figure out next steps?" I asked praying that she would say yes, so I didn't have to know she was home in that shithole.

"I'm pregnant, Annie. I'm not pathetic. I'll be fine, and I can take care of myself. And apparently this baby wants to stick with me too. So, I guess I'll add it to the list of people I keep alive."

I just looked at her for a minute. I wasn't used to her talking to me like that, but I also knew that the amount of grace I was capable of extending to her was limitless. If she needed me to be a verbal punching bag, I was ready to let her have at it.

"I'm sorry," Becca said, shaking her head and closing her eyes. "You don't deserve the lashing. I'm just...so...incredibly...tired." Becca's voice shook at the last words, and my eyes began to water.

We didn't say anything else after that. I waited until Becca was sound asleep before I went home for the night. I showered off the hospital smell and clued my parents in as much as I could without sharing details that weren't mine to share. They were worried about Becca and immediately jumped into solution mode, but I gently reminded them not to over-step. They had known Becca forever, and they knew that pushing her in any direction she didn't want to go was never going to work, so they reluctantly agreed to let me tell them if and when their help was wanted.

Before I headed up to my room, my mom reached out and hugged me hard for several minutes. I let myself soak in her love. I cried. I let myself be a child in her arms, even though my innocence was vanishing rapidly with each day that passed. It felt good to be small for just a few minutes longer.

...

I walked into school on Monday morning feeling numb to my surroundings. The things that had felt important mere days ago, suddenly passed through me like air through a sieve. Becca was in the hospital, and I didn't give a fuck about anyone or anything else. The school felt empty without her, and I realized how much I had taken her, and everyone else that was important in my life, for granted. Like they would always be there. Like nothing bad ever happened to me or my people.

Miss Jones had a sub that morning, and I figured it had to be because she took the day off to be with Becca. I was glad to know that Becca wouldn't be alone all day, but the jealous monster in my brain shook her head from side to side, looking for a reason to feel like I was being replaced by someone older, cooler, and all-around better. Someone who was actually there for her friends when they needed her.

I floated through the rest of my morning like a zombie. Nobody knew about Becca, and it infuriated me that no one seemed to notice she was gone. I guess people missed school for all kinds of reasons, all the time, but still. It felt like they should know how special she was, and they should be tearing the air apart with questions about her absence. My feelings didn't make sense, but feelings rarely do.

When Drew sat down next to me and gave me a kiss on the cheek, I wanted to slap him. It wasn't his fault that I chose to spend the day with him on Saturday instead of being with Becca. It wasn't his fault that he had no idea what she was going through right now. And it wasn't his fault that he was cheery and bright on a day when I wanted to do nothing but cry and sleep. But the fact that he couldn't read my mind or read my emotions irritated me, and I blurted something out without thinking it through.

"I can't do this."

Drew looked at me like I just told him that sugar wasn't sweet.

"Can't do what? Science? Me neither." He smiled at me like life was a bowl of pudding when life was really a flaming pile of shit. Thoughts of all the things I had avoided seeing between us flashed through my mind. Drew coming down the stairs with Stella. Drew brushing off Becca's text asking for help. Drew looking around to see who was checking him out and doing flashy things and taking me to busy places that made me more uncomfortable than anything. Drew was so handsome and so charming, and he wasn't a bad guy. But I also didn't have a real connection with him beyond my own made-up infatuation. For the first time, I was shocked into seeing him without my rose-colored glasses duct taped to my face.

His clueless smile grated on me. I knew that I wasn't being rational or fair to him, but I didn't have it in me to be better in that

195

moment. Tension was building up in my body, but not the sexy, romantic kind that I had enjoyed before.

"I think we need to break up, Drew. I just have a lot going on right now. And I think I need to focus on myself. You are amazing, and I've had so much fun with you, and I hope we stay friends. I hope you understand. I'm so sorry."

There was an unmistakable glimmer of surprise in Drew's eyes that told me all I needed to know about his ego. Becca never really liked my relationship with Drew anyway, and she was probably right. He was too good for me, or I was too good for him, or maybe 'good' and 'bad' are arbitrary labels that mean nothing, and people just are what they are and do what they do. I was starting to see that life was a lot more 'gray area' than it was black and white. And for someone who had spent most of her life pining after the prettiest fish in the sea, when real life hit me, it was surprisingly easy to cut him loose. For the first time in my life, I didn't immediately question my sanity or feel insecure about my choice. But I couldn't stay there next to Drew either.

I walked up to the front of the class and asked to be excused, citing a stomachache. One of the perks of being a good student is that the teachers never question you when you want to leave class for one reason or another. I stepped out into the hallway and started walking until I ended up at my car. I drove to Rosie's daycare and looked in the window at all the babies and toddlers and imagined that one of them was Becca's. Or mine. The thought was terrifying.

Rosie saw me peeking in the window and squealed with delight. Her teacher opened the door.

"Don't you have school right now, Annie? Do you need to pick up Rosie for something?"

"No, it's my lunchbreak, and I just missed my girl and wanted to come see her quick. Is that okay?" I smiled at Rosie who was jumping up and down and waving her arms in the air for me to pick her up.

"Aww…What a sweet big sister! Come on in!"

I sat down on the squishy rainbow floor mat and Rosie sat in my lap. She tilted her head back to look in my eyes and said, "I forgot something for you, Annie!"

"What did you forget, baby?" I beamed at her serious little face.

"This!" Rosie grabbed my face in both of her little hands and gave me a kiss right on the nose. My heart exploded with love for her. There was nothing I wouldn't do for Rosie. She was my little starlight. The thought of Becca knowing this kind of love made me smile. I hoped that she would grow to love her baby, regardless of the circumstances, and I had a feeling she would.

Maybe things would turn out okay eventually.

TWENTY-SIX

I DECIDED NOT to skip art class. Partly because I wasn't looking for an unexcused absence, and partly because I wanted to see Shea. We basically spent the whole night together Friday night, and he had opened up his wounds for me, and the fact that I hadn't seen him or spoken to him since, besides the awkward drive by with Drew, made me feel like an asshole. After how badly I failed Becca and how spontaneously I dumped Drew, I was ready to resolve as many situations that made me feel like an asshole as I could.

I'm not sure why I thought it would be easy—like I would just attend art class, and Shea would be relieved and delighted by my presence. It didn't really happen like that. For the first time ever, Shea was in class before I was and the seats next to him were already taken. *Well, shit.*

He didn't look up at me when I came in and sat down, even though I could see his face through the circle of easels. I immediately had the sinking feeling that he hated me. And I was no longer fooling myself that I didn't care about Shea. I definitely did. A lot. I made a point not to stare at him, and instead tried to focus on our model of the week, a quiet girl named Amelia who spent lots of time sketching horses in her notebooks.

When I looked at my blank canvas, all I could see was Becca crying, Drew's smug look of disappointment, and Shea's brown eyes averting their gaze from me. My phone buzzed in my pocket, and I took it out.

There was a message from Shea:

SHEA: *You look sad today.*

I looked up at him, but he still wasn't looking at me. He was sketching away effortlessly and glancing up now and then to study Amelia. I texted back.

ME: *How can you tell from way over there?*

I clicked 'send' and watched as he looked down toward the bottom left corner of his easel. I figured he must have had his phone sitting there. *Bold move having your phone on display in this class.*
My phone buzzed again:

SHEA: *Since you asked, your face is basically screaming "I need a hug and a nap." Where's Becca today?*

I still hadn't seen Shea look in my direction, but apparently one sneaky glance was all it took for him to read me like the horror novel I was. The fact that he asked about Becca should have made me anxious because of the secret I was holding inside, but it actually made me smile. I didn't want people to know what was going on yet, but I did want people to care about her as much as she deserved.

ME: *She's out with the flu. :(And thanks for noticing how shitty I look. How come when you're feeling bad and someone tells you how bad you look it makes you feel better? Like, I should be offended right now, but instead, I just feel justified in throwing my pity party. Lol*

I watched Shea read my text and crack the tiniest hint of a smile. I beamed at my blank canvas. Shea texted back.

SHEA: *You bravely attended my pity party the other night, so I owed you one. Now draw something before Ms. Young starts sending you magical vibes. :/*

I snorted and tucked my phone away.

When class was over, I took extra time packing up my stuff, hoping that if I was slow enough, Shea would pass by me, and we could talk on the way out the door. Students shuffled out and I joined the pack, and I could feel Shea's energy as he approached my back. Just as we were about to walk through the door, I turned my head around and met his eyes. His dark gaze sent heat through my core, and he let out a half smile that took my breath away. For the first time, it didn't make me feel guilty. It made me feel electric.

I couldn't hold back the giggle in my throat, until I turned back around to see Drew standing in the hallway, waiting for me. My heart sank. I felt Shea's warmth fading from me as he walked past me down the hall with the rest of the students. He didn't look back.

"Hey, can we talk?" Drew was leaning up against a wall and didn't approach me. I went to him.

"Yeah, can we go somewhere else though?" I asked him, feeling exposed standing there in the hallway.

We stepped outside into the gray afternoon, and the cold leached through my light sweater and made me shiver.

"So…what happened between Saturday and today? I'm just surprised, that's all…I thought we were having fun together. Did I do something wrong?" Drew looked at me earnestly, and I realized that all his questions were fair, and I actually seemed like a crazy bitch for dumping him out of the blue.

"No, Drew. You didn't do anything wrong at all. You actually did everything right. You always do everything right. You're so...charming, and hot. I definitely have fun with you." I took a pause, unsure of how to explain myself when I hadn't fully processed it all yet. "It's just...I have some things going on right now that are really confusing me...and I'm just feeling like I need to spend more time with my friends and focus on what I'm going to do after graduation, and...I don't know what to say. You're perfect. I'm just not there right now, and I feel like we...just aren't the right fit. If that makes sense." I looked at him, hardly believing the words that were coming out of my mouth and hoping that he would understand.

Even after these weeks of being Drew's official girlfriend and the confidence boost that came along with that, there was still a part of me that expected him to laugh in my face at how pathetic I was compared to him. Maybe that was part of the reason I broke up with him. I would never get over the feeling that this was probably all an elaborate joke. I was tired of feeling that way.

"Okay. Thanks for explaining. I'm still not sure I totally get it, but if it's what you want, it's what you want. It's been fun, Annie. I hope you get your stuff figured out."

Drew's response felt a little cold, but it was also fair. I didn't exactly expect him to fight for me or beg me to stay after a short stint of holding hands and making out. Drew wasn't a bad guy. But I didn't have time to sit around and ponder him anymore. Becca was getting out of the hospital soon, and I needed to be there.

"I'm sorry, I've got to go now. I'm…sorry. In general. Thanks for everything."

Awkward until the end. It's my superpower.

I ran back into the school to grab my jacket and my bag, and then I got in the car and drove to my Becca.

…

"Where have you been, Becca? We've been *so* worried about you!" Becca's mom shouted in our direction from her perch on the faded green recliner across the room. I held Becca's hand as we walked through the door and into her house. I didn't want her to be here, but it's what she wanted, and I had to respect that.

"Nothing to see here, Ma. Just recovering from the flu. Annie took care of me for a few days." I felt a pang of guilt knowing that I didn't actually take care of her when I should have.

"Well next time you're going to have the flu, maybe you could get groceries first instead of leaving us high and dry here. Your dad and I work our asses off, and we don't need you coming and going and not doing your part."

I could have spit in Sandy's face. Becca was so used to the casual insults and disrespect that flowed from her parents that she didn't even bat an eye. She just shuffled to her room with me in tow. I was supposed to be caring for Becca, and here she was, guiding me down the hallway like a mother hen.

"I don't know why you want to stay here, Becca. Honestly. You deserve better, especially right now," I said as I closed the door to her room, still seething.

"Why especially now? I'm pregnant; I'm not dying. And you might not understand this because your life is a lot different from mine, but as shitty as this house is, and as shitty as my parents are,

202

this is where I live. This is my room. This is my stuff. And being a charity case is not appealing to me—*especially* not right now."

Becca was the strongest person I knew. And as tired as I knew she was of being strong, it was the only way she knew how to be. And if being at her house made her feel more in control of her life right now, then I could understand that. I had to understand it if I wanted to be there for my friend in the way she needed.

"I hear you, Becca. Just know that you have options and support when you want it." I waited a beat. "Do you want to talk about what happened?" I asked her gently because I knew that extracting details from her would take some time. But I wanted her to know that I was ready to listen when she was ready to talk.

"No. I don't. I'm sorry, I just…can we talk about you for right now?" This was a thing Becca did when she didn't want to talk about hard things. The moment she got home from the hospital wasn't the time to fight her on it.

"I broke up with Drew today."

"You did? Good. Why did you do it? I thought you liked him?"

"I did—I do like him. But I like you more, and I want to spend more time with you. And also, Drew and I just didn't fit together."

Becca looked at me with anger in her eyes. I was confused.

"I'm not a fan of Drew. He seems like a douche. But also, if you broke up with your dream guy because of me and my current situation, I will *literally* kill you, Annie."

I put my hands up in front of me as if it would stop that train of thought from pulling into the station before my words could.

203

"No! It wasn't you. I mean, it was partly you, but not in the way you think. I mean, I want to be here for you. I'll never forgive myself for being with Drew instead of you when you needed me. But also, I just kind of blurted it out today that I wanted to break up with him. He's obviously just not the right thing for me, which I guess you saw early on, but it took me longer. Also…I kind of have feelings for someone else, and that's really confusing for me right now too."

Becca gave me a knowing smirk.

"It's Shea, isn't it?"

I blushed, unsure of why I felt so embarrassed to admit it.

"We hung out the other night. Like the whole night. And he told me what really happened with his dad, and it's not what you think. His dad was super abusive, and Shea finally fought back. He beat him up bad, but his dad was the one who…took care of the rest. Shea feels guilty for things he said and did, but he's not a bad guy. He's actually really thoughtful, and kind, and when he looks at me, I feel like he really *sees* me. Also, he reads books. Like he actually *reads* for fun. Like he has hobbies that aren't kicking balls and smashing his head into things. He asked about you today, by the way." I found myself blabbering on about Shea, and it felt good to say my feelings out loud.

Becca listened and I could see the approval in her eyes. It looked like she had known all along how this situation would turn out, and she was just waiting for it to unfold as predicted. She had known Drew wasn't right for me from the beginning, whether or not I was ready to see it for myself.

"The night we were all at his house, Shea couldn't take his eyes off of you. The tension between the two of you was honestly

204

nauseating. But far be it for me to tell you who to be into..." Becca looked pleased with herself, and it made me smile. We laughed together and felt a little newer and a little brighter for a moment.

Our laughter sputtered out and I had to ask the one thing that had been on my mind since I got the call that Becca was in the hospital.

"So...what's the deal with you and Miss Jones? I feel like if I'm getting replaced as your bestie then I need to know." I was trying to keep it light, but I was desperate to know what was going on with Becca and our math teacher.

"Zoey is a friend. She...gets me. We talk about stuff, and I feel like she understands how I feel. I could tell right away when we walked into her class that she was going to be somebody for me." Becca looked calm and hopeful talking about Miss Jones, and that was a good sign.

"When I realized I was pregnant, I didn't know what to do, and I know I should have told you, but you had a lot going on, and I thought maybe I could tell you after I had dealt with things. Zoey was really cool about it. She talked me through some options. I should have let her help me. But I'm an idiot and I thought I could make this all go away on my own. I got scared right before I..." Becca choked up and didn't say the words, but I knew what she meant. "...I texted you. But you were with Drew. You looked so happy. I just...tried it myself. I called Zoey right before I passed out. I didn't know who else to call. I can't tell my parents right now. I just can't. I'm going to keep working and saving money for my own place. I'll figure it out."

It felt good to know more. And it felt reassuring to know that Miss Jones was just a supportive teacher and not my replacement.

"You *will* figure it out, Becca. We will figure it out together. But not tonight. You need to sleep."

I tucked her in and kissed her forehead like I did with Rosie when I put her to bed.

The older I get, the more I realize that the unconditional love and affection we receive as babies and toddlers doesn't stop feeling good just because our bodies are bigger, and our minds are busier. And giving love feels even better than receiving it.

Loving Becca was one of the great privileges of those years of my life.

TWENTY-SEVEN

W<small>HEN</small> I <small>PULLED</small> into my driveway, it was dark, but the porchlight was on. I could see my dad sitting in one of the Adirondack chairs, carving a decoy, as he was prone to do when he wasn't at the shop or out hunting or fishing or taking care of Rosie. I walked up and sat in the chair next to his and was comforted by the smell of wood and the sound of a sharp knife carving shapes out of it.

"Hi, Dad."

"Hi, baby. You hanging in there?" My parents knew that Becca had been in the hospital and that she had some self-inflicted injuries, but they didn't know that she was pregnant and that she had likely been raped and that she tried to end the pregnancy herself and failed.

"I'm okay. Becca's back at home, and she's doing better." I didn't know what else to say. My heart was aching for Becca. I was scared for her and also felt like suddenly we weren't kids anymore and that the real world was a scary place to live in.

"You're a good friend, Annie. I'm so proud of you." He lifted his eyes to meet mine, and the seriousness in them made my stomach drop. "But I also need to know if there's something going on with Becca that you're not telling me."

I wasn't ready to tell her secret, even to my dad. Not until she was ready.

"Becca's just been really stressed, and she hurt herself. I'm going to make sure she gets some help from the school counselor."

I lied. There was a stretch of silence that made me squirm in my seat.

"Some things have gone missing from the shop since Becca started working there." His words took the breath out of my lungs. Becca was a lot of things, but she wasn't a thief. She would never steal from my dad. The fact that he suspected her made my blood boil.

"You don't seriously think Becca would steal from you, do you?" I snapped.

"Annie, I take meticulous care of that shop, and I know that some things have gone missing. I'm not blaming anyone in particular, but if there's something going on then I need to know about it, for everyone's safety. Do you understand?" His voice was calm but firm. My defenses were still up, but I was curious.

"I'll talk to Becca," I said. "And…please don't fire her. She needs this job." I looked at my dad pleadingly, silently begging him to understand me without asking more questions.

"I'd never fire Becca. I'm actually giving her a raise. She obviously needs help right now. But Annie, I can't help her if I don't have all the information. So, I need to you to be honest with me when you can." I had never loved my dad more than I did in that moment.

"Thank you, Dad." I walked over to his chair and hugged his neck. The truth would come out soon enough, and in the meantime, Becca was keeping her job and my dad loved me. That was more than enough.

"I broke up with Drew today," I blurted out. I didn't want to talk about it, but I also didn't want to hold onto any more secrets than I had to. I hoped he wouldn't ask for details or look disappointed, and he didn't.

"You were always too good for him, anyway," Dad said matter-of-factly, and I rolled my eyes and smiled at him.

"Goodnight, Dad."

...

The next day was Halloween, and I woke up with knives in my brain and shadows in my vision. It was a migraine, not an elaborate costume, which would have been preferable. I ran to the bathroom and vomited, and then crawled back in bed and howled for my mom like a toddler. She came in and took one look at me before calling the school and telling them I would be staying home sick. My migraines were few and far between, but when they hit, they knocked me on my ass.

Mom closed my curtains and handed me two red and blue pills, which I took with a sip of water before lying back down and trying my best to play dead while the torture passed. Something in the cocktail of medicine helped me fall back asleep and when I woke up in the early afternoon, I was relieved to feel hunger instead of nausea, and drowsiness instead of stabbing pain.

I crawled out of my crypt and opened my curtains to a gray and windy day and checked my phone to see a text from Becca.

BECCA: *Happy Halloween, witch. I've had enough blood and guts for this week...*

BECCA: *JUST KIDDING! Scary movie night tonight?*

I smiled a wide smile seeing Becca's dark humor returning, and her love of all things Halloween not totally diminished by recent happenings. Every Halloween the local movie theatre showed old horror flicks back-to-back from 9:00 p.m. to midnight, and even though almost nobody went to see them because people were out trick-or-treating or going to parties, the theatre showed them anyway just out of tradition. Becca and I had never gone, but I couldn't think of a better way for us to get out of the house without having to actually face the public yet.

ME: *Let the horror continue! Comet theatre tonight at 9?*

BECCA: *Only if I can dump my peppermint patties in my popcorn without you throwing a fit.*

ME: *I can't make any promises.*

BECCA: *Fine. See you at 8:30, because you're a psychopath.*

ME: :)

At 8:15 p.m., I put on a chunky green sweater, threw my hair up in a bun, and left my house to pick up Becca. I arrived at her house at 8:29 p.m. because...me. She opened the door before I knocked because...her. I knew there was going to be a big Halloween party at Stella's house, but after breaking up with Drew, I didn't exactly feel like I was invited anymore, and also, I had no real interest in going. It felt good to say goodbye to the 'fear of missing out' that I had always worn over my heart like an ugly sweater.

When we pulled up to the theatre, I was relieved to see only a few other cars around, mostly across the street in front of the bar. We walked into the theatre, which was small and old and had ugly dark red carpet and drapes and cheap décor from the 1970s. It smelled musty and tired. Delores, the theatre's owner, was like an extension of the theatre itself, with her box-dyed black hair, red velvet jacket, and yellowed teeth from sixty-odd years of smoking. She was never *not* at the theatre. I wasn't entirely convinced that she wasn't an apparition, just haunting the popcorn and out-of-date candy because it was simply the thing she'd always done.

"Have fun, girls," she rattled as she took our eight dollars in her veined hands and gestured to the door leading to the only screen in the place. The theatre was empty, and I hoped it would stay that way. We were early, but there were already black and white images flashing across the screen of women screaming with exaggerated horror in their eyes. Good ole' Delores clearly wasted no time getting the party started.

It must have been 9:00 p.m. because one film wrapped up and another began. *Frankenstein.* A classic. No sooner did the film sputter to life than a beam of light flooded in from the door being opened in the back of the theatre. So, someone would be joining us tonight after all. I chanced a glance to see who it was, and my heart fluttered in surprise as I saw Shea making his way down the aisle, wearing fitted black jeans and a white t-shirt under a black zip up hoodie.

We made eye contact, and I could tell by the look on his face that he wasn't expecting to see me here tonight. For some reason he looked more like he wanted to run away than stay, but he was already locked into his path and his purpose. I could see how awkward it was going to be for him to have to choose to sit on his own somewhere in the theatre or sit next to us. I had mercy on him and waved him over.

"Hey! What are you doing here?" I asked stupidly and loudly. Because who was I going to bother?

"I guess I'm doing the same thing you are, although I didn't peg you for a horror fan—hey Becca." Shea gave Becca a nod and she gave him a cheesy grin and waved.

Now that she knew about my feelings, I could feel the playfulness coming off of her in heady vibrations. Normally that would have made me want to slap her and hide under a chair, but given the circumstances, it made me happy.

"I'm really not a horror fan, but Becca is my date tonight, and I'm nothing if not an accommodating date." I nudged Becca, who nodded and shrugged. "I know there aren't very many seats to choose from tonight, so feel free to sit next to me if you want."
Shea sat down one seat away from me and tossed his feet up onto the back of the seat in front of him. He then opened up a packet of peppermint patties and dumped the whole thing into his bag of popcorn.

"What is wrong with you people?" I looked at him incredulously and Becca air high fived Shea.

"What?" Shea looked confused.

"Peppermint in your popcorn? You are both psycho." I shook my head, and Shea shook his at the same time.

"Life is to be lived, Annie. Don't knock it 'til you've tried it." He extended his bag of popcorn over to me.

I wanted to refuse him, but he was so handsome, and so charming, and before I knew it, I was chewing on minty popcorn. I don't know if it tasted good or not. I don't remember. I just remember the image of Shea's full lips smirking at me as he put a handful of popcorn in his mouth and how much I wished that popcorn was me.

We sat back in our seats and forgot about life for a while, as Baron Victor Frankenstein diligently worked to create a living human from a bunch of dead spare parts. When we were halfway through 'Dracula' starring Bela Lugosi, Becca nudged me and pretended to snore, which was my sign to get her home and in bed. I was mildly relieved because I had never been a night owl, but there was also a part of me that was enjoying my proximity to Shea, and I didn't want to leave his space. I looked over at Shea and saw him starting to nod off, and I figured he was probably ready to leave too.

I slapped my knees with my hands and said, "Welp," which in Minnesotan means 'it's time to go.' We walked back out into the dimly lit entryway, which was still uncomfortably bright in comparison to the dark room we were emerging from. Becca's eyes were puffy, but she still looked beautiful. Shea's dark eyes looked almost amber in the golden light, and I knew exactly how pale and frumpy I looked. I've always turned white as a sheet (verging on bluish green) when I'm tired.

"So, where's your boyfriend tonight? You didn't feel like being arm candy on Halloween?" Shea asked it casually, but I couldn't help but feel the sting of being referred to as 'arm candy.'

Even though my relationship with Drew was over, I couldn't help my insecurities bubbling up to the surface, and the anger that followed as it occurred to me that that's how Shea and everyone else probably thought of my relationship with Drew. A big joke.

"Apparently you didn't notice, but Annie is busy being *my* arm candy tonight, thank you very much." Becca swooped in with a sassy response that I appreciated, but I still felt the sting of Shea's words.

"Drew and I broke up," I said. It wasn't a secret.

"Oh, man, sorry." Shea didn't sound sorry at all. He actually smiled. He should have stopped there, but he kept talking. "Drew's an asshat for breaking up with you, but you two weren't a great fit anyway so it was only a matter of time, right?" Shea's tone was light, but his words confirmed my insecurities and cut into my soft shell like a sharp knife through a poached egg.

My cheeks burned with anger and shame. Not only did Shea refer to me as 'arm candy,' but he just *assumed* that Drew was the one who broke up with me. Everyone at that party tonight was probably walking around assuming the same thing. *Poor Annie, dumped by Drew after only a few weeks. She was never good enough for him anyway.* Looking back, I realize that I could have taken Shea's words a million different ways. But in that moment, all I was capable of was defensiveness. I had done a lot of growing up recently, but a lifetime of insecurity and approval-seeking takes longer than a few months of growth experiences to heal from.

"Actually, I was the one who broke things off with him, but thanks for assuming it was the other way around. Bye, Shea."

Before Shea could say anything else, I grabbed Becca's arm and pulled her out of there and into the icy night. I dropped her off at her house and drove home faster than usual so that I would beat Shea back to our shared corner of the world and not have to pass by him again. I lay in bed that night and swore off men for the rest of my life. Or at least the rest of the school year.

As if I had that much self-control.

TWENTY-EIGHT

"SO...DID YOU have a good Halloween?" Drew asked me as his thumb scrolled across the screen of his phone.

Things were officially awkward between us now. There wasn't really anything left to say, and yet, there we were, still lab partners. Neither one of us was going to be the asshole that asked to switch seats. At this point, it was easier to just pretend like nothing had happened and move on.

"Yeah, it was good. Becca and I just went to the movies. Pretty chill." I replied, also not looking at him, but feeling the remains of tension tugging between us. "How was the party?"

"It was good. Stella always puts on a good night. She and I both ended up dressing as zombies, so everyone thought we were together."

I'm pretty sure my internal eye roll at that comment bruised a rib. Then again, fair enough. *I* broke up with *him* and left him without a date to the party, after all.

"That's cool" was all I could muster. And then, half a beat later, "Shea was at the movies with us last night, too." I blurted it out like a petty idiot.

Shea had pissed me off, and at this point, I was not interested in speaking to any boys whatsoever, but I didn't need Drew to know that. It felt good landing a little dig, even though, in retrospect, I was only burning myself.

Drew didn't reply at first. And then, "Tyler dressed like a piece of bacon at the party, and he got so drunk that he fell on top of Kamila, who was dressed as some kind of slutty dish soap, I

216

think? Her dress was made from balloons and most of them popped when he landed on her, and I've never been so in fear for someone's life."

I couldn't help but chuckle imagining that scenario, and honestly, I would have liked to witness the fall of Kamila, not because she was mean, or ever did anything to me, but because I was a jealous teenager who wasn't evolved enough yet to be genuinely happy for someone who was prettier than me. Except for Becca, of course.

Without thinking, I looked over at Drew at the same time as he looked at me, and for a second our eyes twinkled at each other. For a brief moment, I had the feeling that maybe I had been wrong and that he did really like me and maybe we would have made a good couple if I hadn't let my insecurity fuck it all up. Drew looked away from me again, and I remembered myself and vowed to trust my gut. I knew that I probably wouldn't ever get a chance to find out what could have been if I had just pushed through my doubts, and I was pleasantly surprised at how okay I was with that.

. . .

Seeing Shea in art class was hard. He stayed focused on his work, and I tried to focus on mine, but my brain was determined to play reruns of Shea and me dancing together, and him telling me his secrets, chewing on popcorn, and calling me arm candy. I could see his jaw clenching from across the room, and I couldn't tell if he was stressed, furious, or just focused on the task at hand and not worried about me at all.

"Annie, can I speak to you for a moment, please?" The sound of Ms. Young's voice snapped me out of my trance, and I looked up to see her gazing at me from her desk, with a kindness in her eyes that made me feel like I didn't need to fear imminent failure, expulsion, or public humiliation. I stood up and walked over to her desk.

"I need some help in the supply room, would you be willing to carry some paint for me?" We weren't using paint that day, so it seemed like an odd request, but far be it for me to question an authority figure, even if she *was* a little batty.

I had never actually been in the supply room before, and it was much larger than I expected. It had floor-to-ceiling windows and rows of neat shelves with all kinds of art supplies, meticulously labeled and organized by color and category. It was a stark contrast to the stereotype I had in my head of artists' tendencies. Apparently, open-mindedness and creativity don't automatically equal clutter and instability.

"So, which color do you need?" I asked, looking around the room, feeling a primal satisfaction at the sight of clean paint jugs organized in rainbow order.

"I don't need any paint, Annie. But I would like to have a chat with you if that's okay. You're not in trouble."

I should have seen this coming since I hadn't managed to produce anything substantial over the last two months of class. I braced myself for the onslaught of criticism, followed by modest encouragement, and gentle warning of impending failure.

"Yeah, sure. I know I'm not an artist, and I haven't exactly been giving it my all either. I'll try harder," I said trying to soften the blow to my ego by criticizing myself first.

"Annie…no. I absolutely do not want you to try harder. Art is not about trying hard." She paused and looked out the window before speaking again.

218

"Do you know why I love art, Annie?" She smiled, and I shrugged. "It's because it's for everyone. Everyone is an artist. What comes out of our hands and our hearts and our souls is not supposed to look the same because we are not the same. Do you understand?"

I didn't understand because to me things were either good or bad. My art was categorically bad. I nodded anyway.

"The first step is noticing. Noticing how things look, and how they make you feel. The next step is enjoying the process. Simple as that. I can give you tips and tools and materials and methods and maybe you'll be a natural at painting realistic, classical portraits, and maybe you won't. But if I can help you enjoy the process of *creating something new*, then I've done my job, and you've done yours. I'm not looking for perfection—I'm looking for an honest expression of you, Annie. I hope you'll consider giving it a try."

Ms. Young was looking at me now, and for the first time, I saw her as more than an eccentric adult in a floral duster. This was a woman who really saw people for who they were, and she looked on them gently and lovingly. Me included. She was someone with her own story and experience, one that I never came to know, but now wish I would have. Ms. Young had peace in her heart and a willingness to share that peace with others, and she gave me something I needed that day.

There, in the supply room of Concord High School, I realized that maybe it was time to stop focusing on everyone else and start focusing on finding myself and stepping into my own talents. Maybe I'd start by chipping away at my tunnel vision and noticing something new, even if it might turn out to be something scary. And then maybe I'd move on to enjoying the process. I needed to

219

write more—but not just journal—really write. Something purposeful. And maybe I'd go back out and doodle on my canvas and see if something might appear that looked a little bit like me.

TWENTY-NINE

I SPENT THE next six weeks with Becca, and alone with myself. I took Becca to a couple doctor's appointments, and we got to hear the baby's heartbeat and see its tiny little legs kicking on an ultrasound. I held Becca's hand, and she held mine, and in those moments, we weren't worried about the next steps or what the world would think when they found out. We marveled together at the miracle of life and did our damnedest to turn a blind eye to the horror that caused it.

As Christmas approached, Becca's belly was expanding, but she was curvy and cool enough to hide it well with oversized t-shirts and a 'try me, bitch' attitude. If anyone suspected, they didn't say anything. Or at least, they didn't dare say anything to her, or to me.

Hanging out in Miss Jones's classroom after school became a regular occurrence for both of us, and Becca was frequently late to work at the shop, but my dad never mentioned it. He knew she was hanging on by a thread. And if he didn't already suspect, then pretty soon, he would find out just how fine that thread really was.

Becca's plan was to wait as long as possible before telling her parents and the rest of the world, so that she had a chance to save up as much money as she could in case her parents kicked her out, and she needed to rent a place. She would be turning eighteen in January, so she needed to find a way to support herself and her baby fast.

Of course, I told her time and time again that she could come stay with me and my family for as long as she needed, but she was adamant that she wanted her own space, and I could understand that. Deep down I knew that she felt safer knowing my family was there for her always, but I also knew my friend, and she was going to do everything she could to take care of herself, just like she always had.

By Christmas, fall felt like a distant memory, as the amber leaves were buried deep under several feet of sparkling powder. Most mornings in December, when I looked out my windows, the trees were coated in thick hoar frost, and it amazed me how something so natural could seem so otherworldly. Like nothing so magical could simply exist in nature without the help of fairies and a big imagination.

During my alone time, I even found myself writing poems about the seasons, and drawing unintelligible little sketches in the margins. I made a mental note to show Ms. Young, partly so I could (hopefully) score some extra credit, but also because it would feel good to watch her beam with delight at my creations, such as they were.

The more time that passed after the breakup with Drew, the easier and less awkward our encounters in science class got. It wasn't just that time was passing, though. I was distracted with new things, like my own goals and my own vision for my life. I was so far from having it all figured out, but with every journal entry and conversation with my parents about career options and moment spent thinking about logistics for Becca's life with her baby, Drew and our brief relationship history felt smaller and smaller. I was growing in confidence, but this time, it was for all the right reasons.

Drew started spending more time in public with Stella, and I was pleasantly surprised to find that I wasn't jealous of her. They looked so natural together that I couldn't help but wonder if his heart had been with her all along, even though he told me they were just friends while we were dating. I passively wondered what their history together was, and what secrets they might be keeping.

I didn't have time to resent either of them, because as much as I tried to fight it, my heart was still focused on Shea. The more time I spent *not* talking to him, the more I wanted him. Desire was building up inside me, and I found myself trying to find excuses to be near him. I knew that at some point I needed to talk to him again or risk driving myself crazy.

Along with my newfound confidence came the realization that I probably overreacted when it came to what Shea had said at the movie theatre. He hurt my feelings, but I didn't exactly extend him any grace. Especially not considering everything he had been through, and how much he had opened up to me and trusted me with his own feelings just days before. He was going through an impossible time, and I shut him out over one silly comment that didn't land beautifully. It wasn't fair of me, and I knew it, but I didn't know how to admit it yet.

. . .

Christmas morning, we woke up to a blizzard, and I was devastated. Becca was supposed to be spending Christmas with us, but I couldn't see three feet in front of me outside, and there was no chance anyone would be willing to drive in that weather. I begged my dad to go pick her up, but he was too smart to give in to my pleas, even though I could tell that his heart was breaking a little too.

He had gotten to spend a lot of time with Becca at the shop in those few months, more than he normally would have if she was just hanging out with me at our house on occasion. And I could tell that he was even more fond of her than he used to be. It felt good knowing that even if I ended up going to college far away next year and Becca wasn't able to come with me, she would be well looked after and loved by my parents in my absence. I still didn't know what my plans were, but I knew I would go to school somewhere so I could achieve whatever it is people are meant to achieve between ages eighteen and twenty-two. Maybe I'd be a writer. Or an artist (just kidding).

Despite my disappointment at Becca's absence, there was no avoiding the pure joy that it brought me to watch little Rosie experience the magic of Christmas morning. She ran to the tree in her jammies and could hardly squeeze complete words out through excited breaths and colored cheeks. We spent the day in a real-life snow globe, enjoying the warmth and love of a peaceful family.

By dinner, the storm had died down, and the sky was black and quiet. My mind trailed over to Shea, as if the blizzard lifting opened up a clear path from me to him. I wondered how he had spent his Christmas. My heart ached as I imagined him alone in his house. After dinner, my mom didn't pack up any food for him, and I didn't ask to bring any to him. Maybe enough time had passed that she wasn't thinking about him as much as I still was.

Rosie was sleepy, and she asked me to take her to bed, which I did with more love in my heart than I thought anyone could feel. I thought of Becca and her baby. I smiled knowing how much love would be flooding into her life soon, even if it was in this way, at this time. My parents stayed up to watch *It's a Wonderful Life* together like they did every year.

As for me, I made my way up to my room for the night. Or so I thought.

THIRTY

I CHANGED OUT of my sweater and leggings and slipped into my white Christmas jammies that I had received from 'Santa' that morning. They were silky and special and made me feel grown up as I crawled into bed in an actual matching pajama set instead of my usual big t-shirt and underwear. It was only 8:00 p.m., so I took my time brushing my hair and washing my face and settling in with a new book (also a Christmas gift from the big man up north).

Just as I opened the creaky new hardcover and found page one, my phone chimed.

SHEA: *Merry Christmas, Annie. I left a gift for you on your front porch. I hope you like me. I mean, it.* ;)

My stomach leaped into my throat and my face tingled with anticipation and delight. *What could he possibly have given me? Has he been thinking of me, too?* It turns out there is always room in a teenage girl's heart for romantic surprises, no matter how determined she is to 'work on herself.'

I slipped downstairs, past the living room where my parents were deep into their movie and their apple pie. I opened the front door to see a rectangular package leaning up against the house, wrapped in brown paper with a big red bow on it, and a white envelope taped just under the bow with 'Annie' written on it in small, capital letters.

I snapped a mental picture so I would never forget how special I felt. I didn't need to open the package to know that I was already experiencing a singular moment in time. I slipped past my parents again with the package held tight to my chest, and climbed the stairs to my room slowly, so I could savor the anticipation before uncovering the mysterious gift Shea had left for me.

I sat on my bed with the package in front of me and decided to read the note first:

Annie,

Merry Christmas. I hope it's not too late to apologize to you for the stupid things I said on Halloween. I was so jealous of how much you seemed to like Drew—to be honest, hearing you weren't together anymore made my night…before I went and fucked it all up.

BUT, just to be clear, I stand by what I said. You and Drew aren't a good fit for each other because you are way too good for him. You're too good for me, too, but I'm choosing to ignore that fact for now.

I was jealous and selfish and ashamed of myself and the burden I put on you by telling you about my life with my dad and the things that I did. It's no excuse for being an indelicate jerk, and I'm sorry.

I hope you like what I made for you. Nothing could compare to the real thing, but I did my best.

Shea

(P.S. I know I haven't earned the right to say this to you, but you are so beautiful, Annie.)

I read the note several times before it finally soaked in that it was real. Sweet Shea. *I* was the one who had been selfish. I had

227

shut him out over a couple of comments that had landed right in a sore spot I hadn't outgrown yet. I pushed him away over nothing, even after the intimate connection we had shared. I had looked him in the eyes as I drove away with Drew the day after he bared his soul to me. I had given him zero grace or understanding when he accidentally said the wrong thing. I had invaded his life and demanded his help and attention and then tossed him aside after he was vulnerable with me because I was too worried about myself to think about how I might be hurting other people. Other people that I happened to want to make out with.

I closed my eyes and reminded myself that I wasn't the same insecure girl I was months before. I felt deep things for Shea. And I wanted to let him feel them for me too, without me getting in my own way.

I took my time peeling back the paper to reveal the back of a large picture frame. When I flipped it over, I was looking at…myself.

It wasn't a sketch of me posing in the art classroom—Shea was gone the week I posed, anyway. I was looking at an oil pastel drawing of me with my hair down, looking out of the picture with every shade of blue and gray in my eyes, and a facial expression that was subtle and kind. Around my bust there was a slash of red, with fine straps reaching over my shoulders. I was wearing my homecoming dress. The background framed my face with abstract light dappling through trees—golden like the fall—colors that were woven throughout my red hair, which appeared to be ever-so-slightly blowing in a breeze. Freckles dusted my nose. Light danced off of my cheekbones. The image stole the breath right out of my lungs.

Shea had drawn me from memory. And it was so skillfully done, and so refined, that I didn't even feel worthy of being its subject. Except that maybe I did. Because when I looked at how Shea saw me, I saw depth and beauty and kindness and light. I had never felt more beautiful. Not even on the night that I actually wore that red dress and kissed the boy that I had thought was the boy of my dreams, not realizing at the time that I was getting it all wrong. I had picked the wrong one. I wouldn't be making that mistake again.

I laid the drawing carefully on my bed and made my way downstairs where I threw my coat and boots on and told my parents that I was going to bring Shea some Christmas dinner. I told them not to wait up—that spending some time with him was the right thing to do, considering the reason for the season, etc. They didn't question me. I wouldn't have cared if they had. My mind was made up.

I grabbed a Tupperware full of ham and potatoes and marched through the shin-deep snow to Shea's house. His porchlight was on. By the time I got there, my silky pajama bottoms were half wet from the snow. I knocked on Shea's door. A minute later the door opened, and I was gazing straight into the warm, dark eyes of the boy who had my heart, despite what I had been trying (and failing) to tell myself all those weeks before.

"I brought you potatoes," I said. Because 'Hi' or 'Merry Christmas' just wouldn't have been my style.

"Thanks. Did you…get my present?" Shea asked, suddenly looking shy.

"I did," I said, not sure how to fully express how beautiful it was, or how much it meant to me.

"Okay good," he said, "…and did you get my note?" Shea was looking at me now with hope in his eyes, waiting for me to either relieve him of his shame or crush him entirely.

"I did," I said, this time, with a furrow in my brow.

I let a beat pass, and Shea started to speak again. "I understand if you don't want to see—"

I dropped the potatoes on the ground and reached my arms up around Shea's neck and kissed him before another apology could fall out of his mouth. Shea grabbed my waist and pulled me in out of the cold, closing the door behind us and pushing me back against it with the firm weight of his body. My knees buckled under me, but Shea was strong, and he was holding me so close that I didn't drop an inch. My head spun with the taste of Shea's lips and the heat of his body and the pounding of my heart against his.

Shea pulled back from me and looked into my eyes, silently asking for confirmation that this was what I wanted. The heat between my legs at the sight and smell and taste of him wouldn't have let me walk away from Shea even if I had wanted to.

"Would you like to come upstairs with me?" he asked, quietly, and I nodded.

Shea grabbed my hand and pulled me up the staircase and to a large room on the left that was modestly furnished with wood furniture and white bedding. Books lined floating shelves, and a desk sat under the window. There was a small lamp on it that illuminated the room just enough to see small flecks of paint on the desk. The light cast long shadows onto the floor made by the bedframe.

Shea didn't close the door behind him. This was his house, and he lived alone. The only other people here were ghosts, and if they wanted to get in, they certainly wouldn't be stopped by something as material as a door.

We didn't speak. Shea reached up and brushed his fingers along my jawline, and kissed me again, softly this time. I was desperate for him, but he was taking his time. He bent down and kissed my neck all the way down to my collarbone and his delicate touch sent shivers across my skin. The silk of my pajamas was suddenly too much of a barrier between Shea's skin and mine. I needed him closer.

As if reading my mind, Shea turned me around and kissed my neck from behind, reaching around to the front of my shirt and unbuttoning the buttons until my bare flesh was exposed. He traced his fingers along the centerline of my stomach like a question. I grabbed his hand and lifted his palm to cup my breast and inhaled sharply as the throbbing between my legs became nearly unbearable.

"Take your clothes off," I whispered through hurried breaths as my pulse pounded throughout my body.

Shea obeyed. He lifted his t-shirt off to reveal his perfect body, no less toned or tanned than the last time I saw him with his shirt off over the summer. He dropped his pants down around his ankles and kicked them off and to the side before coming back to me and pressing himself against my body and kissing me again, harder this time. The heat of him melted my goosebumps away.

I wanted Shea. I wanted all of him. I wanted to know every part of him, and I wanted him to know all of me. Shea reached his hand below my waistband and glided his fingers around to grab my bare ass underneath my pants. I let my pants drop down and my breath caught in my throat as Shea lifted me up and laid me down easily on his bed.

My legs were wrapped around his waist when he pulled back once more to look into my face.

"You definitely want to do this?" he asked as if his life depended on me saying yes.

"Yes. I want this so much, Shea." I looked at him earnestly, so that he would believe me and not hold back.

Shea kissed his way down my body until he got to my hip bones, where he lingered for a moment, before sliding his mouth all the way down to the apex of my thighs. I groaned with a warm feeling I had never experienced before, and my body started a delicious tightening almost immediately. It felt too good for me to be embarrassed by where Shea had his tongue. The sensation was almost more than I could bear. I needed more.

I pulled him back up, and I could taste myself on his lips. I reached down and slid my hand under his boxers and took the length of him into my hand. He gasped at my touch, and I couldn't help the satisfied smirk that stretched across my face. I pulled his boxers the rest of the way down so that we were both completely free of our clothes.

I had never been completely naked with a boy before. The nerves of my inexperience danced with the carnal instinct of my desire in a way that was both terrifying and electrifying. I wanted more.

"Please," I whispered looking him in the eyes once more.

"I don't have anything," Shea said, and I knew what he was referring to.

"I've been on birth control for ages, it's okay. For my period, not because...you know. This," I said, feeling a little embarrassed about my lack of experience and hoping it wouldn't turn Shea off. It didn't.

"Okay," Shea whispered into my ear.

Shea brushed my cheek with his thumb and leaned into me, and the entirety of him slid into my body in one deliciously painful and satisfying motion. I felt his fullness drive into me again and again, slowly at first, and then faster until every muscle in my body contracted and released into a beautiful shower of sparks. Shea let out a final thrust as I came apart under him, and I watched as satisfaction tore through his body in the same way it did mine. I wrapped my legs around his waist and kept him there inside me, not ready to let go of the feeling of Shea yet. We were both out of breath, and I could hear my heart pounding in my ears as we bathed together in our mutual release and satisfaction.

When I did finally let Shea out of me, my legs were trembling. Shea pulled a blanket over our naked bodies and held me close against his chest, a place that I had actually been to before, but under different circumstances. He traced his fingers through my hair, and I listened to the steady rhythm of his heart. I wanted to stay in his arms forever.

I was in love.

This was right.

THIRTY-ONE

NEITHER ONE OF us said anything for a while. Somehow it felt like all the feelings that had been building between us were made crystal clear in the moments between me dropping potatoes all over Shea's porch, and Shea taking my virginity in a sweet but powerful way. I wondered if it was Shea's first time too, but I doubted it. He definitely knew what he was doing. I blushed in the silence, replaying what had just happened over again in my head.

Without a word of warning, Shea climbed out of bed from beside me and walked out the door with his perfect ass staring at me as he went. Once he was out of sight, my rational mind started to catch up with me and I realized the gravity of what had just occurred. I sat frozen in bed, unsure of what I was supposed to do next. Get dressed and leave? I knew I couldn't spend the night because my parents knew where I was, and they would be expecting me back. I didn't need my dad knocking on Shea's door to find me naked and ravaged by him.

I heard the wooden stairs creaking and knew Shea was on his way back up. He slipped back into the room, this time with a towel around his waist and a pint of Chubby Hubby ice cream in his hands. Like magic, Shea's presence sent a wave of calm confidence through me.

"Ice cream just feels right sometimes, doesn't it?" Shea smiled at me like I was the only girl in the world.

"Sometimes?" I replied in mock surprise. "I dare anyone to give me an example of when ice cream *doesn't* feel right." He jabbed the spoon into the ice cream and set it into my outstretched hand.

The cold pint was a refreshing contrast to the sticky heat that was still swirling around my body.

"You're not having any?" I said looking for a second spoon and seeing none.

"I've already had dessert," Shea shrugged, and I blushed with embarrassment and rolled my eyes, so he knew how gross he sounded. Gross…but hot.

"While I appreciate that you had ice cream on hand and had the good sense to bring it up to me, I don't think I can trust someone who turns down eating some of it when offered…it's just a huge red flag for me, in general." I shrugged back at him. Flirting with Shea was easy and delightful.

"So, you're saying *that's* going to be the reason you don't trust me?" Shea chuckled and raised his eyebrows in shock. "Not the, you know…other things?" I saw a hint of fear and sadness flicker in Shea's eyes. I knew the look well. I didn't want to taint this moment by talking about reality, but I had also never felt closer to Shea, and I wanted him to know how much I cared about him. I set the ice cream down on the bedside table and crawled out from under the covers. It felt strange to be completely naked in front of someone other than my mom or Becca, but Shea had already broken down my inhibitions, and I wanted to let him see me. I straddled his lap and held his face in my hands.

"Shea McAteer, I can't say I'm not disappointed that you turned down ice cream. But I do trust you. I always have, even when I didn't know anything about anything. You're a good person. And the way you make me feel…it's…" Shea didn't let me finish my sentence. He kissed me again, and his soft lips set my insides on fire all over again. I tried to speak, but my thoughts were washed away with the tides of Shea's mouth on my skin.

Shea went down on me again, and this time, he didn't come up until I fell apart. I laughed and sighed and couldn't believe how good it felt to be savored by Shea. The lost boy from my childhood, who secretly grew into the most dashing prince when I wasn't looking.

"So...I'm guessing you've...done this before?" I asked, not wanting to know the answer, but needing to know, too. Shea was quiet. I could tell he didn't know how to respond. A few too many seconds passed, and I was ready to tell him to forget that I asked, but he turned to me and looked me in the eyes.

"Yes. But it's my first time with someone that I..." Shea trailed off and took a deep breath and I didn't wait for him to finish the sentence. I knew what he meant. I felt it too.

"Me too," I said and smiled. Shea hugged me and I counted his heartbeats, telling myself I would go home when I reached twenty and then fifty and then one hundred.

Sometime before midnight, I forced myself back into my clothes and out into the cold. Shea led me. He walked me home and kissed me long and hard behind a tree before delivering me back to my doorstep.

"Thanks for bringing me Christmas dinner tonight, Annie," Shea said, and I laughed.

"Sorry about the mess," I replied. Shea's eyes twinkled, and his mouth turned up in the corner and I saw forever. I reached up and gave him one last peck on the cheek and turned to open my front door. When I looked back, Shea was backing away from me with his hands in his pockets and a grin on his face. I spent the next hour writing every detail down in my journal, so I would never forget how I felt in that moment. Once it was all safely on the paper, I forced myself to get some sleep.

. . .

The next morning, I woke up just as the sun was considering its ascent, and I took several minutes to enjoy the deep warmth of my heavy comforter safely shielding me from the cold blue light of winter morning. I shifted my body gently beneath the covers, savoring how sore I felt, and the glowy feeling of knowing how I came to feel that way and by whom.

Something had changed last night. It now felt like unless my skin was touching Shea's, I was too far away from him. I lay there and began to indulge in my memories of us, and groaned as my phone dinged, alerting me to a text message and dragging me kicking and screaming back to reality. My grudge didn't last long, because when I looked at the screen, I saw the message was from Shea. My heart hammered in my chest, hoping for the best, but automatically assuming the worst, because it was just in my nature. Maybe he regretted last night. Maybe he didn't want to see me again. Or…maybe not. I opened the message.

SHEA: *Meet me down at the lake in 30 minutes. x*

I lit up with anticipation at being in Shea's space again so soon, and I leaped out of bed, suddenly immune to the harsh cold of my room. I threw on some leggings, a long sleeve t-shirt, my long puffer jacket with the fur hood, and some thick socks and boots just for good measure. Not my sexiest look, but I'd be trudging through several feet of snow to get down to the lake, and Shea had already seen everything there was to see. The thought made me smile. I ran a brush through my hair, tossed a hat on, went to the bathroom to brush my teeth, and toss a little light mascara on, and stepped quietly out the back door, so as not to alert my sleeping family. I felt like a different person today, and I wasn't ready to look them in the eyes yet for fear they would see the whole of last night play out across my face.

I stepped outside just as the edge of the sun peeked over the horizon, making the trees glitter and shine like a winter wonderland. The fresh snow was sparkling with warm pastel colors, and the sky was a radiant blue, incomparable against the clean, white landscape.

I looked down and forward, and my eyes trailed along a narrow path that someone had shoveled all the way from my back door, across the field, and into the trees that led to the lake. Shea had shoveled me a path. It must have taken him hours. The kindness of the gesture was more than I was used to or would have ever expected, but this time, instead of questioning it and finding a way to reframe this story for the worse, I allowed myself to savor it. I set out on the path carved out by the person that my heart desired, and walked easily through the frosty morning, right in the direction of my dreams.

My breath billowed around me—it was the only disruption for miles to the clear winter air. I liked watching the sun filter around and through my breath, illuminating the edges of where my living energy met the rest of the world. Such simple, perfect moments are generous gifts to our souls—they give us life and color and humanity and pure existence. Sometimes the memories of these moments are the only peaceful visions we have left after everything else has come crashing down around us.

Shea could hear my feet crunching in the snow as I approached, and he turned to face me, with a sheepish smile on his handsome face, and a steaming mug in his hand. He was wearing jeans and boots, with a red plaid jacket that looked too thin for the freezing temperature, but his cheeks were ruddy with heat and his hair was tousled from the effort he had just put in shoveling all morning. I couldn't take my eyes off him.

"Are you just going to stand there looking cold or are you going to come sit down with me?" Shea gestured to my left, where I saw a small table with two chairs set up, along with some donuts in a box and a little fire burning alongside. There were two more steaming mugs sitting on the table.

I couldn't even speak. I just looked at him and back at the table and chairs and back to him. He walked over and grabbed my hand and led me over to a seat at the table. His hand was warm, and it swallowed up my cold hand so sweetly. He sat me in the chair closest to the fire, which was radiating just enough heat to keep me comfortable. He sat on the other side of the table and smiled.

"I don't even know what to say, Shea. When did you have time to do this?" I said, looking around, and then I noticed the extra mug on the table. "Wait…are we expecting someone else to join us?"

"I hope not," he laughed softly. "One mug is coffee, and one is hot chocolate. I wasn't sure which you would like. And there was no way I could go back to sleep after seeing you last night. I figured I might as well shovel."

I blushed at his thoughtfulness. I didn't know how to react but being with Shea felt so natural that I didn't really worry about saying or doing the right things. I took a few sips of the hot chocolate and then dumped a little coffee into it.

"So, a mocha girl then. I'll remember that for next time," he winked as he said it.

"Next time? How often do you plan to spend all morning shoveling snow and making me breakfast?" I laughed.

"As long as you'll let me," he said with a smile, but he sounded serious. I picked up a donut and took a huge bite.

"It's a date," I said, my mouth full of donut and happiness. We both laughed.

"So, just FYI, I do have one more surprise for you when you're done with the sugar overload element of this date," he said.

"Don't tell me a singing clown is going to pop out from behind the tree or something," I said sarcastically.

"Way to go and ruin the surprise, Annie!" Shea shouted at me in mock offense. "A guy can't even plan a special date these days without girls cutting the fun out from under him."

"Girls, plural? How many girls are you currently seeing, Shea?"

"Oh, you know, there are about six ladies waiting for me in the chicken coop, but none are as beautiful as you are. Except for maybe Henrietta…her black feathers are to die for."

"Note to self—ask Henrietta for her feather-care routine." I tapped my chin, and I noticed how Shea's eyes crinkled in the corners as he smiled.

I chanced a wink at him. *Is he blushing?*

Just then, Shea stood up and walked over to my chair, bent down and scooped me up effortlessly into his arms, then sat back down in my seat with me in his lap.

"All this talk about girls made me feel too far away from the only one I want."

I tipped my head back and my hat fell off as Shea ran his fingers into my hair and pulled me in to kiss me. His lips were so soft and so gentle, but so pleading, as if he could kiss me forever and it wouldn't be enough. I sat up and straddled him and took his face in my hands so I could study his strong features and look into his dark eyes which glowed with an intoxicating combination of sadness and longing and joy. I kissed his forehead, and his temple, and moved my way down to his ear and his neck and back up to his mouth which took mine again desperately and sent a delicious pulse down between my thighs.

"Annie," he whispered in my ear, "I…" He leaned back away from me.

"Did I do something wrong?" I questioned, desperately hoping I hadn't, but suddenly feeling unsure.

"God, no. You couldn't be more perfect. It's just, I… I really wanted to do this date properly. I want you to know that I respect you. And I want to kiss you and touch you and have sex with you and that's honestly all I can think about all the fucking time, but I also want to do right by you. And I want to show you that I'm not just the creepy dude next door with a hard-on for you. I have feelings for you, and I want to do things for you and take care of you if you'll let me. And surprise you with singing clowns if that's what you want. Though I think the surprise I have coming is better."

Shea looked at me intently, like he was so utterly exposed that a single word from me could give him wings or shatter him to pieces. I kissed him softly and then whispered in his ear.

241

"Let's have the surprise then."

Shea smiled wide and stood up out of the chair, lifting me up with him and spinning me around a few times before setting me back down on the ground in a giddy daze. He stepped back behind a tree and came back out a moment later with a light blue box. He handed it to me with anticipation on his face, along with the ever-present touch of sadness.

The box was surprisingly heavy. I opened it to see a pair of white ice skates. I looked up at Shea who nodded his head toward the lake, which I just noticed had a patch of bare ice that had obviously been cleared off by Shea earlier that morning.

"We're going ice skating?" I said feeling both like a happy child and a nervous teenager who was well aware of her own clumsiness.

"We are. And there's something I want you to know. About the skates. They were my mom's. She used to come skating out here all the time, and she bought these new ones just before she got sick. She never got to wear them. They've been up in a closet for the last ten years. I just...if you don't want to wear them or think this is weird and morbid, I totally get it. But she's been gone for such a long time now. And I think she would like it if someone skated out here again. Someone who makes her son happy in a way he hasn't been since she died."

Tears glistened in Shea's eyes, and he let one of them fall, without even wiping it away or trying to hide it. His vulnerability made my heart ache and also made me realize that there was nothing I wouldn't do to make him smile.

"I love them, Shea. This is one of the most special gifts I've ever received. The other ones being the painting you gave me, and

242

that thing you did with your tongue last night." I blushed at the last part, but I knew I had said the right thing as I watched Shea's eyes twinkle with mischief and pride. "Thank you," I said sincerely this time.

I sat in the chair and Shea knelt down in the snow to take off my boots and put the skates on, tying them neatly and effortlessly. It was a task I could have done myself (although, admittedly, I would have probably botched the job on the lacing), but I didn't fight him, and I let him do what he wanted to do. He wanted to take care of me this morning, and I wanted to let him. Shea carried me down to the lake, where he set me down and then ran back up to grab his black hockey skates, which he slipped on as he sat next to me on the ice.

My legs were wobbly, and I shrieked every time I slid a little farther than expected, but Shea's hands were steady on mine as he guided me around slowly. He skated backward in a strong, fluid motion and pulled me along with him.

"So, you didn't tell me you were a professional ice skater, in addition to all the other things you're apparently amazing at," I said, staring at the ice in front of me and trying not to break my focus or my arm.

"When I was little my dad and I used to come down here and play hockey together. My mom skated with us too. When she got sick, she sat over there and cheered us on. Sometimes you did too, Annie, but I'm sure you don't remember—it was a long time ago."

The inkling of a lost memory came back to me as he said it. The little brown-haired boy next door skating around with his dad smiling. The woman with the kind, blue eyes and no eyebrows with her warm hat and soft scarf and blanket smiling at me. It was so long ago that the memories were only flashes, but they were real. I pulled myself closer to Shea, so I could feel his warmth.

"My mom loved you, you know. She always said, "Why don't you go ask Annie to come out and play with you?" but I was too shy to ask. But any time I went outside to play I secretly hoped you would too, and whenever you ran over to me with your little braids bouncing on your shoulders, it made my day. You were always so bright and adventurous. I loved playing with you. Still do." Shea looked a little embarrassed at having admitted his childhood crush on me. All it did was make me wish I had noticed him sooner.

We skated in silence for a while, and then Shea kept speaking, quieter this time.

"After Mom died and I got older, there were so many more reasons to keep myself away from you. You were perfect, and my life was a mess. I went from hoping I would see you, to avoiding you altogether. I saw you down at the dock sometimes, and I just stayed away. I didn't want you to have any part of my shitty life. I'm still not entirely sure that my bad luck isn't contagious."

I hugged Shea, and he slid us to a stop. And then I kissed him. My kiss knocked him off balance and we fell down at the same time, our legs all tangled and the pine trees around us echoing our laughter back to us. We just lay there next to each other on our backs, looking up at the blue sky, and letting our laughter turn to chuckles and then to quiet breathing.

"I like you and your shitty life. And this date was perfect. And you're perfect. I don't know what it is you see in me when you could have any girl in the world, but I do know I've never felt more seen in my life, and when you look at me, I feel like I'm going to burst into flames but in the best way."

244

Shea reached over and grabbed my hand, just like he used to do when we were little. Every new moment I spent with Shea was bridging the gap between the then and the now. Even though this was all so new, I was beginning to realize it wasn't really. A foundation was set between us a long time ago, and we were just playing catch-up. The thought made me feel safe.

"So...speaking of shitty lives," Shea said, breaking the silence, "what are you hoping to do with yours? Not that yours is shitty obviously—not a great transition there on my part..." Shea was rambling, and I enjoyed listening to him flounder around. It made a welcome change from *me* being the one putting my foot in my mouth. Shea sighed and slapped his forehead.

"What I'm trying to say is, what do you want to do in life? Or next year at least?"

I didn't know what to say because I hadn't really decided. It seemed like everyone had a plan after graduation, and I was stuck between lofty dreams or something practical. It felt like such a big decision to make for someone who was really just starting to get to know herself for real.

"Honestly, Shea, I don't know. I'll probably go to college and study something like communications or business or something...just something practical that I can apply to a job when I figure out whatever it is I want to do. I've applied to a few colleges nearby. I'm pretty confused at the moment, and I know my parents are getting pretty desperate for me to make a decision, so I'm not left working at the sports shop next year instead of doing what nice, smart girls are supposed to do. It's just a big decision." Even before Shea responded I felt like a weight was lifted. Saying the words out loud—'I don't know' and 'I'm confused'—made me feel like at least I was acknowledging the thing.

"So…I know you didn't ask for my two cents…" I could feel Shea looking at me now, but I kept looking at the sky in case whatever he was going to say was going to sting for one reason or another. "But going to college for the things you just said sounds kind of like a…detour from what your real passion is. Isn't an English program an obvious choice for you? Or hell…write a book—whatever you want."

A light was burning bright in my chest as he spoke my dreams out loud to me. I had shoved them aside for years, reminding myself that writing was a hobby and not a real or reliable way to make money. Maybe I could be an English teacher, but that's not really what I wanted. I would be paying for my own college, and I didn't want to waste all that money on a hobby-turned-pipe dream. Still, Shea seeing my passion and believing in me meant everything.

"Maybe I will," I said smiling at Shea. "Maybe we can travel together and write about it." I knew as I spoke the words, the likelihood of that actually happening was basically zero, but Shea took the bait, and we started planning our imaginary trip—setting aside hard decisions and cruel realities for another place and time.

Such sweet innocence is too fleeting.

THIRTY-TWO

THE DAYS BETWEEN Christmas and New Year's Eve were beautiful. Eventually, Becca made it to my house, but other than her hanging out, it was just me and Shea together on our own, private winter island. My parents asked me why I was spending so much time at Shea's house, and I had to tell them the truth. Well, not the whole truth. But enough. That we liked each other. That he was so kind and smart and such a good guy. That he made me happy. My parents didn't pry further, because I was almost an adult, and they were practicing the delicate art of respecting my freedom. Or maybe they just didn't want to know. If they worried about Shea's questionable history with his dad, they didn't say anything. It felt good to be trusted.

Becca came over to Shea's with me a few times, and it felt so easy and natural when the three of us were together. Becca and Shea had the same sense of humor, and they ganged up on me to laugh at my expense, but in the purest way. Shea made us so much pie I'm pretty sure I gained my freshman fifteen before even setting foot on a college campus. Shea savored my body, and I savored his. I started writing a poem for Shea, and I planned to give it to him as a surprise when it was ready.

Sometimes Shea painted on my back, and I had to guess what it was before he helped me wash it off in the shower. I never got it right, but the shower with Shea more than made up for my disappointment at losing the game. The days passed slowly and beautifully.

One afternoon while we were all sitting around in Shea's living room drinking hot chocolate, Becca got quiet. I looked over at her and she looked at me with fear and determination in her eyes as she said, "Shea, there's something I want to share with you, friend to friend. Okay?"

My breaths shortened as it occurred to me what she was about to do. Keeping this secret from Shea had been hard, but I would have kept it locked down forever if that's how long it took for Becca to be ready. Shea nodded at her gently. He was a good listener, and I knew he would be understanding.

"Of course, Becca. You can tell me anything." Becca took a deep breath and let out a big sigh.

"I'm pregnant. Really pregnant, actually. Like 18 weeks along. Please, don't tell anyone." Becca's voice quivered on the last words, but she held herself together. Saying those words out loud to someone new took a huge amount of courage, and it was all I could do not to run over and hug her right then and there.

Shea didn't say anything for a moment. I could see the shock sitting just inside his carefully maintained facial expression. After a second of silence that felt like an hour, I saw the shock retreat even further into his body, as he consciously replaced it with compassion. Shea stood up and walked over to where Becca was sitting and kissed her lightly on the cheek and grabbed her hands in his.

"Congratulations," he said with a wide smile on his face. He didn't ask questions. He didn't make judgments. He gave Becca what she needed and that was respect. It occurred to me that Shea was probably the first person to congratulate Becca. Her pregnancy was unwanted, but it was real, and she deserved to be celebrated for becoming a mother regardless of the circumstances.

Becca smiled at Shea with tears in her eyes and stood up and hugged him. She cried on his shoulder for a while, and I watched as two pieces of my heart gave each other comfort. Once Becca had collected herself, she stepped back and let out a small laugh. Shea and I did too.

"So, who wants some cake?" Shea shouted brightly, clapping his hands together.

"Me!" Becca and I shouted in unison. "What kind do you have?"

"Depends—what kind do you want? We are going to have to make it ourselves, so..." Shea had a twinkle in his eye that reminded me of my grandpa, in the best way. We spent the rest of the afternoon baking and eating a giant chocolate cake.

Life was so, so good until it wasn't.

. . .

Every year the PTA hosted a New Year's Eve party at the country club for high school seniors and their families. It was an event that most students and their parents looked forward to, partly because of the opportunity to dress up and celebrate, but mostly because of the free, three-course dinner and complimentary beer and wine. I begged Shea to come with me and my parents, and he agreed, even though I could understand why he might be reluctant to go, given the likelihood that he would either be treated like a murder suspect or a sad little orphan boy by most of the people in attendance. I still wanted him with me.

I had a short, black cocktail dress with long sleeves, which I paired with black tights and trendy black velvet pumps. I arranged my hair in a low bun and opted for a nude, glossy lip, and a smokey eye. When I looked in the mirror, I looked so much older, and it felt good—like my appearance was matching the woman I was becoming. The doorbell rang, announcing the arrival of Rosie's babysitter, and I went down the stairs to find my parents looking surprisingly vibrant in their cocktail attire. It might have been the clothes, but looking back, I think it was more likely the joy and excitement they shared at seeing each other dressed up and beautiful for a night out together, which probably hadn't happened in years.

We drove over to Shea's house, and I got out to knock on his door. My jaw hit the floor when he opened the door and stepped out in a black suit that hugged him in all the right places, and his dark hair pulled neatly back into a messy bun. His chestnut eyes twinkled in the headlights that were shining straight at us, reminding me that I couldn't make out with Shea until later that night. We flashed each other a knowing smile and got in the backseat like friends, even though by that point we were already so much more than that.

"Is Becky coming tonight?" my dad shouted back to us louder than necessary. I imagine this situation was as awkward for him as it was for me.

"Yeah, she didn't want to, but her parents are making her go. Free drinks and all," I said, trying not to sound sarcastic and disparaging and failing. Becca's parents were selfish and terrible.

"Well, good. You'll be glad to see each other," Mom said keeping the conversation above ground.

We stayed quiet the rest of the way, but Shea brushed his pinkie finger against mine on the seat between us, and my insides

250

lit up. I couldn't wait to get him back home and feel him everywhere it was possible to feel another person. I suspected he was thinking the same thing.

The country club was already bustling when we pulled into the parking lot. The warm light from inside the building cast long, golden arms reaching out across the blue-black snow. My parents led the way, and Shea grabbed my small, cold hand in his big warm one, making me smile and hope the whole world would see us together. The compacted snow squeaked and crunched beneath our fancy shoes, and when we entered the large dining room, we were met with the distinct smell of chicken, booze, and snarky competition.

I immediately spotted Becca sitting alone at a round table while her parents chatted up with the same town bar staff that worked at every event. Her parents were both dressed in jeans and button-down shirts, and their faces were already red and shining as they laughed too loud at things their friends behind the bar said. Adults were allowed two drink tokens each, but Becca's parents were chummy with the bar staff, and they already knew going into this night out that Steve would slip them extra drinks no questions asked. It appeared like they were already well into their cups by the time we arrived. If my parents hadn't been there, I would have probably asked Steve to hook me up too.

Becca huffed a sigh of relief as Shea, and I approached her table and sat down.

"Becca, you look amazing. I mean, no surprise there, but still," I said genuinely amazed by her effortless beauty.

"Are you kidding?" She rolled her eyes at me, and then whispered in our direction, "Absolutely nothing fits. I had to drive to Pine Lakes last night and pick up this glorified sack of a dress from Walmart."

Shea looked at me and shrugged like he wouldn't know the difference if we drew a diagram for him, and I shrugged too because, to me, Becca looked like a mix between Jackie-O and Joan Jett.

Becca just *tsked* at us and took a drink of her sparkling water.

I could tell that Becca was anxious because she always bounced her knee and chewed her lip when her thoughts were spinning. I couldn't blame her. This sucked. She kept looking at the exit.

Before I could mention it, Shea said, "There's an empty table for five up there by the stage…would you ladies care to join me at it? Annie—maybe you can set a couple of seats aside for your parents?" Shea to the rescue. We all stood up to shift far away from the bar area.

Becca looked relieved, and she disappeared into the crowd in the direction of the new table without a second thought. Shea and I followed close behind, and I caught my mom's eye and gestured to the table we were headed to, just as one of the country club employees stepped up on stage to let us know that it was time to eat.

Everyone settled into their seats as the first course arrived— wild rice soup and a side salad comprised of wet iceberg lettuce and an unseasoned wedge of tomato. I finished my soup and ate a couple bites of lettuce, so that I looked like a grown-up, even though I'm pretty sure nobody actually enjoys house salad at any age. I'm still convinced that it's one of those things that just exists out of sheer habit and determination to appear better than you actually are. Like napkin rings. Or tonic water.

Just as our main course of chicken cordon bleu and wet California blend vegetables arrived at the tables, Melinda Matthews (radiant mother of Drew and PTA President) stepped onto the stage and adjusted the microphone to accommodate her modelesque form in heels. I glanced around the room and saw Drew and Stella sitting together a few tables away, looking gorgeous together with Stella's parents, and Drew's dad looking up at the stage proudly.

"Good evening, everyone! It's my honor to welcome you all here tonight on behalf of the Concord High School PTA." Melinda clapped indicating that the rest of us should clap as well, while she gestured around the room at the other PTA members in attendance who nodded and smiled with appreciation for themselves.

"Tonight, we celebrate a new year in which our children will graduate high school and enter into adulthood. I know I speak for all the parents here tonight and those who are with us in spirit," she glanced at Shea as she said it, and I could feel everyone's eyes shift in our direction, "how extremely proud we are of our babies."

I cringed inside but didn't let it show. I could feel Shea shift uncomfortably behind me, and I felt for him. I was glad to have him by my side tonight, but I also felt a little guilty for pushing him to be here. Another part of me wanted people to look at him and surround him with the love I knew he deserved. Gossip about Shea's dad had died down recently, but I knew that there would probably always be a cloud hanging over Shea's head, no matter how much time passed. That's just the way small-town life is.

Melinda breezed through the rest of her speech, thanking people, and plugging the local businesses that supported the event. Paulson's Sports Shop was among the 'silver sponsors,' which meant my dad must have been politely coerced into paying out of his humble earnings simply because he happened to be a business owner. None of the businesses in a town as small as Concord really needed the advertising, they got in exchange for donating to community funds, but it was expected of them anyway, so they did it, sometimes with pride, and sometimes begrudgingly. Dad gave a quick smile with no teeth and nodded in the direction of the rest of the room as his name was mentioned.

Melinda wrapped up her official speech but tacked one more thing onto the end.

"Now, I know that my son is going to hate me for this, but if I could just indulge myself for a moment here, I would like to say how proud I am of Drew, and his girlfriend Stella on what wonderful people they are becoming. We are so proud of all you have achieved, and you are a credit to our family and our community."

Melinda teared up and people around the room clapped and cheered. Melinda fanned her face with her hand like she had just won Miss America.

I was just waiting for someone to come out of the kitchen with a sash to place over her head. I looked back at Becca and Shea, and Becca's eyeroll could have stopped traffic. Shea was smirking, and he winked at me. Unlike me, Shea didn't seem to be bothered by other people's flashy self-esteem. I didn't understand. I just told myself that he was probably judging everyone on the inside and turned back around to watch the spectacle.

254

Just as the dessert was arriving at the tables, Becca leaned over and told me she needed to pee. We got up together and went to the bathroom, which was empty because everyone was currently stuffing their faces with assorted mini cheesecakes.

"Oh my god, my stomach is killing me from sucking it in all night. This is awful," Becca said as she leaned against the sink and let her belly hang out. She sighed as she rocked her hips from side to side.

"Honestly, I don't know how you're pulling it off, but you can*not* tell at all. And you look so stupidly beautiful it's kind of annoying." She lifted her smoke lined eyes to look at me through the mirror. She made an exaggerated model face that she meant to be funny, but it was actually just stunning. I rolled my eyes at her, and we laughed.

"Okay but I really do need to pee," Becca huffed as she stood up and walked into the first stall. "This baby is pushing on my bladder—I feel like I need to pee every five minutes."

Before I could warn Becca, the door was opening behind me, and Melinda Matthews walked in. She looked at me with wide eyes that told me that she had heard everything Becca just said. Becca came out of the stall a second later and looked from me to Melinda, and then she walked out of the bathroom without stopping to wash her hands. I tried to follow her out, but Melinda grabbed my arm.

"Did I just hear what I think I heard? It's okay to tell me, Annie."

I wasn't sure if I saw fire or ice in Melinda's eyes, but either way, I was uncomfortable. I didn't know what to say. The secret was coming out soon anyway. But Becca had her reasons for hiding things, and I wasn't about to start talking before she was ready. She clearly wasn't, since she had just run out of the bathroom without me. "I'm not sure what you heard, but it's really not my place to say anything about anything, Mrs. Matthews." It was all I could say. I tried to step away, but she held on tight to my arm. When I looked down at her hand, she seemed to come to her senses, and she let go.

"Enjoy the rest of your night, sweetheart," she said to the back of my head as I walked out of the bathroom in search of Becca.

THIRTY-THREE

"BECCA'S GONE. I can't find her anywhere." I looked at my parents feeling small and helpless.

"Annie, what's really going on with Becca? We can't help her if we don't have all the information," my mom whispered to me, not unkindly, as the dessert plates were being cleared.

Lying was futile at this point, and I needed my family's help. Now that Melinda was in the know, I knew that it would only be a matter of hours before the whole town was talking about it. I leaned into my mom and looked at her seriously. I spoke so softly that no one other than my own mother would be able to understand me.

"Becca was…assaulted. I think. Maybe over the summer. I'm not sure when. She won't talk about it. But…she's pregnant now. That's why she was in the hospital before."

I didn't give more details about the hospital visit, but my mom gave me a knowing look. I could see from the look on my dad's face that he had read my lips. Red anger crawled up his neck, probably at the thought of whoever did this to Becca, or maybe shame that he hadn't pushed the issue when he first suspected something was wrong. My mom looked concerned but determined. Like this was just another thing that could be managed. It occurred to me how much we need our moms, and how often I had taken mine for granted.

"Nobody knows about the baby. Well now, I guess, a lot of people will know, because Melinda Matthews just overheard Becca in the bathroom. At least it looks like Becca's parents haven't received the message yet." I looked over to where Jim and Sandy were still stuck to the bar like fruit flies on corn syrup. "Becca doesn't want them to know because she thinks they will kick her out and she's saving up for her own place before that happens. I need to go find her."

My parents agreed to let Shea and me go out and look for Becca, and they would stay at the party and make excuses for us in the unlikely event that Becca's parents started wondering where she was. When we left, Becca's parents were happily eating the extra cheesecakes at their table by the bar, apparently none-the-wiser…yet.

Shea and I jumped in my mom's car, and he drove while I tried calling Becca's phone a few times. The country club was just on the edge of town, and it was so cold outside that it only made sense that she would head deeper into town somewhere. We stopped by her house first, and it was empty. We stopped at the sports shop next, but the lights were off, and the door was locked. I didn't have a key.

We sat in my car for several minutes, with no idea where to look next. Shea suggested we call the police. In my mind, that was a last resort. I didn't know who Becca's attacker was, and at this point, everyone in Concord was a suspect. Just as the thought of her occurred to me, I received a text message from Miss Jones.

UNKNOWN NUMBER: *Hi, Annie, this is Zoey Jones. Becca is here with me. She's okay, but she's shaken up.*

Zoey Jones was a good person, and Becca trusted her, so I did too. She gave us her address and Shea sped over to her small, gray-blue duplex on second street. She let us in. Becca was sitting on the couch with a dead expression on her face that gave me chills. She didn't even look at us as we entered. I sat by her and grabbed her hand. It was like ice.

"It's going to be okay, Becca. People were going to find out soon anyway. I'm sorry I didn't warn you about Melinda—she just kind of showed up behind me right as you started talking and…" Suddenly things felt wrong. The way Melinda reacted felt weird. My mind was spinning. Something was really, really fucked up here, and the thought felt like worms crawling under my skin.

"It's not okay, Annie. Now he's going to know. Melinda is going to tell him. What if he finds me? What if he tries to hurt me or the baby? I didn't have enough time to hide yet. I'm not safe anywhere now. Now that he knows." Becca was a pale shell. Her eyes were wide and frantic.

"Becca, I think it's time that you tell us who did this to you so that we can help protect you. We can have him arrested and charged. We will find a safe place for you and your baby to live. We will take care of you. You're not alone." Miss Jones was gentle but firm.

Miss Jones made it feel like we were in control, and like everything was going to be okay. The fog of terror started to lift from my vision, and I could see a potentially happy ending to this nightmare.

"No." Becca looked at Miss Jones with fire in her forest green gaze. "There is one thing about this whole fucked up situation that I can control, and that's *my* baby. This baby has a mother. No father. And I won't breathe his name until the day that I die because if nobody knows, then neither can my baby. This little

259

person doesn't deserve to live life knowing part of them came from a monster. I won't do that. And that's final."

We were all quiet for a while. I knew there was no point in trying to convince Becca otherwise, and Miss Jones seemed to know Becca well enough to know the same.

"I can't go home now. Jim and Sandy are going to hear the news soon enough, and let's face it, I can't really hide this very much longer anyway." Becca rubbed her growing belly with her hands. "I need to find a place to live."

"I would love to have you stay here with me," Miss Jones said, reaching across to grab Becca's hand affectionately and give it a light squeeze, "but there are rules about teachers and students, as you know." Becca looked at Miss Jones with understanding eyes. They were still looking at each other when I jumped in with what I thought was the obvious solution.

"Becca, you know that my family would love nothing more than to have you with us. Please come stay with us—it's the best thing to do right now. I know my parents will be on board, no question." I looked at Becca pleadingly. She needed to accept the help. I wanted her safe and with me. Becca shook her head, and I couldn't understand why she was so determined to push me away. Selfishly, my feelings were hurt.

"Annie...I don't think I'd be safe there. Anymore." My stomach dropped. Why didn't she feel like she would be safe at my house? It was basically her second home. We had been her safe haven since she was little.

"It's just...I think if the devil wants to find me, your house is the first place he'd look. That's all." She started to cry.

Her desperation broke me, and I started to cry too. There had to be somewhere safe for her that wasn't a women's shelter. I wasn't ready for us to leave each other's side yet. And I wasn't ready for her to be alone out in the world. I knew that she wasn't ready for that either, even if she would have done anything she needed to because she was a survivor.

"Stay with me," Shea's voice came from behind me like a warm breeze. "I have plenty of space and no visitors. Except for your nosy neighbor, who keeps bringing me hot dish for some reason." He smiled and the room brightened. "I don't want or need money, and you can have your own room and bathroom. I'll even put extra locks on your door if it makes you more comfortable. Nobody will find you with me, and if they do, I'll kill them." Shea shrugged like the thought of killing a rapist was actually pretty appealing. If I didn't already know his heart, it would have scared me.

I looked from Shea to Becca and watched as she nodded slowly. She trusted him. She always had. It was decided—I was getting a new neighbor, soon to be two.

THIRTY-FOUR

I CALLED MY mom and told her our plans. We left Miss Jones and drove to Becca's house to collect as much of her stuff as we could fit in the trunk. Becca left a note on the counter, which read:

Staying at Annie's house for a while. They need a nanny for Rosie — they hired me. Can always use the extra money.

Becca

Becca always knew what to say to make her way in this world. Jim and Sandy were greedy and wouldn't think twice about Becca moving out and getting another job. The only reason they would look for her would probably be to ask for money. I guessed we would find out at some point, but this was good enough for now.

We swung back through the country club parking lot and picked up my parents. Shea was driving with my dad in the front seat, and we didn't take the time to switch anyone around because getting out of town was the number one priority. Becca was sandwiched in the backseat between me and my mom, and my mom wasted no time leaning into Becca and scratching the top of her back with her free hand.

"We told your parents you were going to spend the night with us. They seemed fine with it." My mom had a way of speaking politely about people even when obscenities would be more apt. 'They didn't give a shit' was probably the accurate description of the situation, but she made it sound so much nicer. *Note to self—be more like Mom.*

Shea pulled into his driveway and popped the trunk to gather Becca's things and carry them up to her room. My dad helped. I guided Becca into the house where she would be staying for the foreseeable future. I can't describe how, exactly, but the house looked different now than it did when we were just passing through as visitors. The woodwork was shinier. The walls were more familiar. It felt like so much more than just a house where sadness and Shea lived. It felt like hope.

Once Becca was in bed and my parents had gone home to relieve the babysitter, Shea and I had a chance to sit on his bed and talk.

"Thank you, Shea." I wrapped my arms around his waist and snuggled my face into his chest, wishing I could live there forever.

"Are you kidding? It'll be nice to have someone else in the house. I was seriously contemplating moving the chickens into one of the bedrooms, so it wasn't so quiet in here. Plus, I mean, the chicks are my special ladies, and they deserve to enjoy all of life's comforts, obviously." Shea's tone was serious, but I knew he was being a clown, and I gave him a playful shove.

"Careful who you push around, missy." Shea knelt down on the floor in front of me and pushed my knees apart, sending a shock of desire through my body. He leaned his cheek against my knee and looked up at me like a question.

I looked into his eyes and saw the only man in the world. The one my soul loved. I was angry for all the years that I had been too blind to see him. He was right there all along. And it felt like I would be his forever.

I slid down off the side of Shea's bed and into his lap. I wrapped my arms tightly around his neck and kissed him slowly

263

and surely, as if holding him closer and kissing him longer would make up for all the time we lost when we didn't yet know what love was. Shea inhaled as he kissed me back, and the feeling of being savored by him made me ache for more.

"I love you, Annie," he whispered into my ear. My insides glittered at the words that felt so pure and so natural.

I pulled back and looked my soulmate in the eyes. "I love you, too."

Shea smiled and we laughed together as he lifted me up onto his bed and kissed me everywhere. We made love, quietly and slowly, and fell asleep wrapped in each other's arms. When I woke up, the sun was shining through the window. I had spent the night. And it felt so right that I didn't care who knew about it.

I hoped with all I had that we would spend our nights that way for the rest of our lives.

...

Living next to Becca and Shea was amazing. Becca decided not to return to school, but as soon as she turned eighteen, she tested for her GED and passed with flying colors. No surprise there because she was brilliant. She bought herself a laptop with some of the money she had saved up for rent and was already applying for college courses available online. She was growing rapidly, in more ways than one.

She didn't feel safe working at the sports shop anymore, and my dad wanted her to focus on taking care of herself anyway, so he found a way to employ her remotely, balancing books and ordering inventory, and doing tasks that I think he made up just for her benefit. Becca did the work without questioning its validity, and I could see that as her way of accepting help. I was proud of her.

Spring semester also brought a shift in class schedules, which was a relief, because I wasn't sure how to face Drew after how his mom acted at the New Year's Eve party, and I couldn't shake the feeling that he had something to do with what happened to Becca. The thought made me nauseous, so I tried to ignore it. There was absolutely no way Becca would have let me date him if he had raped her…right? Nothing about any of it made sense.

Despite my burning desire for answers, I respected Becca's wishes, and I stayed the hell away from Drew. I knew if I spoke to him, I wouldn't be able to hold back, so I avoided him like the plague instead and trusted that eventually, things would come to light if they were meant to.

At this point, word was out that Becca was pregnant, and there were all kinds of theories flying around about who the father was and where she had gone. There was a rumor she was at a home for young mothers a few towns over, and another that she was locked in her parents' basement. Becca's sexuality was a major topic of debate, which pissed me off, but I kept my mouth shut. The thing is that nobody seemed to actually care to find out the real truth—they just liked speculating. I figured as long as they were only speculating, Becca was safe, so I kept my head down and let them talk. I was beyond caring what people thought of me, or her, or Shea for that matter. As long as we had each other.

I passed the fall semester art class with a glowing B+ thanks to the kindhearted soul, Ms. Young. She told me I would have gotten an A if I hadn't drawn stick figures for the first several portrait assignments. It felt more than fair. I hugged her on my last day, and she gave me a journal with a note inside:

Art looks different on everyone. Use your creativity to make the kind of magic that only you know how to make. Happy writing.

Holly Young

I applied for the University of Minnesota English program that afternoon.

Spring semester math was still with Miss Jones, but this time instead of sitting next to Becca, I got to sit next to Shea. I'd like to say Miss Jones went easy on us because we were acquaintances outside of school and we shared an enormous secret, but she wasn't. After a few weeks of being too busy ogling Shea to focus on learning math and getting some assignments back with sad faces in red pen drawn on the front, I decided to up my game and find myself a study partner. Luckily Shea was up for the job, and I had another reason to be near him at all times.

Some days after school Miss Jones would come back to Shea's house with us to visit because Becca needed company and she needed support, and I could tell that she and Zoey were building a deep friendship. When they were together, it felt like I was looking at a beautiful piece of modern abstract art, one where the shapes and colors are dissimilar but somehow, they go together in a perfect and unexpected way. While Shea and I went up to his room and "studied," Zoey and Becca hung out downstairs and talked, or sometimes went for a walk outside if it wasn't too cold and wet.

Zoey was a city girl, but she was a natural fit in the country. She always stopped to feed the chickens and asked if she could chop some wood for the fireplace or shovel snow from the driveway. At first, I thought she just wanted to help out some poor, very young adults who were living alone without parents, but as time went on and I saw the glow in her cheeks emerge from the joy of the work, I realized it was something else. She felt at home here. And she felt at home with Becca, too. I would have been jealous if I hadn't also found my own piece of home in Shea. For a few months, we were like a strange little family who had found some peace together in a fucked-up world.

Becca's due date was approaching just as the snow was melting and the first wildflowers began shining their faces toward the sun. Springtime in Minnesota is beautiful. The first warm air in many months arrives and budding leaves begin to soften the edges of the angular tree branches. Springtime in Minnesota is also ugly, as the snow disappears, revealing all the plastic bottles, partially decomposed carcasses, and dirty secrets that were hiding underneath it all winter long.

THIRTY-FIVE

A WEEK BEFORE Becca's due date, my mom planned a small baby shower for her at our house. With Becca's permission, she invited Charlotte, Sydney, and Zoey. When Becca stepped through the door, she looked soft and radiant in a white dress that spread across her belly in beautiful folds.

My mom and I had spent all morning decorating, and the look on Becca's face when she looked around the room made it all worth it. There were fresh flowers everywhere, and pastel balloons and streamers and a three-tier cake that my mom had baked and decorated with intricate white, lacy details. The table was loaded with gifts (my mom and I had gone shopping in Pine Lakes a few days prior and bought baby supplies like it was going out of style).

Charlotte was smiling from ear to ear, always a beacon of joy, and I could tell how happy she was to see our friend. Sydney ran up and hugged Becca before she could even set her purse down, and it brought me joy to see her be surrounded by happiness. Zoey hung back, but there was a look in her eyes that I recognized. It was love.

We settled into our seats in the living room and my mom handed out little plates with fruit and cheese on them, and we started chatting like this was the most lovely and normal thing in the world.

"Becky!!!" we heard a small voice shout from the top of the stairs—Rosie had woken up from her nap, and now that she had graduated to a big girl bed, she could come out of her room whenever she pleased. My mom jumped up to grab her before she fell down the stairs in her sleep sack, and Becca reached out her arms to take Rosie in her lap. Rosie sucked her thumb and snuggled into Becca's shoulder for a few minutes, before making her way to my lap, where she seemed to want to stay.

My mom disappeared upstairs again and came down with a big bundle in her arms. It was a quilt she had made for Becca's baby over the last few months. It was white and pink and blue, and tied off with little pieces of yarn that made it look soft and special. I silently wondered if I would ever grow into someone as talented and generous as my mother, and I didn't think it was possible that I could. We all ooo'd and ahhh'd over her handiwork, and I beamed with pride at being the product of such a graceful person.

My starlit bubble of pride and admiration was interrupted by the doorbell ringing.

"I'll go get that." Mom walked over to the door and opened it, like she knew this was coming. I looked around the room to see if anyone seemed to know who else we might be expecting. Everyone else's expressions were as blank as my own, and I felt a faint tremor of anxiety come from Becca's direction.

"So glad you could make it! Come on in, make yourself comfortable," Mom said with unflinching kindness.

Sandy stepped into the house holding a bouquet of carnations and a small gift bag. She wore jeans, black tennis shoes, and a plain, light pink t-shirt, and I noticed she was wearing lipstick, which I'd never seen on her before. We were all stunned into silence. She looked nervous. I looked over at Becca who had a blank look on her face that I couldn't read.

"There's a seat for you over here, Sandy. Let me get you a plate." Sandy sat down as Mom grabbed her some snacks from the kitchen. Rosie broke the silence.

"Can we open presents now?" She wiggled free from my lap and picked up a big box with a purple bow on it and dropped it in Becca's lap. Charlotte let out a laugh and the rest of us followed suit. The elephant in the room had been carefully shrouded in polite banter for now.

Becca opened gift after gift—clothes and diapers and bottles and blankets and wipes and more diapers, all fresh and new and beautiful. Zoey's gift was a large painting of brightly colored butterflies. Charlotte and Sydney both came armed with enough baby clothes and shoes to dress triplets for a year. I gave Becca a scrapbook with supplies to fill it up, along with other practical things like a grooming kit and a baby bath seat.

When Becca was done opening gifts, Sandy softly cleared her throat, and set her gift bag at Becca's feet. Becca looked down at the bag and then over at me, and for a second I thought she wasn't going to open it. But she did. Inside was a faded pink blanket and a new pack of pacifiers.

"The blanket was yours when you were a baby. I thought maybe..." Sandy didn't finish her sentence. I could see tears forming in her weathered eyes. "There's a card in there too, if you want to read it."

I had never seen her so sheepish before. Normally she was brash and horrible, but then again, I had never seen her sober before either, which today, she seemed to be. I could see her hands trembling in her lap as she waited to receive her judgement.

Becca opened the card and read the note inside. I'll never know what it said. Becca folded it up and slid it back into its envelope and placed it carefully back in the bag, along with the blanket which she had neatly folded. All I know is, after the cake was eaten and the party was over, Becca hugged her mom on the way out. I looked over at my own mom, who looked like she was lit from within. It was a special moment that we never said another word about.

After all the guests cleared out, Shea came to meet us and help us carry all of the gifts back to his house. Our arms and hearts were full. As we walked through the grove and up to Shea's house, I glanced at the road and saw a flash of yellow. Adrenaline prickled at my skin as it registered that Drew had just driven by. He had no reason to be out here. My gut told me something wasn't right with him. But today was a good day, and I wasn't going to make an issue where there might not be one. It could have been someone else. I took a breath and put it out of my mind.

We started lugging things upstairs to Becca's room, but before we got to her door at the end of the hallway, Shea stopped us.

"Nope! Not in there... This way." He pointed to a closed door to the right of Becca's door. Becca and I looked at each other, confused. She had to set the gifts down to open the door, and when she did, she cried out.

"If you don't love the color, I can change it," Shea said, shyly, and I hugged him close as I let Becca walk around her baby's new nursery.

"It's absolutely perfect, Shea. How did you...?" She sat down in the rocking chair that awaited in the corner, right next to a white crib that I recognized as the one Rosie had just grown out of. The walls were painted a creamy white and Shea had installed white curtains and constructed a small dresser that doubled as a changing table. At the bottom of one wall, just under the window and between the curtains, Shea had even painted a little mural of a

271

mama deer with her fawn, with flowers sprouting up around their legs and a butterfly flying over their heads. It was breathtaking. His talent and generosity knew no limits.

Becca stood up and hugged Shea, and when she was done, we brought all her new supplies in and arranged them on the closet shelves. We were ready. All we needed now was a baby.

Life was turning out to be so much more intense than I thought. The things that happened in the novels I read actually happened to real people. Real people that I happened to care a lot about. There were so many bad things in life. So much fear and sadness and evil. But there was so much goodness too. More goodness than evil, it seemed. And I felt ready to face it all with Becca and Shea by my side.

THIRTY-SIX

I'LL NEVER REGRET missing my own high school graduation, because on that day, I was busy becoming an auntie instead.

When Becca's labor started, it was raining outside, and the water fell around Shea's house like curtains. Shea was timing Becca's contractions while I sat next to her and marveled at her body's natural strength and intuition. Becca set my hand on her belly, and I could feel the tightening as her uterus prepared itself to deliver a whole new life into the world.

She grimaced with each contraction, and I felt both helpless and proud to be witnessing one of life's divine moments. When Shea told us it was time, I called my mom and together we helped Becca into the front seat, and Shea and I slid in the back.

When we arrived at the hospital, Becca was wheeled to her room where it was confirmed that her cervix was dilating, and she was well on her way to having a baby. We all settled in, and I texted Zoey to come meet us when she could.

Seeing Becca in the hospital this time was much different from the last time we were there together. The fear was still surrounding us, but it tasted different. It wasn't a hopeless fear. It was an anticipation of the new life that was on the other side of this labor.

The doctor offered Becca an epidural, which my mom strongly recommended, but Becca declined it. I shook my head at her determination to suffer unnecessarily. I still didn't understand then how much pain meant to her. How it gave a tactical sensation to the feelings she carried around inside. Suffering and surviving made her feel stronger. It was as much a part of her as her determined green eyes and her effortless style.

From where I stand now, it all makes total sense to me. Now and forevermore, pain will be my constant companion. But in that moment, 'suffering' and I hadn't met yet.

Becca's face and legs were swollen with the weight of this life and the role she was playing in it. She grimaced as each contraction came on harder and faster, until beads of sweat were dripping from her hairline and her knuckles were white as her fingers squeezed hard around the bars on either side of the bed.

Shea and my mom had stayed out in the waiting room to give Becca privacy, but she wanted me there with her, and by her side was the only place I wanted to be. The doctor came in and checked Becca's cervix again and told her that it was time to push. With each contraction Becca pushed with all her might, and she screamed as the baby worked its way out of her body. Becca grabbed my forearm so tightly that I had a bruise for weeks after. I didn't mind. Tears streamed down my cheeks as I watched Becca struggle and conquer this thing with the power I always knew she had in her.

After hours of hard labor, with one final push, a baby came rushing out to meet us. A girl. With cries so loud and beautiful and hair so dark that there was no question who her mama was. Becca sobbed beside me as they laid the baby on her chest.

"Hi baby, I love you so much," she said to her daughter over and over again. "I love you so much, baby girl. Hi. I'm your mommy. I'm going to take good care of you." Becca was her own little loving family now. The family she never had, and always needed. She was complete. We were complete. That baby girl was everything.

Once she was bathed and wrapped up, we were moved to another room that had more furniture and comforts in it, including a shower for when the time came to help Becca get cleaned up. Visitors were allowed in this room, and although there was a bassinet next to the bed, Becca refused to put her baby down. She just held her and looked at her and smiled from ear to ear, oblivious to the world around her.

Shea came through the door meekly, but as soon as he saw Becca's smiling face he beamed like a proud uncle.

"Any chance I can hold my new little best friend?" he said, looking at the baby like she was the most precious thing he'd ever seen. He had a good eye for precious things, from what I could tell. To my surprise, Becca released her hold on her girl and handed her up to Shea before reaching her hand out to me and asking me to help her over to the bathroom. When we returned from the bloodbath of the post-partum bathroom process, Shea was sitting in the rocking chair with the baby talking quietly to her about things we weren't privy to.

"Have you picked her name yet?" he asked, and I grinned. I looked over at Becca.

"I was thinking of calling her Emily. What do you think?" She looked at Shea with a twinkle in her eyes, and Shea looked at her with the sweetest surprise in his.

"That was my mom's name," Shea said with a sad smile.

"I know it was." Becca beamed and so did I.

"Hi, Emily. I loved you before I even met you. You're going to be my little sunshine," Shea whispered to the baby, his words wrapping around her like warm swaddling clothes.

Just then, my mom came in with Zoey, who had rushed over to the hospital as soon as she could get away from the graduation ceremony. Shea handed Emily back to Becca, who was sitting back in bed, and when she and Zoey locked eyes, something unexpected happened. Zoey walked right over to the bed and leaned down and kissed Becca, and Becca kissed her back. It suddenly became clear to me what had been building up all this time, since the first day we walked into Miss Jones's math class. Zoey and Becca were in love, and now that we were officially 'graduated,' they were safe to be together publicly. Finally.

"Her name is Emily," Becca said, handing the baby up to Zoey.

"Hi, sweet Emily. I've been waiting SO hard to meet you!" Zoey wasn't a natural baby holder, and I could tell that she was afraid the baby might break if she didn't keep her entire body rigid and alert at all times.

My mom put a gentle hand on Zoey's back and guided her to a couch, in a subtle gesture that made everyone in the room more comfortable. After a few minutes Zoey relaxed in her seat, and Emily melted into her arms as if she was as much a part of her as she was a part of Becca. I had a feeling that with time, she would be.

It was a beautiful day the day baby Emily was born, and I sometimes wish we had never left that hospital room.

THIRTY-SEVEN

THIS IS THE part of my story that's hardest to tell. It's the part where I broke. It's the reason I am half a person. This is the part of my fairytale where the twisting black smoke emerges from the forest and swallows up my life. It's the final dose of reality that well and truly makes me grow up in the worst kind of way.

I would say that settling back into Shea's house with a newborn was lovely and magical and easy, but it wasn't. Babies are hard. I remembered this from not so long ago when Rosie was born, but at that time, I had had adult parents who were responsible for her care, and it made the whole thing seem easier than it actually is.

Becca was happy, but she was exhausted, and motherhood was overwhelming. She was up every couple of hours at night nursing the baby or swaddling her or changing her diaper or just rocking her, unsure of what to do to help Emily stop crying. In those first couple of weeks, I spent the night more often than not, and would get up and rock Emily once or twice, and sometimes Shea would do it too. Shea never minded being woken up. He savored the time he had with Emily, even if it was singing quietly to her at 2:00 a.m.

I had been accepted to the University of Minnesota and was excited to start the English program in the fall. I was already reluctant to leave Becca, Emily, and Shea, but Shea planned to visit me often and even get an apartment with me when I was ready to move off campus. We planned to travel. I planned to write. Shea planned to make art. We were going to take life on together and make an adventure out of it.

Zoey came over most days, now that it was summer break, and she didn't have to be at school all the time. In those wild and blissful weeks, little Emily had four parents who doted on her non-stop. We had found a rhythm—it was a little off-beat, but it still made a song.

Becca wasn't ready to have visitors at Shea's house yet. She wasn't ready for anyone to know where she was. She didn't even tell her parents that she wasn't really living at my house, and they never questioned it. I think they were relieved to be rid of their official duties as parents, and all parties involved settled into a 'don't ask, don't tell' policy when it came to anyone's whereabouts or activities. Becca's parents did come to meet Emily a few days after she arrived home, but the meeting was scheduled in my parents' living room and lasted no more than fifteen minutes. I think it was more than Becca expected, and it was enough.

...

Saturday, June 11th, Emily was up in her nursery taking her mid-morning nap, and Shea and Becca and I were scattered across the living room furniture, soaking in the quiet house. Becca and Shea were resting their eyes for as long as they could before it was time to start the cycle of feeding and playing and rocking all over again. I had gotten a full night of sleep and was working out the finishing touches of my poem for Shea—the one I had started months before but didn't get around to finishing until now.

It was warm outside, and the 10:00 a.m. sun was shining in on us. I started to sweat, and if I hadn't been so focused on what I was doing, I would have moved to a cooler seat, but I just lay there and melted into the couch like limp rubber while my pencil scratched against my notebook paper.

Just little hands, in winter mitts.

I set my notebook aside and let out a sigh, feeling a moment of fullness at having written the last line of a poem that meant so much to me. Then, there was a knock at the front door. Shea and Becca opened their eyes to little slits, but nobody jumped up to answer it. I figured it was probably Zoey—we were expecting her sometime around lunch, and I peeled myself off of the couch and opened the door wide.

Before I could close it, Steve, the bartender—of all people—stepped through the door. Shea instinctively snapped to attention and stood.

"Can I help you?" Shea asked, looking taller and fiercer than I'd seen him look since before his dad died. Shea's eyes darted to Becca, and the look on her face told him all he needed to know about who had just entered his house.

"Well, I think you can help me, actually," Steve said. He was standing in the middle of the living room, with the same Hawaiian button down he always had on when he was behind the bar. He had a sheen on his face that made me think he had already been drinking that morning.

Shea was inching toward the bottom of the staircase as Steve talked.

"I'm here to see my baby." Steve winked at Becca, and my stomach lurched.

Becca stood up from where she was sitting. Her hands were trembling. I was frozen to my spot, feeling like I was in a waking nightmare. So, Steve was the disgusting creature who had raped my best friend.

I wanted to throw my fists at his body until he died, but I knew I didn't stand a chance against a grown man, and I wasn't brave enough to stand up to him anyway.

"That baby will never have anything to do with you, so you can just go ahead and get the fuck out of here right now before I call the police." Fear and hostility burned in Becca's eyes.

I glanced back at Shea, who was now holding a baseball bat that he had kept leaning at the bottom of the stairs. I slid my phone out of my pocket and silently dialed 9-1-1.

"See, that's where you're wrong, honey bun… With tits like that nobody is going to believe anything you say. You've got slut written all over you." Becca seethed and Shea tightened his grip on the bat. Becca looked like she was about to take a run at Steve, but Shea spoke up first.

"Get the fuck out of my house right now. I'll kill you before I let you get close to Becca's baby." Shea had fire in his eyes. I could see the veins in his biceps rippling and his shoulders twitching, ready for a fight.

I prayed that Steve would just leave the house, but he just rolled his eyes like Shea was a mosquito threatening an elephant. His cockiness made me cringe. I didn't dare lift my phone to my face, but I prayed that someone was on the line and listening.

"How did you even find me here?" Becca asked, her voice sounding smaller and weaker. I could see how scared she was, and it made me shiver as I realized how dangerous Steve really was. All the times I had stood near him. Pretended I liked him to get drinks from him. It made me queasy.

"Where do you think? My nephew had no problem telling me where to find you when I threatened to call him out on his bullshit if he didn't. He's always been such a pussy."

My heart thudded in my chest. I didn't know for sure who Steve's nephew was, but I had a feeling who it might be, and it made bile rise in my throat. *The family photo at Drew's house. Oh my god. Of course, it was Steve. Did Drew know about this?*

"Get. Out. Now," Shea said, taking a step closer to Steve.

Steve pulled out a pistol and pointed it at Shea's head. He had the audacity to laugh.

"You see, the thing is, *Shea*... Nobody gives a shit about you, or whether you live or die. Everyone in town thinks you're a murdering cunt anyway. You're just another piece of trash like your dad was. And I'm really not interested in letting a little orphan shithead with a baseball bat stand in my way."

Steve walked toward the stairs with the gun still pointed at Shea, but Shea didn't budge. Shea took one look over at me with love and fear in his eyes. Before Steve could push his way up the stairs, Shea took one hard swing, right at Steve's exposed side. Steve buckled over as the wind was knocked out of him. Shea lifted the bat up again and prepared to take another swing.

Then, the pop of a single shot rang out from Steve's gun.

Shea dropped to the floor.

I dropped my phone and *screamed.*

The sound of a second shot from somewhere behind me clapped through my skull and Steve dropped to the floor next to Shea.

I looked over to see Becca holding a gun in her hands, trembling from head to toe. I ran to Shea. He was already gone, but

I think I started CPR anyway. Blood was pouring onto the floor from his head, and I didn't hear or see anything after that.

What I do know is that I wailed because my throat was sore for days afterward. I also know that at some point, the police arrived. So did Zoey. I know that the paramedics had to pry Shea's perfect body from my arms as they loaded him into the ambulance. I know that my soul was ripped in two, and the remaining edges were rigid and dangerous.

Half of me died that day.

There are no words that can accurately describe how deep the well of grief is if you've never experienced it before. It is both a profound emptiness, and a heavy limb that you carry with you in every waking moment. It is deeper than the ocean, and as inescapable as a tomb. Joy is still visible, but it's not tangible anymore. It slips through your fingers like silver, never sticking anywhere for more than a second before the weight of your pain shadows your eyes, and your brain, and your heart and your stomach.

The detectives made me tell the story again and again, and I was forced to replay the image of Shea's beautiful light being carelessly extinguished in front of my eyes like he was nothing. To me, he was everything. And to be honest, I *wanted* to tell the story, because I couldn't shake the images from my mind anyway. I didn't want to let any piece of Shea go. I wasn't ready. We didn't have enough time. This wasn't how our story was supposed to end.

My dad underwent questioning as well because the gun Becca had was from his sports shop. They wanted to know why he didn't file a police report for a gun stolen from his store, and he showed them the inventory records where the gun wasn't listed. Becca had obviously spent some time covering her tracks so that my dad wouldn't be implicated. She had been preparing to defend herself in any way she could for quite some time. My dad had clearly known that Becca had stolen a gun and never said anything. I imagine he planned to, but maybe he had felt better knowing she had some way to protect herself. Not everything in life is black and white.

Becca blamed herself for Shea's death. No one else did. But I don't think Becca will ever forgive herself for not pulling the trigger a second sooner. Just like I'll never forgive myself for opening that goddamn door.

When tragedy strikes, suddenly every little moment of your life comes into question. As if torturing yourself with 'would haves' and 'should haves' and 'if I'd only knowns' could bring the love of your life back to you. Suddenly every moment of your life somehow becomes wrong, or to blame. It's the worst kind of torture.

Now that the police were involved, Becca had to give details about the circumstances surrounding her pregnancy and the events that followed. I sat with her as she prepared to tell the story she had been keeping inside for nearly a year, and my heart pounded as I prepared to hear words that might confirm my suspicion that I was part of the reason any of this happened in the first place. More fuel to add to the fire of my guilt and despair.

The fluorescent lighting in the detective's office was harsh and unfeeling. The detective behind the desk looked kind but also shrewd. The chairs were covered in cheap gray fabric. The desk had fingerprints on it. I passively wondered who had been here before us, and what horror had occurred in their world. I suddenly felt connected to every other person who had sat in those seats, like we were all a part of a big, silent club, where the dirtbags and the victims and the evil people and the sad people go to tell the man behind the desk the cause of their pain.

Becca held Emily close to her chest as she told her story. I was an empty shell beside her.

THIRTY-EIGHT

"ANNIE AND I spent the whole day at the beach that day. We were just...hanging out, like all the high schoolers did over the summer." Becca paused and looked over at me, and then back at the detective. She cleared her throat.

"I always knew that Steve was a creep. I'm not an idiot. He was an old guy serving alcohol to teenagers. He was gross. But we just took what we could get from him. Free alcohol on the beach. It was worth batting your eyelashes for, right? I wasn't scared of him. Like what was that fat fuck really going to do to me, you know? He got an eyeful, and I got a daiquiri, and everything was kosher." Becca cleared her throat and wiggled in her seat, and I reached my arms out to take Emily so she could relax a bit, but she held on tight to her baby.

"Annie and I drank all afternoon. We both got pretty drunk, but her more than me because I've always been able to hold my liquor better than her. It's in my genes, I guess. Annie and I were dancing and she faceplanted in the sand. Before I could help her up, Drew Matthews came out of nowhere and scooped her up like it was the most natural thing in the world." Becca looked at me again, and I gave her a nod. I was okay with her saying whatever she needed to say, even if it made me look stupid. I *was* stupid. I deserved it.

"Annie had had a crush on Drew since forever. I'm not sure why. But because I love Annie, I gave her a second with Drew before going to check on her, even though I've always felt like Drew's a bit of a creep. I don't know why. I just have. Turns out I was right about that."

I reached over and squeezed Becca's hand. My head was spinning as I relived the night that for the longest time had felt like a life-changing night for me. It was the night that Drew and I connected for the first time, even if it was embarrassing as hell. It turns out that in my selfishness, I didn't see that so many more terrible things happened. Things that I could have possibly prevented if I hadn't gotten drunk and abandoned my friend on the beach.

"Just as I was walking over to check on Annie, she vomited all over the place. Then she mumbled something incoherent and passed out. Drew was understandably grossed out. Annie's mom was supposed to pick us up, but I didn't feel like I could call her to come get us when Annie was passed out. I didn't have a car and I was too drunk to drive anyway, and the beach was clearing out fast. After a few minutes of trying to figure out what to do, Stella called Drew over to one of the bonfires, and he gave me an apologetic look and went over to her. They eventually disappeared with everyone else.

That's when Shea appeared. To be honest, I didn't know him very well at the time, but I knew he lived next to Annie. I hadn't noticed him all day on the beach, either, but he must have been hanging around on the fringes. He came over and asked if we were okay. Clearly Annie wasn't. Shea was walking straight and speaking clearly, and he didn't smell like beer. I trusted him to get Annie home safely, and he did. I'll always be grateful to him for that, and for every single thing he did for me after that. He was…" Becca started to cry softly, and she didn't wipe the tears away as they ran down her cheeks.

My heart ached for Shea. It ached for him so badly. But by this point my tears had run dry. I had already become sorrow itself. We all waited quietly for Becca to continue, and I painstakingly held myself together, for her sake.

"Shea wanted to make sure I got home safe too, but I told him I wanted to walk. My house was only about ten blocks away, and I'm a night owl. Walking at night was something I did a lot. It helped me sleep. He insisted I go with him. Apparently, I'm not the type to give in to reason. I also felt like fear couldn't touch me. I thought I was untouchable. I was so stupid. I started to walk myself home. I didn't get very far before I heard Steve's voice call my name.

"I turned around to see him closing up the little beach bar for the night. There was no one else around. The last thing I wanted to do was talk to that creep, but I asked him what he wanted. I should have known better, but I didn't. He told me he had some extra bottles of vodka behind the bar and asked if I wanted to take them home with me. I said yes, like he and I were in on some kind of adult secret.

"When I got close enough for him to speak quietly to me, he told me that he kept a secret stash in a box just inside the wooded area that lined one edge of the beach. If I didn't already know he was planning to assault me, I should have known then. But I thought I was invincible. I rolled my eyes at him as if doing so gave me some kind of power, and then I followed him about twenty feet into the woods. Steve stopped in front of a big oak tree. I asked him where the vodka was, and he grabbed my arm and told me he'd show me as soon as I paid him what I owed him. I tried to scream but he whipped me around and slapped his hand over my mouth before I could make a noise anyway. There was nobody around to hear me anyway, or so I thought.

"Steve…did what he wanted…and threatened to kill me if I told anyone. He told me nobody would believe a slut like me anyway. That's when I looked through the trees and saw Drew and Stella running out of the woods toward the beach. Drew made eye contact with me. I know that he saw what happened. For the longest time I wanted to believe that maybe Drew thought it was consensual. That I wanted to have sex with a disgusting old man. And that's why he didn't stop or say anything or help me or call the police. If I had known the real reason he kept his mouth shut, I would never have let Annie go near him. The Matthews family is rotten."

My throat tightened at her words. Drew had witnessed Becca's rape. And he said nothing. And then he chased me down and asked me to be his girlfriend. Why would he do that? My mind was spinning and all I could think was how off-kilter the entire world felt. I prayed that this was just some sick version of the twilight zone and soon someone would call 'scene' and the lights would come on and Shea would walk through the door and hug the life back into my body. This wasn't a movie, and there was no one in the world who could save me from my shame, my anger, or my grief. Especially now that I finally understood what Becca had been saying about Drew this whole time—he was a coward. He wasn't brave. And he wasn't good enough.

"I walked home after that. I should have called the police. I should have stood up for myself. But honestly, I didn't know how much 'self' there was to stand up for as it was. The only person I cared about in the world was Annie. And she was home safe. I went home and took a hot shower hoping maybe I could burn my skin off. I scrubbed myself raw and still. I still… I'll never…"

Becca's face was tight with emotion. I reached my arms out again and this time, Becca placed Emily in my arms. Emily was warm like a baked potato in her soft pink pajamas and holding her precious body gave me comfort. She was asleep, and her little lips were moving like she was nursing and then she cracked the flash of a smile. I held her like my life depended on it. Because in that moment, I think it did. She softened my edges enough to survive another minute and then another.

The detectives asked more details, about where she found the gun, and if she had planned to use it to kill Steve. She told the truth. That from the moment she was raped, she had feared for her life. She took the gun because she was scared that Steve would attack her again or try to kill her so that people wouldn't find out what he had done. She had lived in fear every day. And she had kept the gun with her at all times, just in case.

"I know I'll probably go to prison for taking the gun. But I'm done hiding and I'm done lying. Just do what you need to do with me, but please take care of my baby." Becca had a desperate look in her eyes. She was the bravest person I knew. She and Shea. I handed Emily back to her, and I could see her relax in her seat a little in the way only a mother of an infant does when she has her baby safely in her arms.

The detectives decided not to charge Becca for any crimes. She had suffered enough, and the gun was now in police custody. She had possibly saved three lives that day by doing what she did. My parents met us in the hallway, and as we walked out of the police station together, the Matthews family was walking in.

Apparently, they, too, had some questions to answer regarding Drew's uncle Steve. Drew shuffled inside like a kicked puppy, avoiding eye contact with us at all costs. Drew's dad, Shep, looked straight ahead, dressed in a black suit and tie, as calm and confident as if this were just another day in court. I saw Melinda try to catch Becca's eye and get a glimpse of her niece, but Becca walked straight past and tucked Emily into her body. That baby would never belong to anyone but Becca.

If I was capable of gratitude for anything at this point, it was for the grace of having two loving parents who were grounding beacons of goodness. They didn't take away my despair, but they gave me a safe place to exist alongside it. Those first days after Shea's death were a blur, but the grief didn't kill me, and I have my parents and baby Emily to thank for that.

THIRTY-NINE

SOMEHOW EVEN WHEN the best part of you dies, the sun still rises. New days keep emerging over the horizon thoughtlessly and relentlessly. I woke up the morning of Shea's funeral unable to move my body. I felt like the weight of my grief had pinned my limbs to my bed, and I couldn't even open my mouth to call for help. I didn't even want help. I just wanted to go back to sleep where I might have a chance at pretending that this day wasn't real.

At some point, my mom knocked on the door and then opened it, but my paralysis was unaffected by her presence. She sat on my bed and said my name, but all I heard were gunshots and thuds. My mom lifted me into her lap, and once the tears started falling, they didn't stop. Being alive when Shea wasn't was just more than I could take.

My mom dressed me like she did when I was a small child. She slipped my black dress on—the only one I owned—the one that I wore as Shea's date to the New Year's Eve party. The one that I took off in Shea's bed. The one that had been touched by his strong and loving hands. It hung off of me now like it was on a different person entirely. Because I *was* a different person. And swallowing food was still an overwhelming task, so my clothes were starting to swallow me up in the same way my sadness was. The emptiness in my heart made room for a fierce anger at the injustice of Shea's young life being stolen from him, and from me, and from all the people and places that we were supposed to explore together. I mentally and physically collapsed under the weight of it.

My mom brushed my hair gently and put it in a simple, low ponytail, so it would be out of my face. Makeup was futile. And anyway, the only person I really wanted to be seen by was about to be buried in the ground. I went to the bathroom and threw up in the toilet before I went downstairs. Rosie told me I looked pretty. She was dressed in a little navy-blue dress, and I told her she looked pretty too. She spun in circles, unaware that there were more states of being in this world besides 'playful' or 'fancy.' She hadn't crossed the invisible threshold yet between the 'before' and the 'after.' I so desperately ached for the kind of innocence that I would never see again in this lifetime, except through the eyes of the children who came behind me, running happy and oblivious toward their own inevitable ruin.

The sun was shining when we arrived at the cemetery. Shea wasn't a churchgoer, but there was a small country church a couple of miles away from our house, and it seemed like the most appropriate place for Shea to be laid to rest. Near his mom. And his dad. I hoped that heaven existed, and that Shea's mom was holding him now. Maybe they would go ice skating together, or plant flowers. Maybe Shea would tell her about me, and she would say, 'I told you so' and they would laugh together while they ate cake and waited for me to join them.

The cemetery was just behind the church, which was elevated on a gently rolling hill, with mature trees that shaded the small cluster of gravestones as they looked out over the long waves of prairie grass. Lilacs were blooming nearby. It was warm and beautiful and quiet. A day not unlike Shea.

It felt strange that an entire life could suddenly disappear just because someone else decided to pull a trigger back. It's also strange how a place that used to be as insignificant to me as any other building I passed on my way to school in the morning could suddenly hold everything that mattered to me. Because of that tiny little trigger. Because of the selfish person who pulled it. Because of a million things that a million people did or didn't do, which led me to where I was, on top of the hill, looking out at the fields, and wondering where our souls go when we die. Wondering where Shea was. Willing him to be anywhere but in the ground beneath my feet.

The pastor from the church was a man I didn't recognize. He was very old, and very white-haired, and very patient. The funeral was set for late morning, and when I arrived with my family, there were only a handful of others there, including Becca, Zoey, and baby Emily. I was too paralyzed at first to notice the crowd of people who had gathered behind us. But when I glanced behind me, I was met with the sorrowful gazes of classmates, teachers, and community members, many of whom had gossiped about Shea while he was alive but appeared to want a piece of his tragedy. Our tragedy.

I did see some faces that brought me comfort. I waved Ms. Young over so that she could stand closer to the grave. She had cared about Shea, and I could see that. I wanted the people who cared about him to be close to him. I wanted their pain to mix with my pain. I wanted to feel like I wasn't the only fly in the pudding. I wanted the world to mourn Shea with me.

When the pastor approached the head of the gravesite, the quiet whispers rippling behind me ceased. The only sound was a gentle breeze, and the sound of someone quietly crying. I think that person was me, but I can't be sure.

"Today we gather to lay to rest the body of a young man whose life was good and valuable and deeply cherished. I met Shea McAteer as a young boy, when he attended this very church with his mother, Emily. He was a clever, joyful, and generous child. When his mother became sick, Shea cared for her like someone twice his age would be expected to. He was careful with people and their feelings. He was fearless in the face of hardship. It's my understanding that he maintained those qualities until the very end of his time on this earth."

I clung to every word coming out of the pastor's mouth. Each word gave me another little piece of Shea that I hadn't had before. I reached for them like they were swirling scraps of debris after an explosion and held them desperately in my heart.

"The last time I saw Shea was just over there at his father's funeral. Life had not been kind to Shea, but it never hardened him. He remained gentle and forgiving, even after everything he had been through. I don't know if Shea was a believer or not, but I do know that his character reminded me a lot of the person I encourage my parishioners to emulate every Sunday. Shea was a good boy, and I will miss him."

The old pastor's tissue-paper skin crinkled around his eyes, and I could see the gentle folds cradling tears inside them. I'd never heard anyone speak about Shea as a child before. I desperately wanted to get to know this man and hear the stories he had to tell. Months later, I did just that. He was a treasure—a gift from the heavens and another tiny piece of Shea.

After the pastor finished speaking, Becca stepped up in his place and looked down at the paper she held in her trembling hands. Zoey was standing nearby, holding Emily in her arms, and looking at Becca with love and compassion in her eyes. Becca's voice was shaking, but she projected loudly so that everyone could hear what she had to say.

"Shea was a hero. He was my hero. He saved my life, and my baby's life, not only by protecting us from that monster, but by giving me and my baby a safe place to live. He didn't just give me a room. He gave me a home. He made things special for me. He made me feel comfortable and wanted. He made me feel like I could do this life. He made me feel seen.

"That was his gift. Seeing people. Loving people. Even when the universe was hell-bent on hating him. Watching Shea and Annie fall in love was one of the greatest joys of my life. I had never seen two people more perfect for each other or happier together."

Tears were streaming down my face as I watched my best friend speak these words out into the world.

"Shea and Annie were meant to spend the rest of their lives together. That was stolen from them. Shea was my friend and my only real protector in this world, and that was stolen from me, too. I'm angry and I'm sad and I'll never stop being so fucking grateful for this beautiful person who fearlessly and open-heartedly sheltered me and my baby from the storm."

Becca reached over and set a white paper butterfly onto Shea's casket. I willed my body forward and set my journal next to it with the orchid pressed inside. Then the men came to lower the casket into the ground and a wail escaped my body. I wasn't ready to let go. I wasn't ready for this to be over. I wasn't ready. I stayed at the grave site long after everyone else had gone. My dad stayed too but he stayed far away from me. He waited patiently and gave me the space I needed. Like he always did.

I reached into my dress pocket and took out a folded piece of paper that had the poem I had written for Shea on it. The one I had just finished moments before he died. I never got to read it to him. But I needed to do it. I wiped the tears off my face with my bare arm and looked down at the words on the page:

Little hearts and little hands
And little humans making plans
Could not have guessed that they would know
Whereto the winds would blow the sands

Or why the light shone on the snow
Like moons and stars and things that know
My soul saw yours – and yours saw me
And fated love began to grow.

And when we grew together, see
Our branches twisted like two trees
Who knew that they were duty bound
To live one life, just you and me.

And when your heart song my soul found,
I could have dropped onto to the ground
And let myself become of it
And all the love that flowed around

Once my flame by yours was lit
I did no longer give a shit
About the world or space or time…
Just little hands in winter mitts.

I could barely see through the tears, but it didn't matter. I knew what the poem said. I folded it and set it on Shea's grave. Then I stood up. And looked out over the fields. I didn't know where my life was going to go next, but I wasn't ready to let go of Shea yet.

Right then and there, I vowed to make our dreams live on, someway, somehow.

FOURTY

So MANY THINGS came to light after the funeral. There were investigations into Steve's past, which led to surprise discoveries about the rest of the Matthews family. Drew's perfect life suddenly came crashing down around him, and the scale of the scandal meant it was flashed across news networks all over the country.

We found out that Shep and Melinda had known about Steve's proclivities and had been covering for him for years. Drew and Stella had reported to them that they had witnessed Steve assaulting Becca, and apparently the family had decided that Becca wasn't worth stirring up trouble for. Drew was instructed to tip his dad off if he heard that Becca had told anyone about what happened, or if she was planning to file charges against Steve or make a formal complaint in any way, and it turns out that getting close to me was a convenient way to get that kind of information.

According to Drew, he really did have feelings for me before and after the incident, and he was genuinely surprised and heartbroken when I broke up with him. It felt good to know that the whole relationship wasn't a complete lie, even if there was nothing that could redeem the Matthews family in my heart or mind. Drew had failed my best friend in her hour of need, and as much as I want to forgive him for that, I'm still working on it, and probably always will be.

Melinda said that she later regretted covering for Steve, and that she hoped she could make amends to Becca, and Steve's other victims someday. She confessed that the guilt she felt was overwhelming, and that the pressure she felt from her husband to keep up appearances despite the despicable things she and her children had to do to maintain their family's reputation was more than she could handle. Shortly after speaking her truth to the authorities, Melinda Matthews filed for divorce.

Shep Matthews said as little as possible to avoid incriminating himself. Upon further investigation, it was revealed that Shep had secrets of his own, which included money laundering, blackmail, and a 49% ownership of the strip club two towns over which, it was later discovered, employed several underage girls. Apparently, Steve had played a key role in recruiting 'talent' for the club, and frequently took advantage of vulnerable young women, who began to come forward and tell their stories when the whole thing became public. Shep was duly prosecuted.

As much as I genuinely hated Drew, I felt sorry for him too. I think he was just as blind-sided by the whole thing as the rest of the town was. Drew knew he had a creepy uncle, and he did what his parents told him to do. It wasn't a good excuse, but it *was* a reason—one that it was possible to understand, even if incredibly difficult. Now his uncle was dead, he had been publicly shamed, his parents were divorced, and his dad was facing serious prison time. It actually made me glad to see that Stella stayed by his side through it all. As far as I know, they went to college together somewhere in Wisconsin and married each other a couple years later.

Becca decided to pursue a degree in social work. She didn't wait to graduate before making a difference, though. She started holding meetings once a week in the country church's basement, where victims of sexual assault could gather and support each other. Sometimes family members were invited to attend the meetings, and I would go and support Becca. It always surprised me how many women were there, and it also surprised me to see who some of the women were.

Janet, our sweet elementary school librarian who was nearing eighty, had been sexually assaulted by a college professor as a young student, and still suffered from the emotional trauma that she had suppressed for her entire life because she was afraid of the judgement she might receive if anyone found out what had happened.

Katie, a girl a year younger than me, was there with her mom, and they held hands as she described the abuse they had both endured from her stepfather.

Becca created a safe space for women to share their pain and work through their feelings of shame and guilt and anger and sadness and fear. Women of all ages acknowledged and supported one another in a beautiful sisterhood that transcended the evil that was done to them. So much healing happened because of Becca and seeing her transform lives while healing herself made me proud and happy and comfortable thinking about spreading my own wings and leaving this little corner of the world in fair condition.

After Shea's death, because Becca wasn't family or a legal partner, Shea's house was put up for auction by the State. As much horror as that house had seen, it was also filled with some of the most beautiful moments of my life, and it was Shea's and it pained me to think of someone else living there or destroying it or buying the land and forgetting about it. Becca wanted to stay there with Emily, but she didn't have the money to buy the house. She stayed with my family for a while and planned to move into Zoey's rental house in town by the end of the summer. Zoey came over often, and I watched as their love grew deeper and deeper each day. As much as my heart broke for my own loss, it made me happy to see that happy endings were possible for some people. Especially ones who deserved it as much as they did.

...

In late July, I turned eighteen. I spent my birthday with Becca and Emily down by the dock. It was painful to be in the place I was when my heart first opened itself to Shea. I kept imagining him coming up out of the water, facing away, the sun glistening off the beads of water that rolled down his hair and his tanned body. I imagined him turning around and smiling at me with warm playfulness in his eyes. Then I blinked and the image disappeared. I jumped in the water and stayed there in the cool silence for as long as I could. I felt like maybe if I stayed long enough, time would turn back, and I would see Shea's shadow arch over head as he dove into the water, and we could start again. I could love him sooner. I could kill Steve before he killed us. I waited until my lungs burned, and I had to break through the surface again to breath or stay down and die. I eventually did pop my head above the water, but I think I'm still waiting to take a full breath.

As Becca and I walked back up to the house, I felt older than my eighteen years. I felt both harder and softer. Like nothing could hurt me anymore, but also, at any moment, a feather might land on me, and I might shatter into a million pieces.

We stepped inside the house, and my mom handed Becca a letter. Becca opened it and said nothing before handing it over to me. I looked at it passively and then when I saw what it was, my mouth dropped open.

It was a check. For the exact amount that Shea's house was for sale for. The signature on the check made me feel such a muddled soup of feelings that I didn't know if I should shout obscenities, jump for joy, or cry like a baby. Melinda Matthews wanted to pay for Becca to own Shea's house.

Becca's first reaction was to set the check on fire. She wasn't one to take handouts, especially not ones that were driven by guilt and shame. But then, an amazing thing happened. Sweet little Emily cooed in her baby swing, and when Becca looked at her, her face softened. She looked at the check, and back at her baby, and back at the check. I watched as Becca did a new thing. She put the check carefully into her wallet. Several days later she owned the house. Zoey moved in with her shortly after, and they've been raising Emily there together ever since. Emily's room still has Shea all over it and that will always feel right.

My people were settled, and it felt like some pieces that were broken were being glued back together. Some of them looked even more beautiful than they did before they broke—an enigma that I can't stop seeing in the world.

As for me, I declined the offer to attend the University of Minnesota. I know this would have made Shea angry—me giving up on a dream of mine, but I just wasn't ready to face college after what happened, and I'm still not sure what I think life should be. I know that things rarely fit into neat categories. I know that most people aren't just good or bad, and that we are (almost) all doing the best we can. I know that for every evil that exists, there are a hundred more angels smiling their faces on creation. I know that death isn't the end of love. I know that I will never feel complete, and my journey will be finding a way to live with that. I know what love feels like, and I'm hopeful that maybe there is more of it out there. Because it's the thing we all live for. It's the thing Shea did so well. It's the best gift I've ever received.

Shea didn't have a plan, but he always talked about Alaska. I thought maybe I would start there. When I was ready, I looked for his maps and smiled at his little drawings that adorned the margins, and I made a list of all the places he had circled. My dad loaded me up a duffle bag full of outdoor gear, most of which I didn't know what to do with, but I planned to figure it out. And probably get cold and wet in the process. When the worst has already happened, you find that a lot of things aren't as scary as they used to be. I packed some empty notebooks too. I wasn't going to college, but I was still going to write. Maybe I would start by telling Shea's story. Our story.

When I disembarked the tiny plane in Sitka, Alaska, a gust of cold, wet wind knocked me onto the tarmac. Then the sun came out, and I felt Shea smile on my skin. I laughed as I stood up and walked in the direction of nowhere in particular, in search of nothing at all.

EPILOGUE

I WALK INTO the generous air conditioning of the lodge after a long afternoon guiding hikers along Angel's Landing. Zion is my third national park job in five years. I don't have a plan, but I've got time and space and life, and if Shea taught me anything, it was that nobody is owed any of those things. To exist fully in the present moment is the highest form of being. I don't think too much about tomorrow or the next day. These days I get up early to watch the sun rise over the canyons, and sometimes I even find myself smiling when the first rays of light hit my skin.

I write a lot. I write about Shea, but I write about other things too. Things I observe. Things I feel. It feels necessary and good, so I know I'm on the right path. Taking the time to get to know myself after having to grow up so fast is one of the best decisions I've ever made. Shea would have loved this life for me. He would have loved this life *with* me. It still stings. But the anger of losing him has shorter visiting hours than it used to, and I'm proud of that. Shea would be proud of me too.

"Hey Annie—phones for you." Shannon hands me the chunky, off-white landline that has been at the front desk since the 90's, and I'm surprised that anyone would call for me here and not just call my cell (although, to be fair, reception is pretty hit-or-miss in Zion).

"This is Annie," I say.

The voice on the other end is low, gentle, and a little nervous. I listen to what he has to say and find that for the first time in a long time, I am *very much* thinking about the day after tomorrow. The butterflies that used to fly freely through my abdomen are suddenly reawakened, and their wings have grown since the last time I felt them.

"I look forward to seeing you too. I honestly can't wait. Thank you." I head to my room and cry.

...

It's Monday morning, two days after I received the call in the lodge, and thankfully it's quiet in the park. My suggested meeting place is on a trail near the lodge; a short, breezy hike that is easy for a newcomer to find, but far enough out of the way that I'm confident we won't be interrupted by my coworkers or curious passersby.

As I round the last bend and meander down into the canyon valley, I see a man squatting down, gently inspecting the rocks being smoothed by the clear blue river water. Behind him, the golden light illuminates the orange and red and pink striped canyon walls, and I find myself not wanting to make my presence known, and instead just wanting to watch him be himself for a while.

The rocks betray me, and as a few pebbles roll down the hill beneath my feet, I slide down with them and barely manage to stay upright. I always did know how to (not) make an entrance.

He stands up and turns to face me, and when we lock eyes, his face lights up with all the warmth and beauty of a kind soul. He is tall and angular, handsome, but understated. His clothes are plain and practical, but his dark hair and bright, hazel eyes are vibrant and full of life.

"You must be Annie. You have no idea how hard it was to find you." He smiles and looks around himself, maybe at the incredible scenery, or maybe just because my staring face makes him feel uncomfortable.

"Hi. It's…amazing to meet you…Nick."

"I've never done this before, so I'm not really sure how it's supposed to go. Maybe I'll start with 'thank you?'" He smiles at me earnestly.

"I'm also a first-timer, so you're in good company," I laugh. Nick's energy makes me feel safe. There's just something about him, and I have a feeling about what it must be.

"So…do you want to hear?" he asks.

I nod as unexpected tears sting the corners of my eyes. I don't hold them back.

Nick unbuttons his shirt to reveal a long, vertical scar along his broad chest. I touch my hand to it and let the tears fall. He pulls me into a firm hug and places my ear at the scar's center where the *thump, thump, thump* of Shea's heart brings life to the beautiful human holding me.

"I was so desperate to thank someone for this gift, but my donor didn't have family that I could find. The people living in his old house told me about you. They said you two were close."

"We were." My voice cracks on the words.

The thought of Becca speaking to this man about me, and Shea is more than I can handle. I let out a sob and Nick hugs me tighter. He is patient. I listen to the steady beat of Shea's heart, and I don't let go for a long time.

Eventually, though, I say goodbye to Nick. But when he glances back and smiles at me as he walks away, I can't help but think that it won't be the last time I see his face or listen to his heart.

READER'S GUIDE

1. How might things have been different if Becca had gone to the police right after she was attacked? Why didn't she?

2. What role does family reputation play in small-town life?

3. What does it mean to be a good person?

4. What is a soul mate? Are soul mates pre-determined by fate or is loving someone a choice?

5. Is Drew an antagonist? What about his mom, Melinda?

6. What is art? Can anyone be an artist?

7. Is experiencing some form of grief or trauma necessary to fully understand it?

8. Was Shea responsible for his father's death?

9. Are most teenagers ready to choose a career path right out of high school? How important is it to make a practical choice over a passionate one?

10. Will Annie ever be able to love someone in the same way she loved Shea?

ACKNOWLEDGEMENTS

Finishing my first novel is like letting out a big breath I have been holding in for years. Thank you to PWH Publishing for your belief in me as an author and to Dr. Meghan Hurley-Powell for making this book everything it is with your editing prowess, your encouragement, and your sparkle.

This book might not have happened if it hadn't been for my first readers and best friends, Jenna and Jessica, who devoured each chapter as I wrote it and demanded more. They gave me the confidence I needed to keep going and brought so much joy and excitement to the process.

Special thanks to my husband, Liam, for loving, supporting, and creating space for me to live out my dreams. You and the girls are everything to me.

Mom, thank you for helping me believe that I'm the luckiest girl in the world, deserving of all things beautiful and good, and that nothing is out of my reach.

Dad, thank you for the stories and the magic and the music and the woods.

To my grandparents, teachers, and everyone else who came before me and modeled creativity and patience and love, this book and everything I produce hereafter is made with gratitude for you.

To my children and everyone who comes after me, my creative endeavors are in service to you, with hopes that you follow your heart and know that you are worthy of your wildest dreams.

I love you all.

ABOUT THE AUTHOR

Haley is a native of the Perham, Minnesota area, and after some extensive travel around the world, she has settled with her husband and two daughters in Katy, Texas. She is the artist and owner of Haley McMillan Creative Studio and can usually be found in her studio splashing paint around, playing guitar, dancing, or dreaming up her next story.

WHAT'S NEXT?

Stay tuned for Haley's next book, *Margot James is Fine*.

After getting dumped at the altar, a thirty-one-year-old bereavement coordinator and former foster kid, Margot, is left untethered and alone. When her co-worker convinces her to go on her honeymoon by herself, she is reluctant, but okay with the idea of running away. She has no idea the things that are in store for her in St. Lucia, or the ghosts from her past that will threaten to derail her happiness.

An exploration of love, trauma, and healing, *Margot James is Fine* is a must-read chick lit novel that delivers emotion, humor, and romance with all the trimmings.

Printed in Great Britain
by Amazon

22667247R00185